The girl walked naked out of nowhere on a winter night and to psychiatrist Paul Fidler it was as if one of his own obsessive visions of disaster took human form, bringing nightmares to life.

Piquantly lovely, she belonged to no known racial type. Of high intelligence, she spoke a language no one could be found to understand. Most remarkable of all, commonplace objects like clothing and cars were a mystery to her.

Has she truly been cast adrift from her own familiar world into another branch of the universe?

Such was the frightening that gradually seemed to be answer Paul could come up it implied things that he h dared to dream.

QUICKSAND

John Brunner

DAW BOOKS, INC.

DONALD A. WOLLHEIM, PUBLISHER

1301 Avenue of the Americas
New York, N. Y.   10019

He holds up, warning, the crossed cones of time:
Here, narrowing into now, the Past and Future
Are quicksand.
                                    —Randall Jarrell
                        The Knight, Death, and the Devil

FIRST PRINTING, JULY 1976

1 2 3 4 5 6 7 8 9

PRINTED IN U.S.A.

1

For a long moment after opening the door of the sitting-room Paul Fidler was literally frightened.

—The wrong door? The right door with the wrong room beyond it!

His hand had reached for the bell-push on the wall, a foot past the doorjamb, and encountered books on a shelf. Startled, he had looked instead of taking for granted and seen the big table in a new place, the chairs in a new arrangement, everything moved to a different location.

—Mrs Gowler at her tricks again?

She was a widow of fifty, childless, to whom Chent Hospital had become a sort of outsize extended family; she had spent ten years here, sometimes as a patient, sometimes as a member of the maintenance staff doing cleaning work and washing-up, because she had nowhere else in the world to go and nobody to care whether she lived or died. And once or twice a year the signal would come that her lucid phase was ending: one would walk into a room and find everything topsy-turvy, perhaps even the carpet turned over. Meantime Mrs Gowler would have gone humming to her next task, unaware of any departure from routine.

But this wasn't her doing. All that happened was that two sorely needed, long-awaited new bookcases had been delivered and someone had spent the afternoon filling them with medical journals previously kept on the table in untidy stacks.

—Glad I'm the first to arrive for tea. The look on my face just then must have been a sight! Talk about reversion to infantile behaviour!

But that wasn't a subject he cared to dwell on. As a child he had sometimes been haunted by the fear that he would waken one morning into a world of strangers: parents who didn't recognise him as their son, a school which didn't remember having him as a pupil. And once, much later, it had all seemed to come true.

—Shut up. What a fuss about some new furniture!

Sighing, he recalled that the bookcases now covered the bell-push. Glancing around to see if there was a substitute, he grimaced.

—If only the change extended to that hideous wallpaper. . . . Not in this year's budget. Anyhow: have to wait for a change of matron before we get some good taste around this place.

On the side-table, a little hand-bell. He picked it up and gave it a shake. Simultaneous to the tenth of a second, the clock in the tower overhead ground towards striking, and he cringed. For most of the day he'd managed to avoid noticing it, but last night, during his turn of duty. . .

Bang boom *clink*. Pause. Boom *clink* bang. Pause.

—Christ. Doesn't it get on anyone's nerves but mine?

Clink boom bang. *Clink* bang boom. And with a sense of relief from unspeakable torture he heard it progress into the calm sequence of the hourly chime: bong bong bong bong.

—No wonder that poor fellow that Matron told me about tried to climb the clock-tower in '63. Probably wanted to silence the cracked bell.

Speaking of bells . . . He was just about to ring a second time when Lil, the cook's helper, put her head around the door.

"Oh, it's you, Doctor. Sorry—that thing's going to take a bit of getting used to. Not so loud as the electric. Tea up in a couple of shakes!"

Waiting, Paul put his hand randomly into the bookcase hiding the bell-push, drew out and opened a magazine.

—Chlorpromazine three times daily? What's new about that? Oh: this stuff fluphenazine enanthate. Relief for up to twenty-eight days from a single injection. I should know about this; it sounds useful. Only . . .

Only somehow the words wouldn't assemble into a meaningful pattern. Recollection of the letter in his pocket kept getting in the way.

"Your tea, Doctor!"

Lil standing there impatiently with the cup and saucer, two biscuits balanced precariously beside the spoon. He accepted the tea, already stewed sour although he'd got here a minute early. Stirring it listlessly long past the point at which the sugar dissolved, he let his eyes roam to the window.

Most of the day a lid of grey cloud like dirty cotton-wool dressings had lain over the district, shedding halfhearted rain at intervals. Now, with not long to go before sunset, a cold wind was brooming the clouds eastward and wan sunlight was leaking through.

—Does that view seem as horrible to other people as it does to me? Lord, I must stop this, or I'll be back to another of those childhood obsessions: the endless questions about solipsism and how do you know that what I see as red is the same as what you see as red?

When he first came here, he'd liked this country: irregular, dramatic, as if the red rock underneath the red soil were heaving itself up preparatory to the titanic effort of building the mountains of Wales. A landscape appropriate to castles, fit setting for heroic deeds and grand gestures.

—I suppose it takes a Paul Fidler to make it a backdrop for failure.

He checked that thought instantly, but it wouldn't depart from him. Everything in view seemed to reinforce it. The parklike grounds had once been a fine estate, and still were scrupulously tended, partly by the patients as a valuable form of occupational therapy. But now rather than a vast garden they constituted a sort of no-man's-land dividing the hospital from the ordinary life of town and village beyond. Ignorant of that, one might admire their stately beauty; informed, Paul associated to wire entanglements and minefields.

And the hills leaped about the flat-floored valley: they had once appeared grand to him. Now they seemed constricting, a planned wall excluding the greater world. Some barely grey-green, some, in this month of February, spined with naked trees, some forbiddingly dense with conifers, they encircled town, hospital, Paul Fidler. Through this window, though not from his own office, it was possible to see the point at which the single main road breached the ring, but even there he was unable to imagine open country, escape, freedom. For at this angle the two spool-shaped cooling towers of the power station seemed to stand guard over the exit from the valley, watch-posts of the forces prisoning him.

—It's not right for a man to be glad his wife isn't coming home at the promised time.

Fact. Inarguable. All day he'd been edging away from the admission. Now it had sneaked past his defences. And . . .

—Damn it, I can't lie to myself. I *am* glad.

He set aside his tea, barely tasted, and drew out Iris's letter.

For the latest of many times he glanced at the opening lines.

No address. No date apart from the curt "Tues." And no salutation. That fitted. One could hardly call a husband "Dear Paul" like a chance acquaintance, and while the "darling" came readily enough in speech, putting it starkly on paper would by now be so dishonest even Iris would feel the incongruity.

"I'm afraid I shall be away a bit longer than I expected. Bertie and Meg insist on my staying with them another few days and I can't turn them down. I'm sure you won't mind too dreadfully. . . ."

No point in rereading the whole thing. Jerkily he slid it back into his pocket.

—It *is* a relief. Excuses? Why bother? I know exactly why I'm pleased. Not for the reason I gave when she said she wanted to go and would I mind: because I'm more free to study when I'm on my own. But because being with Iris is a daylong and even a nightlong strain.

He felt a little better for this access of candour. But considering all the consequences which must inevitably flow from it was more than he could contrive at the moment; as always happened to him when he was confronted with a point of crisis in his life, possibilities multiplied and multiplied in his imagination until they were beyond counting, and some of them seemed almost physically real, they were so vivid. He simply stood at the window and stared out, noting without paying much attention that the wind from the west was now bringing up cloud of its own to close the gap of lighter sky which had briefly relieved the greyness of the February day.

◆ 2 ◆

"What's wrong, Paul? Has the cata got your tonia?"

He started and swung around. There were exactly two things he disliked about Mirza Bakshad, and both had just happened to him: the man's capacity for moving without a whisper of sound, and his delight in excruciating deformations of English.

"Oh . . . hullo, Mirza."

The Pakistani plumped himself into the best armchair and stretched elegantly. "The bookcases turned up, I see," he commented. "Not before time, either. . . . Lil! *Li-ill!*"

Still without moving from the window, Paul watched the girl bring the tea and biscuits.

"Iced!" Mirza noted with satisfaction. "My favourites!"

"Saved them for you specially, Doctor," Lil told him, and giggled out of the room.

—Blast Mirza. Doesn't anything ever go wrong with his life?

But the twinge of bitterness didn't last in Paul's mind. Mirza was diabolically handsome, indecently intelligent and quite without false modesty: how could anyone help liking him?

—Although, of course, Iris . . .

The Pakistani sipped his tea, grimaced, and put the cup on the arm of his chair. He touched the trace-line of moustache along his upper lip as though making sure it was still there, and fixed his bright black gaze on Paul.

"You really do look under the weather. What's the matter?"

Paul shrugged, kicking around a hard chair to sit on.

"You closemouthed English," Mirza sighed. "It's a marvel you aren't all stark raving bonkers in this country. Or are you? Sometimes I get the impression . . . Well, I'll guess, then. A rough session with Soppy Al?"

He meant Dr Knox Alsop, the consultant with whom Paul worked most closely.

"No, he wasn't in today," Paul muttered. "Put it off to tomorrow. Some committee meeting he had to attend."

"Then it's probably Hole-in-head. Hm?" Mirza cocked his right eyebrow to a disturbing angle.

One of these days Dr Joseph Holinshed, medical superintendent of the hospital, was going to learn about the series of punning nicknames Mirza had coined for his superiors, and feathers would fly. As yet, though, he seemed to have remained aloof from earshot of them.

"It's partly him," Paul conceded. A frigid exchange with Holinshed was becoming almost a daily feature of his work, and this morning had conformed to the pattern.

"Only partly? Holy Joe is the largest single obstacle to getting one's work done around this place, and occasionally I experience this urge to lock him accidentally in the disturbed female ward overnight. Then perhaps he'd catch on to what's really happening." A casual gesture implying dismissal of a whole range of alternative possibilities. "That leaves your lovely but unsociable wife. What's she done to you this time?"

"Changed her mind about coming home tomorrow," Paul admitted reluctantly.

There was a short silence, during which the two men faced each other directly, Paul wanting to turn aside but somehow lacking the will-power, Mirza biting down on his lower lip in an expression eloquent of concern.

He said at length, "What can I say, Paul? If I speak my mind I risk making you think I'm offended because of the way she treated me. I'm not—enough of the attitude customary at home under the Raj leaked through my arrogant skull for me to half-expect women like her to snub wogs like me. It's what she does to you that bothers me. She wants to boss you about, and that's bad."

"Now look here, Mirza!" Paul began, and realised with an appalling shock that it stopped there; the words he needed to counter the charge didn't exist.

He was saved from having to bluster, however, by the arrival of others of the junior medical staff: Phil Kerans, Natalie Rudge, Ferdie Silva. At once, with the more-than-British tact of which he was invariably capable, Mirza was away on a ludicrous fantasy about Holinshed, and they were laughing together, allowing Paul to sit by quietly and even crack a passable smile of his own.

—Without Mirza, what the hell would I do?

Sufficiently distracted to swallow his sour cool tea without tasting it, he considered his colleagues.

—Relating to other people: a jargon phrase we use to blanket the spectrum love-to-hate. But human beings don't follow tidy lines on graphs. They diverge at odd angles into n dimensions. Where can one plot the location of indifference? Somewhere in mid-air above the surface of the paper? It leads neither to affection nor to detestation. It's a point in a void.

Not that he was totally indifferent to these coworkers. Just . . . somewhat indifferent.

—A state worse yet?

Take Irish Phil Kerans. At forty-plus he knew he was

never going where Mirza certainly and Paul presumably were going, to consultant status. He'd do a reasonable job in this or another hospital until he retired: an average, neutral person. He seemed no longer to resent the fact. Paul matched his own probable future against Kerans's, and could draw no conclusions from the comparison.

—Natalie?

When he had first seen her it had been from behind, and he had immediately been attracted by her sleek black hair glistening under a fluorescent light. It had been a shock when she turned to be introduced and he saw the bad complexion and receding chin which made her not downright ugly but just plain. Yet she had an amazing talent for warming the cold withdrawn personalities of chronic geriatric cases.

—Do I like her? As with Phil, the answer is: yes/no. A reaction equidistant between liking and disliking but far off the line which would lead me to either.

So too with Ferdie Silva, like Mirza an immigrant but unlike him of European extraction, born in British Guiana: a sallow, stolid man whose chief attribute was the unspectacular one of patience.

—I can't work up enthusiasm over someone's patience!

Then: over what? Anything? Not today, not now. His brain had congealed before the prospect of accepting what Mirza said straight out, what he himself knew intellectually but dared not let seep into total awareness for fear it would overload his mind with pseudo-real visions of the consequences. Best to spin out uncertainty as long as possible.

He felt poised in this instant of time, as an impossibly slow spinning top might poise before falling. He could almost sense the rotation of the earth, carrying him past the successive doorways leading to his alternate futures. It was within his power to move forward into whichever he wished, to go on putting up with things as they were or to make a clean break and any of half a dozen fresh starts, or to set in train events leading to a break being forced on him. He could picture with painful clarity the likely form that each of those futures would take. Only the act of choosing between them was beyond his present ability.

Passive, he absorbed snatches of what was being said.

"I think young Reynolds is on the mend. He got quite animated telling me about the right time to plant flowers this afternoon. I must find out if there's a patch of garden he can have."

Groping, Paul attached the name to a person: a youth who had at first lied to his mother about going to work and spent his days riding about on buses, then progressed to refusing to get out of bed.

—To be cured with a plot of ground and a packet of seeds? God, how wonderful to find such an easy solution!

"Watch out for Lieberman next time you're on duty. They found another key under his pillow this morning."

—Lieberman the master locksmith. See something locked, open it. Anything. When he tried the cages at Dudley Zoo they sent him here, and now . . .

Paul jangled the heavy bunch of keys in the side pocket of his jacket.

—What's the difference between me and a jailer? No prizes for the first correct answer.

"Paul, you're looking pale today. Anything the matter?"

Natalie, eyes monstrous behind pebble-thick glasses, was regarding him.

"I didn't get much sleep last night," Paul apologised hastily. "It was my duty. And that bloody cracked bell . . . !"

"If you didn't live out in luxury you wouldn't notice it," Phil Kerans said. "Since the first week I was here I've simply learned to ignore it."

"Can't ignore it now," Ferdie Silva put in, glancing at his watch. "Time to move along."

There was a chinking of piled cups, a stubbing of cigarettes. It was just about sunset, and the wind had risen enough to moan in the mock battlements of the building.

"I have an idea for augmenting our budget," Mirza said. "Let's rent this place to a horror film company. *Dracula Meets the Headshrinkers* would pack them in at the local flea-pits!"

"We're packed in tightly enough here," Natalie said. "How near are we to capacity, Paul?"

Paul started and thought back to the chart on the wall of his office. "We have a couple of discharges due for to-morrow," he said. "Which will leave . . . uh . . . eighteen bed-spaces empty."

"It's a record," Kerans grunted. "I hope you're keeping quiet about it, or they'll send us twenty new admissions."

The clock chimed. Natalie gave an exaggerated wince and looked for Paul to respond, which he did belatedly, and then she was gone. The rest of them moved in her wake.

"How are you fixed for work this evening, Mirza?" Paul

inquired as they emerged on the landing. "Time for a quick one before supper?"

"I wish I could," Mirza answered. "I think you need company. *But.*"

"It's not your duty tonight, is it?"

"No, it's Natalie's, I think." Mirza gave a consciously mock-wicked grin. "I have a date, though, and it's too . . . ah . . . tentative to risk making her hang around."

"Another new one?" Abruptly Paul found himself trying to imagine Mirza through a woman's eyes: tall, lean, his skin not much darker than a heavy sun-tan, his English far better than most Englishmen's, his features classically regular . . .

—God damn.

"I've told you before," Mirza said, smiling. "It's prophylactic. I gather Holy Joe is winding up to a session on the mat because he doesn't approve of my goings-on—what else could you expect, though, of someone named after the idiot who turned down Potiphar's wife? But if push comes to shove I shall tell him what I've told you: I'm insuring against a breach of ethics. Your poor repressed womenfolk nursing their desire to be raped by a nigger would be all over me, and I couldn't stand them off if I didn't . . . ah . . . make adequate provision elsewhere."

The self-deprecating mockery left his tone abruptly.

"Paul, this girl had a friend with her when I met her the other night—rather a dish. But you wouldn't be interested, would you?"

Paul shook his head and tried to swallow, finding his mouth was desert-dry.

"A marriage like yours is no basis for a proper understanding of women," Mirza said, so clincally it was impossible to take offence. "Try looking at it from that point of view. It may be a consolation. . . . I'm sorry, Paul. Believe me, I really am very sorry indeed."

He touched his friend lightly on the shoulder and was gone.

After the first pint of beer Paul thought about a second and went to the toilet while making up his mind. Tiredness leadened his limbs—pressure of work had kept him in the office far later than the official quitting time—but at least he had a more concrete reason for not going home yet than the mere prospect of a cold empty house and a meal out of cans: a sad drizzle of rain was muttering at the pub's windows.

—On the other hand, why stay in this dismal dump?

In the hope of waking himself up a little he splashed his face with cold water. Wiping the wet away with the automatic roller-towel—overdue for changing again, hanging fully out of its white enamel dispenser like a lax pale tongue from a dinosaur's mouth—he stared at himself in the mirror.

Not a remarkable person, this Paul Fidler. Rather a round face without great character, his eyes turned to echoing circles by puffy dark lower lids and exaggerated half-moon eyebrows. Dark brown hair above the face, crisp and rebellious; below, a decent medium-priced suit, white shirt, green tie. . . .

—To look at: a Kerans-type second-rater in the making?

The trend of his thoughts alarmed him. He dropped the towel as if it had stung him and thrust his way back to the bar. He needed to take the pressure off. He ordered a Scotch and carried it to the corner table where he had been sitting before alone.

—I have this sense of *waiting*. But . . . what in hell for?

The fact that the feeling was familiar didn't make it any more palatable. It had reverberated along his life-line in advance of almost every major event of his existence, pleasant or unpleasant, each pulse spawning in his imagination a horde of possible worlds: failing to win the scholarship he banked on, being ploughed in his medical course, losing Iris after becoming engaged to her against all his expectations, being turned down for this post as psychiatric registrar at

Chent. Sometimes, between sleep and waking in the morning, those unrealised possibilities became so real he mistook them for memories and carried nightmare into the daytime.

—And during my breakdown, of course, they *were* real.

He tossed back half the whisky to douse that idea. Somehow things had worked out for him in the end. So far.

—But this time, not. The next big event looks like being squalidly commonplace: the collapse of a marriage.

He stared about him, vaguely searching for some jolting incongruity in his surroundings to provide temporary distraction, but the Needle in Haystack boasted nothing out of the ordinary except its peculiar name. The only reason he came here was because it stood handy to the hospital. Thirty years ago it must have been a village local and might have been interesting; now the town of Blickham had linked itself to Yemble with a pseudo-pod of straggling postwar houses and the latter counted for a suburb rather than a village.

The best the pub could do by way of a surprise was to show him a smart young executive type in a fleece-lined carcoat buying Nurse Davis another sherry. Nurse Davis was from Trinidad, a cocoa-coloured girl with immense dimples in her cheeks, and her escort's family would probably have a fit if they got to know.

But this led him straight back to the proposition Mirza had made after the tea-break, and there, as when following so many other trains of thought today, he stopped at a blank wall.

—In principle, damn it, why object? I know practically for sure about Iris and that suave bastard Gellert. . . . But the desire isn't there. We are the hollow men. Tap my chest: I boom with empty echoes.

The after-work clientele had dispersed to go home and eat and the ones who would stay until closing time had not yet begun to arrive. Only a few diehard regulars and himself remained. The staff were watching television; from Paul's corner the screen was a narrow white blur and the sound a mere irritating grumble. Nurse Davis and her companion left. A wake survived from their passage.

—Wake: a funeral ceremony. Did coldly furnish forth the marriage tables. Should I have another? Lunch was ghastly and I didn't even eat the biscuits at teatime. The hell with it.

Hiding her annoyance at missing the next two minutes of the TV programme, the landlord's wife pushed his glass up to

the udder of the inverted whisky bottle and replaced it next
to the soda syphon. He had expected her to take the money
he'd laid down and say nothing, but she spoke after all.

"Had a bad day, have you, Doctor? You look a bit peaky."

"Hm? Oh . . . yes, I do feel rather tired."

—She must have all the hospital gossip, since so many of
the staff drop in every day. Is there gossip about me too?
What does it say?

Almost, he asked her point-blank, but she was gone to the
till with his jingling coins.

Sitting down again at his table, he fumbled out cigarettes
and was about to light one when the outside door slammed
wide. Everyone froze. Everyone stared. The man in the
doorway was an apparition.

Hatless, his head was wrapped in a scarlet scarf of blood
from a cut on his scalp. One eye was vastly swollen into a
black bruise. Three scratches were crusting on his cheek.
Mud fouled the legs of his trousers, his shoes, the hem of his
damp fawn raincoat. He held his left arm cradled in his right,
swaying at the threshold and seeming terrified that he might
brush the jamb with the hurt limb.

"Harry!" the landlord's wife said faintly, and her husband
thrust up the bar-flap and strode toward the intruder.

"My God, what happened to you? Been in an accident?
Flo, get him some brandy!"

Customers on their feet now included Paul, walking
mechanically around this table, those chairs, to get where he
was going.

"Ambulance," the man said in a petulant high whine. "Oh
Jesus, my arm."

Shaking, the landlord guided him to a padded settle and
made him sit down. He rapped at his wife for being slow
with the brandy.

"Harry, there's Dr Fidler," she countered, glass in hand
but making no move to fill it.

Paul was trying to make sense of the man's condition. A
car smash? Presumably; perhaps he'd run off the road into a
ditch and got muddy climbing out. . . .

He found his voice and addressed the hurt man. "Yes, I'm
a doctor. Let's have a look at you." And to the landlord,
aside: "Get me a bowl of warm water and some disinfectant
and anything you have in the way of dressings. Hurry!"

The other customers had burst into excited chatter. Paul
snapped at them to stand clear, eased the man into a lying

position with his head on a cushion the landlord's wife gave him, and dropped on one knee.

—Funny. Those marks on the cheek: from nails? The way the grooves are arranged . . .

But those were the most superficial injuries. He tugged the clean handkerchief from his breast pocket and lightly separated the hair beginning to clot with blood. The man flinched and started to draw rapid hissing breaths to distract himself from the pain. The cut looked worse than it was; he must have an X-ray, naturally, but probably there was no fracture. As to the black eye: one ordinary shiner, like the scalp more spectacular than dangerous.

—Which leaves that arm he's nursing.

The landlord produced the bowl of water and announced that his wife had gone for plaster and cotton-wool. Paul leaned close to the hurt man.

"Can you straighten that arm?"

A headshake, breath gusting between clenched teeth.

"Have you any other pain except your head, face and arm?"

Another headshake. Good: the depth of his breathing certainly indicated he could hardly have injured his rib-cage.

"Is the pain worse above or below the elbow?"

With his right forefinger the man pointed towards his shoulder.

—So: presumably a fractured humerus. Just possibly a dislocated shoulder . . . ? No, the joint feels normal enough.

Paul rose to his feet. "Get me some sharp scissors, please," he told the landlord. "Or a razor blade would do."

"Here!" The injured man struggled to sit up. "What for?"

"Lie still," Paul soothed. "I shall have to cut the sleeve away and look at that arm."

"But this is my best suit, and I only bought the raincoat last Thursday!" Very pale from shock, the man nonetheless forced himself into a sitting position, so swiftly that Paul could not prevent him.

"But you said your arm is too painful to straighten," Paul sighed. "And anyway if you try to get your coat off you're liable to grind the ends of the broken bone together, and that would be sheer agony."

"It's broken, is it? You sure?"

"I can't be completely sure till I get a proper look at it, but I think it must be."

"But I only bought the coat last Thursday," the man protested again. His eyes, rolling, fell on the landlord's out-stretched hand proffering a packet of razor blades, and he made a weak attempt to open his coat with his good arm before Paul could intervene.

The fly of his trousers was undone, letting the white of underpants show through.

Some of the bystanders giggled and exchanged nudges. Paul wanted to bark at whoever thought this was funny, but he was too busy steadying the hurt man, whom the pang from his arm had shaken severely.

"I warned you," Paul said. "You can always buy another coat; arms are a bit harder to come by. I'll be as gentle as I can, but I'm afraid this is going to be painful whatever I do."

Unwrapping the packet of blades the landlord gave him, he was struck by a thought. "You did phone for an ambulance, didn't you?" he demanded.

The landlord blinked. "Well . . . no, actually I didn't."

"Why on earth not? Look at the state the fellow's in!"

"But I thought you could just take him across to your hospital," the landlord countered. "It's only a few yards along the road."

"Hospital!" The hurt man reacted. "There's a hospital that close? Then why are you fooling around in here?"

"I'm afraid it's no good to you," Paul answered. "You need proper surgical facilities. We'll have to more you to Blickham General."

"I'll phone up right away," the landlord muttered in embarrassment, and pushed his way to the back of the bar.

Dazed, the hurt man didn't seem to have heard Paul's last words. He complained obstinately, "But if there's a hospital just down the road . . . You come from there?"

"Yes."

"What's wrong with it, then? A hospital's a hospital!"

"Mine isn't equipped to handle emergencies like yours," Paul said, his patience stretching to the limit. "You'll need that head X-rayed, for one thing, and your arm splinted, and you may have other injuries for all I can tell. We don't have the facilities."

"So why in hell do you call the place a hospital?"

"It's a mental hospital!"

"Then that explains it," the man said, opening his eyes as wide as the bruising would permit.

"What?"

"How the hell do you think I got in this mess? I was attacked, damn it, I was beaten up! One of your blasted loonies must have escaped!"

"The ambulance will be here in a few minutes," the landlord panted, returning from the phone.

"Better get the police as well," said a sour-faced man from Paul's left. "There's an escaped lunatic about."

—Enter rumour, painted full of . . .

"Nonsense!" Paul snapped. "I came from the hospital directly I finished work. Certainly none of our patients is missing!"

"Ah, but you'd say that anyhow, wouldn't you?" the sour man grunted. "Besides which you've been in here two hours. Saw you come in. That's plenty of time for a bloodthirsty maniac to break out." He rounded the words with a horrid relish, and Paul's patience ended.

"You married? Got a family to look after you when you get old?"

—Safe ground. Happy family men don't spend whole evenings in dreary pubs like this one.

"What's it to you?" the man countered belligerently.

"Only that most of my patients aren't maniacs—just lonely old people who don't want to get out because nobody on the outside ever treated them better than they get treated inside. Understood? Now shut up and let me find out the truth behind all this!"

—I should be ashamed. But people like him make me sick.

Working on the layers of cloth, coat, jacket, shirt, slashing each and laying bare the broken arm, he questioned the hurt man and received answers punctuated with gasps.

"I was driving back towards Blickham—go easy there, damn it! Name's Faberdown. I'm a rep, see? Fertilisers and cattle cake. Firm transferred me here last month and I don't know my way about very well yet—Christ, I said go easy!

Got behind schedule taking a wrong turning. And when I came to those woods up there, half a mile back, I had to stop and get out, follow me? It was dark, nobody to take offence. And while I was stretching my legs a bit . . ."

He broke off, not from a pang of pain this time.

—Curious.

Paul was lightly palpating the injured arm. As far as he could tell it was a perfectly clean break and ought to heal without complications, but it needed splinting before he was put in an ambulance. Separating the three sleeves from the rest of the garments at the shoulder, he prompted: "Yes, what happened?"

The man swallowed hard. "Someone rushed towards me. Just went for me, like that. I didn't do anything, didn't say anything, *no* reason. Clawed my face like you see, punched me in the eye, and when I tried to fight back picked me up the way you see on telly and chucked me at a tree!"

The bystanders were hanging on every word.

—Lapping it up, aren't they? If they saw the sort of things I see every day of my life . . .

Paul stifled that reaction. He looked Faberdown over, trying to sum him up. Thirties, a bit of a phony—Irish thornproof suit for the "country gentleman" air, a not-quite-genuine old school tie in case the gentleman bit needed reinforcement. Running to fat. A load for anyone short of a professional wrestler to "chuck" at a tree.

"Would you recognise your attacker again?"

"It was all over so quickly . . ." Once more the salesman swallowed convulsively. Then the reason for his previous hesitation emerged with the reluctant admission: "About all I could tell was that it was a woman."

"A woman? Did *this?*"

"I couldn't be bloody well mistaken, could I? Not when she didn't have a stitch of clothes on her!"

—Oh my God. Tomorrow's headline: Naked Woman Maniac at Large.

The door of the bar opened. "Ambulance!" said a cheerful man in a peaked cap.

"Over here," Paul called, and added with a surge of gratitude, "You made damned good time getting here."

While they were loading the salesman on his stretcher—he wanted to object, but by now shock had so weakened him he complied even as he was insisting he didn't need to be carried —the first of the later wave of customers came in and the story had to be recounted to them, and then again for the next arrivals. Paul drew aside wearily, lit a cigarette and ignored the babble as he tried to decide whether there might be a grain of truth in Faberdown's assumption.

—Have we any violent females?

Like it or not, the answer was yes, though a person as badly disturbed as the victim's description, wandering naked through the woods on a wet February night and assaulting innocent strangers, would logically be in one of the horsebox-like isolation cells behind steel bars and three locked doors.

—Lieberman?

It was unlikely. But another homemade key had been found under his pillow this morning, and the locksmith made no secret of his ambition to pick every lock in the hospital.

—It could be, I suppose. . . .

It was not, however, logical reasoning which decided him on action. It was the chance that brought Mrs Weddenhall into the pub.

He knew her only slightly, but she wasn't easily forgotten once she'd been identified. A masculine woman of fifty, tonight wearing a trench-coat over her invariable tweed suit, woollen stockings and brogue shoes, she supplemented private means by breeding dogs at a kennels just outside Yemble, but regrettably that didn't occupy her time so fully she couldn't spare some to interfere in other people's lives. She was a justice of the peace and at the last election had stood for the local council; the electorate had shown sufficient sense to frustrate her.

She came briskly in, demanded in her booming baritone what the blazes was going on, was told, and nodded vigorously. Armed with the bare bones of third-hand information, she approached Paul and addressed him in the patronising tone appropriate to a mere grammar-school product of only twenty-eight.

"I hear one of your . . . ah . . . charges has gone over the hill. If you can tell me exactly where she attacked this unfortunate chap, I'll bring a couple of my hounds along. Soon root her out of cover, I can promise you."

Paul looked at her, not believing his ears. He saw the incipient dewlaps along her jaw, the bulky chest which it was impossible to visualise as bearing feminine breasts, the straight legs four-square planted on the floor in their armour of laced shoes.

"Are you honestly suggesting hunting her? With dogs?"

"Damn' sight quicker than traipsing through the woods around here on foot! Ask anyone who's been fool enough to volunteer as beater for a shoot!"

"Did you see the injured man?" Paul inquired sweetly.

"The ambulance drove off just as I arrived."

"Quite a big man," Paul said. "The woman who went for him must have been powerfully built. Brawny. Muscular."

"All the more reason for doing as I suggest!"

"In short," Paul concluded, ignoring the comment, "I picture her as being rather like you."

He didn't stay to see the effect of the words.

His hand shook as he pushed the key into the lock of his car. The wind had dropped, but that hadn't made the air any warmer—only ensured that the drizzle would stay in this vicinity instead of moving on.

—That woman! I'd like to do to her what Mirza suggested doing to Holinshed!

He let the car roll to the edge of the pub's carpark. There he paused, struck by a minor problem. Faberdown was a stranger hereabouts, on his own admission; he'd said no more than "woods half a mile away." And the pub was sited at a crossroads.

—Must be the Cornminster road. Coming into Yemble by any other route, he'd have passed a house with a phone long before he reached the Needle in Haystack. In which case . . .

The woods Faberdown meant must be a neglected copse which he passed daily going to and from the hospital, with a gateway adjacent into which a car could conveniently be run while the driver relieved himself. It was part of the grounds of what had once been a fine private house, burned to the foundations in the depression years and never rebuilt. Speculation was still rife locally as to whether the owner had fired it to collect the insurance money.

—I wonder if the attack was really unprovoked!

The idea sprang from nowhere, but seemed like such a dazzling access of insight he was about to drive in the direction of Cornminster without further ado, convinced he would find some harmless imbecile wandering in search of kindly treatment. That was ridiculous. The salesman's arm had really been broken and his eye had been blacked with a heavyweight punch.

He swung the wheel the other way, towards the hospital.

—Thank goodness Iris left me the car. Otherwise long

horrible walks in rain like this, endless standing at bus-stops with the feet squelching . . .

She would have been entitled to take it, of course. It had been bought with her money, not his.

He swung past the big black-and-white sign identifying "Chent Hospital for Nervous Disorders"; the gatekeeper peered out with a startled expression meaning what's Dr Fidler doing coming back at this time of night.

The building itself loomed sinister with its mock battlements. Relic of a Victorian miser's dreams of grandeur, it was about as unsuitable for use as an asylum as any in Britain, half make-believe castle, half ill-conceived afterthoughts such as the high-security Disturbed wing in red brick and the inevitable tall chimney crowned with its spiky lightning conductor.

But it had been left for a mental hospital by heirs grateful that the owner had finally been certified insane after making their lives hell well into his eighties, and with the shortage of facilities one had to be satisfied with what one could get.

—Though the impact of it on a patient arriving for the first time must be disastrous! Imagine being delivered here in a state of acute anxiety, for instance, and seeing those turrets and crenellations, and then hearing that iron-studded oaken door go thud behind you! Christ, the effect on the staff is bad enough!

He braked the car with a grinding of gravel and marched up to the forbidding entrance. It was locked after six, but a key for it was among the many which constituted his burden of office. In the hall he found himself face to face with Natalie.

"Paul! What are you doing here? Never mind, I'm glad to see you."

Blank, he stared at her. "You won't be when I tell you why I've come."

"This alleged escaped lunatic?"

"*Is* it one of our patients? I didn't think it could possibly—"

She made an impatient gesture. "Of course not! I've been double-checking because the police insisted, but everybody's safe and sound."

"That's how you heard about it—from the police?"

"They rang up about ten minutes ago. I must say I didn't get a very clear idea of what's supposed to have happened. Something about a man in a car being attacked by a naked madwoman, as far as I could make out. Is that right?"

Paul let his shoulders sag. "Yes, I'm afraid it's true. He came staggering into the Needle with a broken arm."

"Then we can look forward to a month or two of the leper treatment from our neighbors, I suppose," Natalie commented without humour. "Did you only come back to make sure it wasn't somebody from here?"

"That's right. And since it isn't, I suppose I'd better go down to the woods where it happened so that somebody's on hand to stop Mrs Weddenhall turning loose her hounds."

◆ 5 ◆

—I'm sure Natalie thought I was joking about Mrs Weddenhall. I only wish I was.

He clicked his lights up to full beam and accelerated down the winding Cornminster road. The village stopped dead at this point, though on the other roads leading from the junction it straggled a few hundred yards further. In seconds a curve had taken him out of sight of human habitation and he was driving between steep black banks crowned with wet thorny hedges.

—Abstract of insanity: aloneness in a private world. Oh, there is some excuse for a reaction like Mrs Weddenhall's. A cripple can still be a person, but in what sense is a lunatic human? Humanity's in the mind, in the tangle of thoughts spun by the brain, and once that's gone what remains is human only in outward shape. But sometimes one can win back what's been lost. You can't create a person, only let him grow, but you can occasionally, with care and planning and foresight, help shattered fragments bind together, whole.

He felt the car's rear wheels slide on mud and slowed down; better to get there in one piece than not at all.

—All the king's horses and all the king's men . . . They put me back together. I owe them that.

The doom/the dome of the black night leaned on his skull with a crushing weight. For an instant he had, with terrifying vividness, the old familiar illusion: that when he ended this interval alone and once again came on his fellow men, they would stare at him strangely and speak incomprehensible new tongues.

—I built myself a blank black trap like this empty road. I should have had the sense to tell Iris the truth even if it meant her not marrying me. They don't talk about it in my family because it's a shameful thing, and I banked on their silence. By shifts and devious expedients I eluded the admission and uttered those diversionary half-truths: psychiatry is the coming thing, that's the field where the great new discoveries will be made from now on, this is the right branch of medicine for an ambitious newcomer to select. . . . And the worst sophistry of all: passing off my analysis with that ready phrase "Physician heal thyself." What good are clichés in ordering your life? Stick to the stale and sooner or later you wear down into the standard mould. Goodbye individual, hello matchstick man!

He braked abruptly. There was his goal, and he hadn't been joking about Mrs Weddenhall.

In the glare of his lights stood three vehicles, partly blocking the road. Under branches dripping rainwater, a Ford Anglia station wagon, which must be Faberdown's, a police Wolseley with its blue light shining, and Mrs Weddenhall's elderly Bentley with its wired rear compartment used for transporting dogs.

He pulled as far on the verge of the road as he dared, cut his engine, and at once heard a low bark: the sound between a cough and a roar which he'd noticed many times as he drove around Yemble. He jumped out.

And there she was, standing with her dogs on short leashes—two wolf-hounds, rangy, rough-coated, excited at being brought out into the country at night. She was talking to a police constable in a waterproof cape, and Paul caught the tail of her latest statement as he approached.

"But we can't have maniacs terrorising people in the isolated farms between here and Cornminster!"

—Christ, she must be eager to have dashed home and fetched the dogs so quickly!

"Officer!" he called. "What's going on?"

A little relieved at the interruption, the policeman turned. "I shouldn't hang around here, sir," he warned. "We've had a report about—"

"I know all that, thanks. My name's Fidler, Dr Fidler. I'm a psychiatrist from Chent Hospital."

The policeman grunted. "Not one of your patients on the loose, is it?"

"No, of course not. I checked at the hospital to make sure. What are you proposing to do?"

"Well, we're going to search the area, sir. I've sent for extra men and a dog-handling team." A sidelong glance at Mrs Weddenhall. "As I've been trying to explain to this lady here, though it's kind of her to offer assistance we prefer to rely on our own experts."

"And where are they?" Mrs Weddenhall rasped. "Anyhow, like it or not you're going to have as much help as you can use. I told my kennel boy to ring around the neighbourhood and turn out everyone he could reach. With guns." She set her chin aggressively.

—I'm dreaming. I must be dreaming.

Paul swayed a little, very conscious of having drunk a lot of beer and whisky without stopping for his evening meal.

"We can't allow that, and that's definite," the policeman said. "I don't know who you think you are, madam, but this is our business, not yours."

"For your information, young man, I'm Barbara Weddenhall, JP, and if you ever turn up to give evidence in my court I shall remember your face, I can promise you that!"

The policeman blanched and recoiled. Abruptly Paul was furious. "Mrs Weddenhall!" he said loudly.

"Yes?"

"Have you ever had any experience of rape?"

"What?" The horrified bellow was all she could utter; following it, her voice gave out and she simply stood with eyes bulging.

"You ever seen a rapist, officer?" Paul continued, turning to the policeman.

"Well ... Yes, sir. I helped to arrest one a few months ago."

"Was he marked at all?"

"Not half as bad as the poor girl he'd attacked. But ... yes, that was what clinched the evidence. He was all scratched on the face where she'd tried to drive him away."

—Am I doing that poor devil Faberdown an injustice? I hope not.

"Mrs Weddenhall didn't see the victim of this alleged madwoman. I did. And he had three scratches down his cheek exactly where the nails of a girl's right hand would have put them. See my point?"

The policeman rounded his mouth and nodded.

"It's by no means certain the attack was unprovoked. Think it over. There's another condition besides insanity where a woman—or a man, come to that—can display extraordinary strength like what you'd need to pick up a grown man and throw him at a tree, as the victim put it. And that state is mindless terror."

"You think he went for her first, maybe?"

"*Maybe*. That's the important word. You're going to look pretty stupid if you go out with dogs and guns and what you finally come up with is some hysterical teenager."

—Exactly what an innocent teenager would be doing walking nude around here in February, I won't try and guess, but it ought at least to make Mrs Weddenhall reconsider.

There was the noise of another car approaching, and the policeman cheered up noticeably.

"That'll be Inspector Hofford, I expect," he said, and excused himself.

Hofford proved to be a matter-of-fact countryman in a tweed coat, chewing a briar pipe. He heard the constable's account of events up till now, had a short talk with Mrs Weddenhall which Paul didn't overhear but which climaxed in her ill-tempered return of both dogs to her car, and then addressed Paul.

"I gather you don't think the victim was entirely truthful!"

"I'm simply reserving judgment," Paul answered.

"I'll join you in that. Now let me ask you to look over the scene with me. I'm always glad of assistance from an expert, though there are other kinds not so welcome." He jerked his head meaningly in the direction of the Bently. "Got a torch by any chance?" he added. "It's pretty dark in this wood."

"I keep one in my car. Just a second."

He fetched it under the stony gaze of Mrs Weddenhall and rejoined Hofford, who had gone to the gateway beside the copse and was flashing his own torch across the grass beyond.

"Now as I understand it he pulled up to answer a call of nature. He wouldn't have wanted to climb this gate, would he? It's soaking wet and there's moss on the top bar here. Let's see . . ."

The beam of light swung to play along the rusty wire fence enclosing the trees, stopping on a broken post which dragged the upper wire low enough for a man to step over.

"That way, I think," he murmured, and swung his leg across.

Paul was impressed with the accuracy of the guess. Not more than five yards further on, they found a patch where the undergrowth—mainly bramble—had been violently disturbed. His torch showed something round and brown snagged on a thorn, and he bent to pick it up. A tweed cap. He showed it to Hofford.

"Belongs to the victim, I suppose," the inspector commented. "Thank you." He turned it around in his hand and went on, "No blood or anything on it—just rain. Well, some professional advice from you, please, Doctor! Would the woman have stayed nearby or taken to her heels?"

"It's impossible to say. If she was sane and the man did attack her, she'd have run off, but she might not have reached a house before collapsing from shock. It's a pretty exhausting experience, being assaulted by a stranger. Alternatively if she is insane she might be miles away or equally she might be strolling unconcerned across the next field."

"Damnably complicated, aren't we—we human beings?" Hofford turned back towards the road. "Well, I'd better start a check at the houses nearby, make sure nobody has had a weeping girl arrive on the doorstep. And after that I'm afraid we'll just have to comb the area. Filthy night she picked to bring us out on!"

Paul didn't accompany him back to the cars. The running-water noise of the rain on the trees had brought the pressure due to his earlier drinking to an urgent climax, and he seized the chance to slip away out of sight and attend to that minor problem before it began to interfere with his concentration. He picked his way awkwardly to the middle of the copse, brambles tugging at and releasing his legs on every step, and stood shivering a little against a dying tree.

—Mirza and his horror film ... Ought to be here now: *The Hound of the Weddenhalls!*

He had snapped off his torch to conserve the battery, and without it the dank misery of the drenched woods overwhelmed him. Silence might have been better, and absolute pitch blackness. The sodden murmur of rain was like a complaint of nature against his intrusion; the faint voices which carried to him were just faded enough to escape comprehension, heightening his sensation of being cut off in a solitary private universe, and though a gap between the trees afforded a line of sight toward the cars, he could not see the people there as whole persons; they were mere shadows, and incomplete at that, their passage back and forth, their gestures, every movement, curtailed as their voices were blurred. An arm and hand melted into the clawing twigs of a tree branch; a head into the black sky.

—A prisoner in Plato's cave, watching the shadows of the greater world. In another minute, back on the road: who are you, what are you doing here? Inspector Hofford, I'm Dr Fidler and you were talking to me a moment ago! My name isn't Hofford and your name isn't Fidler and this world is a trick and a lie, a vault of illusion and the time for deceit is over....

Shuddering, he turned to retrace his path, hurrying a little because that momentary vision seemed so much of a piece with his surroundings.

"Tiriak-no?"

The voice struck out of nowhere, uttering that single incomprehensible word on a rising, questioning note. Paul gasped and whirled, his torch beam slashing across tree trunks flick-flick and halting. To be spoken to here, and in an unfamiliar language, was a foretaste that his vision would come true.

Then he saw her, uncertainly shading her eyes against the light, and brief terror was swept aside by disbelief.

—She can't be the one! Damn it, she's so tiny! Like a doll!

And yet there couldn't very well be *two* women walking this wood without clothes.

She stood in the beam of the torch, a pallid, somehow pathetic figure. The world paused long enough for Paul to study her and compile an almost clinically thorough description of her in his mind.

—Feet and half her calves out of sight in the undergrowth but the rest perfectly proportioned, so ... Not over five feet at the tallest. Age? Twenties, just possibly eighteen/nineteen but I think older. Take that hand away let me see your face—ah. Black hair cropped very short. Sharp face: sharp nose, chin. Big eyes. Never seen a facial structure quite comparable. Must be white European, but she has the epicanthic fold. Chinese somewhere, generations back? *I've* no idea how long it keeps recurring after the initial incrossing. Small breasts, nipples practically unpigmented, navel not re-entrant so no fat on the belly, all muscle, narrow hips, legs scratched all to hell with thorns and a patch of mud on the thigh as if she's been pushed over and sat on wet ground. . . .

She was still just standing, poised either to flee or to defend herself.

—If you're really the girl who beat up Faberdown, you're a wildcat. You can't possibly weigh more than eighty pounds. And I said: must be like Mrs Weddenhall.

The absurdity of the idea made Paul want to laugh, but memory of the salesman's injuries sobered him. He was by himself with a girl who had probably broken a man's arm with bare hands, and he was going to have to be very tactful indeed. He cast around for something to say and decided on a phrase which promised maximum reassurance.

"Hullo. I'm a doctor. I've come to look for you."

She raised both arms, fists clenched, not menacingly but with an expression of dismay. After a pause she responded, but his tense ear could not identify the words.

"English!" he said slowly and clearly. "Do you speak English?"

Her head lifted in a quick gesture he recognised from seeing Cypriot nurses do it at the hospital: a Balkan negative equivalent to a headshake.

—Deadlock.

He realised suddenly he was shivering. And if he was chilled, how about her? He hesitated, weighing the facts: the salesman's arm against the way she had shown herself when he might have walked past without noticing her.

—Watch it. Don't let superficial helplessness persuade you because you don't like men in imitation old school ties.

Nonetheless, if he didn't act quickly Hofford would have filled the wood with noisy men and that lingering terror on her face would spur her to flight. He unbuttoned his coat carefully, one-handed.

"Here, put this around you," he said, trying to make the tone convey what the words could not.

—That headshake. Greek, perhaps? I don't know what Greek sounds like. But what in hell is she *doing* here?

Cautiously she accepted the coat. Her eyes never wandered from him; she slipped the garment on purely by touch.

—In case I go for her while she's hindered from striking back? What did Faberdown do to her?

The coat came to her ankles and was impossible to button closely. She tugged the belt as tight as she could, drew a deep breath, and seemed to pluck up the courage to abandon her watchful suspicion. Favouring her right foot, she came up to him with her hand outstretched. He took the small cold fingers in his and led her towards the road.

"Inspector!" he called. "I've got her!"

She tensed at the cry but didn't try to hang back. At the low point of the wire Hofford and one of the constables appeared, silhouetted in the light of Wolseley's headlamps. A torch stabbed towards them.

"That's her?" Hofford exclaimed. "Why, she's only a child!"

Beyond the two men, Paul noticed with satisfaction, Mrs Weddenhall was venturing to take a closer look.

—So much for bloodthirsty maniacs to be hunted with dogs and guns. But I bet you won't learn anything from this.

Hampered by the coat, she negotiated the fence, accepting aid from Hofford, and Paul saw the reason for her limp: a cut just behind her right little toe, no longer bleeding but obviously tender.

"More than a child, I think," Paul told Hofford. "But she's definitely a half-pint. Goodness knows who she is or what she's doing here, though. She seems to be a foreigner—doesn't appear to understand English."

Hofford blinked. "Are you sure? Couldn't she just be . . . ah . . . 'mute of malice,' as the phrase goes?"

"That's just it. She's not mute. I'd never have noticed her if she hadn't spoken to me."

A semicircle of frowning faces focused on the girl. She had detached her hand from Paul's and was peering at the things close to her, especially at the cars. Now she raised her eyes to Paul as though asking silent permission, and went to the nearest, the police Wolseley. The driver, reporting her discovery over his radio, watched her nervously.

She touched the door of the car as if she had never seen anything like it, walked to the rear and first examined, then touched, the maker's insignia.

"Don't think she's going to break and run, do you?" Hofford whispered to Paul.

"I doubt it. But I can't figure out what she's up to!"

The girl turned from the police car to look at the Bentley. Two eager dogs returned her gaze. One of them barked and clawed at the car's window.

She covered her face with both hands and began to cry.

She parted her fingers to find out who it was when Paul comfortingly put his arm around her, recognised him and allowed herself to be led back to where the others were standing. Her weeping consisted in small dry sobs; he felt their pulselike tremor come and go.

"Well, the question is now," Hofford said, "what's to be done with her? Your hospital strikes me as the best bet, Doctor, because even if you're right and the man she——" He checked, aware that a phrase like "beat up" sounded absurd applied to a man nearly a foot taller than this slip of a girl and practically twice her weight. "What I mean is, she must be a trifle odd walking around in the altogether!"

Paul nodded. "Can you take her down in your car? I'll follow in my own. And perhaps you could radio in and ask your headquarters to warn the duty doctor that she's coming."

"Yes, of course. Okay, come along, my girl!"

But though she didn't struggle, she flinched away from Hofford's encouraging hand and shrank back closer to Paul.

"Taken a fancy to you," the inspector commented. "Must be the bedside manner, or whatever you call it in your line of business."

"I suppose I could take her in my car," Paul suggested doubtfully. "It's only a two-seater, but——"

"I'd rather you didn't," Hofford interrupted. "She can obviously be a handful, no matter how harmless she seems at the moment. Constable Edwards over there is a class A driver; suppose he brings your car in and you ride with us?"

There was a brief disturbance caused by the angry departure of Mrs Weddenhall, the Bentley's engine roaring and both dogs barking frantically. Hofford sighed.

"That's a relief! You know, for a moment I thought I was going to have to arrest a justice of the peace for obstructing me in the execution of my duty. . . . Right, let's get going."

Having to urge her on at every step, they persuaded the girl towards Hofford's car.

"You'd think she'd never seen a car before, wouldn't you?" he muttered to Paul as he opened the rear door. "Get in first, please—it may reassure her."

Paul slid across the back seat and extended a hand to the girl. Taking it like a shipwrecked passenger clutching a life-belt, she crept in beside him.

—Like a wild animal being lured into a cage, terrified beyond reason but equally afraid to fight back against enemies it doesn't understand. I hope it's not a symptom of claustrophobia; she's bound to have to go into a security cell until she's been properly examined.

She gasped when the engine started. Then, paradoxically, she craned forward to watch the driver's movements at the controls as he engaged reverse and swung the car to face the other way. She followed every action, fascinated.

Paul glanced at Hofford and read on the inspector's face puzzlement as great as his own.

—What's the good of guessing? We'll find out soon enough. People don't just drop out of nowhere into a strange country, without clothes, without a word of the language. A girl like this, tiny and lovely: someone's bound to have noticed her and will remember.

Facile jargon seeped up in his mind.

—Hysteria, perhaps. The effect of attempted rape on sensitive personalities is . . . But there were no clothes to be seen bar that tweed cap, and with his arm broken Faberdown couldn't have got rid of them. . . . Oh, stop it. As Hofford said, people are damnably complicated and it's ridiculous to expect solutions with a snap of the fingers.

At least she seemed to have relaxed a bit. She was gazing first out of one window, then another, as though desperate not to miss anything the car went past. He caught her attention and tapped his chest with his free hand.

"Paul!" he said.

"Pol," she echoed docilely. The vowel was wrong, but then the sounds she had uttered earlier had been wholly alien to English. He turned his hand and pointed at her.

"Arrzheen," she said.

"Did she say 'urchin?' " Hofford chuckled. "That's appropriate enough. I thought 'gamin' myself when I first saw her."

—All right. "Urchin." It does fit.

Paul smiled, and after a short pause she tried to smile back, but the expression wouldn't come.

"Evening, Doc! What have you got for us?"

The speaker emerged from the porter's office: deputy charge nurse Oliphant wearing his forehead scar like a campaign medal, relic of a pub fight in which a drunk broke a bottle on his head. He was given to letting people assume that one of the patients had done it. Paul disliked him for that.

—But it's my own sin: "letting people assume." Maybe that accounts for my strong reaction against it in others.

"An emergency admission, I suppose," he answered wearily. "Where's Dr Rudge?"

"Coming, Paul!" Natalie hurried down the last few steps of the staircase leading to the staff quarters. "Just went to see if Phil had come back, but you'll do just as well."

She saw the girl for the first time, and stopped dead.

"Her?"

"Apparently. Oh—this is Inspector Hofford. Dr Rudge, Inspector . . . Where do you want her put, Natalie?"

"I told Nurse Kirk to get a cell ready in Disturbed Three because I was expecting some hefty Amazon running amok." Natalie hesitated. "Well, let's examine her in the duty office and make up our minds after that. Oliphant, ring Nurse Kirk, will you, and ask her to join us right away?"

Constable Edwards appeared in the doorway, jingling the keys of Paul's car. He took them with a word of thanks, his full attention on the girl's reaction to her surroundings. As she had done in the car, she was studying everything with an expression that mingled fascination with horror.

—Why should she find ordinary things so peculiar? Is she high on a psychedelic, maybe? Oh, stop trying to *guess!*

"Come along, dear," Natalie said. The girl gave a blank stare.

"I should have told you," Paul said. "She doesn't seem to understand English."

"Hysterical aphasia?"

"No, she spoke to me. But it was in a foreign language."

"Hasn't she even told you her name?"

"It's Arrzheen," Paul said, framing the unfamiliar sounds with care. The girl responded instantly.

"Urchin," Hofford muttered in the background, still pleased with his own joke.

"Well, she's taken to you okay," Natalie said tartly. "You'd better come along and keep her quiet. Do you mind, or do you want to dash off?"

"No. . . . No, I've nothing else to do. Inspector, do you want to hang around, or would you like me to phone you and tell you if we've learned any more about her?"

"Yes, ring me up, please," Hofford said. "I might have something to tell you, too; I sent a man to Blickham General to interview the salesman, and he should be reporting in pretty soon—What on earth is that on your hand, Doctor?"

Paul turned his palm up numbly. Where the girl had been grasping his hand so tightly in the car, a smear of almost dry blood. He took hers and examined it. Yes: under three of the nails, traces of more.

"That clinches it," Hofford said with satisfaction. "Thank you, Doctor . . . Dr Rudge . . . good night!"

"How do you spell this name of hers?" Nurse Kirk demanded, looking up from the table at which she was completing the admission record. She was a wiry Scotswoman of definite lesbian tendencies and extreme Calvinist morality; Paul had sometimes wondered why she didn't shatter to bits like an overwound clock-spring. And she added, seeing the girl laid out naked on the examination couch, "Scrawny little thing, isn't she?"

—No, actually she's built perfectly for her height.

But that response rather shocked Paul. Mirza would no doubt already have made half a dozen obscene cracks and reduced old Kirk to a state of hysteria herself, but Mirza lacked the English reluctance to admit the existence of sex.

"Put down a case name," he said tiredly. "No, I have a better idea. Put down 'Urchin.' The police inspector suggested it."

Nurse Kirk frowned at the levity of it all, but did as she was told. Natalie, engaged in reading the thermometer which she had eventually persuaded the girl to keep under her tongue, glanced up and grimaced at Paul. He relaxed a little.

—There are human beings in this world, not an endless string of Mrs Weddenhalls.

"Temperature barely subnormal," Natalie said. "She's not significantly shocked, is she? You noticed, I'm sure."

"Of course, or I wouldn't have let her ride here in the car." Paul hesitated. "I mean, she's not shocked in the ordinary sense—circulation's normal at the extremities as far as I can judge, and I managed to count her pulse while she was holding my hand in the car, and that seemed okay too. But she's not a well person, is she? Have you done the blood-pressure yet, by the way?"

"Next on the list." Natalie shook down the thermometer. "Why don't you attend to it while I get on with the rest? She'll probably take the . . . ah . . . intimate details better from me than from a man."

Paul complied listlessly, unfolding the bandage of the sphygmomanometer while Natalie drew on a rubber glove and proceeded to palpate the girl's abdomen.

"I'm damned," she said after a few moments. "She doesn't like it at all. Look at her, squirming away from my hand. You try!" She stripped her glove off with a snapping sound.

Unwillingly Paul proceeded with what was necessary, and the girl objected less to his attentions than she had done to Natalie's, lying still with her almond eyes fixed on his profile.

—Nothing about this makes sense. If Faberdown did assault her, and it was traumatic, you wouldn't expect her to prefer a man poking about like this. . . .

"Any traces?" Natalie inquired.

"Hm? Oh—no, he didn't get at her. Nothing worse than this mud on her bottom. No bruising, either. Soft ground. Did you—? Oh yes. I didn't notice you dressing her foot."

"You're only half here, Paul," Natalie said. "It's unfair to dump this on you after last night."

"I don't mind. If I went home I'd only lie awake puzzling about her."

"As you like. Oh—*intacta,* by the way?"

"No. But for a long time, and quite normal."

"What Mirza would call well reamed," Natalie commented caustically, and Nurse Kirk scowled.

So to completion: reflexes checked, eyes and ears inspected, scratches washed, mud rinsed away. . . . Finish. They sat her up and clad her in a cotton nightgown, heirloom of who could guess how many previous wearers, and a towelling robe with CHENT HOSPITAL stitched around the hem, which was at least snug. They put a chair beside the couch and she moved to it apathetically.

"A cup of tea," Natalie said briskly. "And . . . Nurse!"

"Yes?"

"Bring the sugar *and* the milk separately."

—Neat. I should have thought of it.

"Are you any the wiser after all this?" Paul said aloud.

"Not a sausage." Natalie took out a packet of cigarettes and gave him one. Watching as they lit up, the girl suddenly giggled.

—Breakthrough! But it only makes the mystery murkier. There *is* something comic about people sucking smoke from a white stick. Only . . . Like the cars, isn't it?

"Did you turn up anything on the physical?" he asked.

"If she were up for a life assurance policy I'd offer her optimum terms. She's downright bloody *fit*. Feel that biceps muscle? I did, when I was putting the sphyg on. Hard as a boxer's. Whatever's fouled her up mentally, it hasn't affected her physique."

"I suppose she *is* fouled up." Paul hadn't meant to speak the thought, but it leaked out past defences lowered by exhaustion.

"You're joking, of course. Granted, her lack of goosebumps indicates she doesn't mind walking around starkers in winter. But most people simply don't behave that way." Natalie cocked her head, listening to footsteps outside. "Ah, here comes our tea."

The girl accepted her cup and saucer—from sheer professional obstinacy, Nurse Kirk had brought one cup without a saucer "for the patient," but Paul left it on the tray—but seemed at a loss what to do with it. She waited for the others to set an example.

Paul offered her sugar. She hesitated. Then she licked the tip of a finger and dipped into the white mound, withdrawing just enough to taste.

—Not so crazy, that, on the assumption that she literally doesn't know what we're giving her. But *that's* crazy.

He showed her what the sugar was for, spooning some into his own cup, and added milk from the bottle the nurse had brought.

—Why the hell didn't the kitchen send up a jug? Kitchen? No, of course not. Not at this time of night. Christ, it's past ten o'clock.

And on the realisation, heard the familiar gurgle of the

plumbing as it coped with the staff-supervised evacuations of the patients preliminary to their bedding down.

—What else doesn't she know about? Toilets, maybe?

Tea, excessively spiked with milk, sweetened, she sipped and eventually drank down. They all three watched her intently. Abruptly Paul realised they were doing something he normally objected to in principle: treating a patient as a thing instead of a person.

—Simply because I can't talk to her. Hmmm . . .

He turned to Natalie with an exclamation. "Chuck over a notepad and a pencil, will you? Let's try and get her to write something down."

—Is she going to have to have this explained too? No, thank goodness.

With something approaching briskness, the girl set aside her empty cup and took the pencil and paper. She examined the point of the former and made a tentative mark with it as if to be sure that was the way it worked, then wrote quickly. Paul noted that she was right-handed but preferred the rare, though not remarkable, grip between index and middle fingers.

She showed him the result, saying at the same time, "Arrzheen!"

He found confronting him four symbols like a child's incomplete sketch for two Christmas trees, a fishhook and an inverted spear.

All the way home Paul kept shivering, although the car's heater was switched on full.

—The way hope seemed to leak out of the girl's face when she realised I didn't understand what she'd written down. My imaginary terrors have come to life in her; she's stranded in a world where nobody can speak to her and nobody knows who she is!

—The curious greedy "ah-hah, they're locking you up too"

expressions of the patients as we took her through the dormitory to her cell. Maybe I should have experienced that instead of being protected and isolated. But it would probably have broken me into little bits.

—She can't be under any illusions about where she's wound up. Things may baffle her but people she does appear to understand. Packed in head to foot to head in what were once fine stately rooms but now stark with chipped plaster, faded ugly paint, bars at the windows and locks on the doors.

The keys in his pocket jingled, not audibly but in memory.

—And I told Natalie this afternoon we had eighteen free bed-spaces. Whose word am I taking for that? Every ward so crammed we only have room for a poky little locker too small to hold a kid's toys alongside each bed. Anything too much or too numerous for the locker to hold: taken and shut away. How do people reassure themselves of identity? Belongings, possessions, mementoes: the solid proof that memory doesn't lie. And bit by bit we chip away the mortar of their lives. Christ, how did I ever wander into psychiatry for a living?

The lamp-post standard outside his home appeared around a bend, and he slowed. There was no need to get out in the rain and unfasten the gate; he'd left it open this morning.

—And that's something Iris won't let me do when she's here. Being with Iris has turned into an endless series of having to get out in the rain because an open gate "looks bad." And might let dogs into the garden.

He halted the car and switched it off. As darkness rushed in, so did fatigue, and he sat thinking along the same lines for another few minutes. This car was a Triumph Spitfire, not because Iris hadn't had cash for something more ambitious but because the car she originally chose was four inches too long for the gate to be closed behind it and there was only a narrow verge—no pavement across which it could have been rehung to open outwards. Moreover, fitting a modern gate that folded by sections would mean sacrificing the present one of stout oaken bars which the daily woman warranted to have been made by a joiner in Blickham with such a reputation that antique dealers from London brought him valuable furniture to restore.

—Funny how one thing leads to another. Suppose the man who made our gate when he was an apprentice had dropped dead before becoming famous; no prestige would attach to it and we could throw it away.... I wish to God the events which culminated in Paul Fidler had followed another course.

He ordered himself out of the car, mind buzzing with conflicting visions of the way his life might have turned out: if he'd chosen another career than medicine, if his breakdown had been permanent, if he'd failed to get the job here at Chent.

—Why can I never visualise things turning out better as clearly as I can visualise the catastrophes I scraped past by a hair? "Everything for the best in the best of all possible worlds!" Hah!

Key poised to let himself in, he hesitated and scanned the house's façade by the light of the nearby street-lamp.

—Façade is the right word and no mistake. How pleased I was when Iris fell in love with it and decided a couple of years at Chent wouldn't be as bad as all that. And it's much worse. Behind the façades—the house's and mine—rot, woodworm, death-watch beetle.

He slammed the door and made the windows rattle.

There was nothing very special about the house in this part of England. It was inarguably handsome to look at, with its black-and-white half-timbering. On the inside, though . . .

He'd driven up from London on his own to be interviewed at Chent, and when that was over he was ninety per cent certain he'd got the job. He needed it; his original idea of sticking as close as possible to a London teaching hospital was foundering because—to Iris—progress was dismayingly slow in the fiercely competitive atmosphere of the capital. Yet he knew as soon as he set eyes on Yemble that she'd dislike living there with equal intensity.

On the one hand: being appointed psychiatric registrar at Chent was going to save him a year on the promotion ladder and make up for that other year lost beyond recall, the one Iris had not so far learned about.

—Bloody fool. I really am a bloody fool.

On the other hand: Yemble was being absorbed into the drab town of Blickham, whose single claim to distinction was an Elizabethan town-hall sandwiched between a garage and the public baths. Eight miles away, Cornminster—charming, largely unspoiled, but offering what to a wealthy attractive girl used to London? A twice-weekly change of programme at the Lido Picture Palace and advertisements for the Cornminster Madrigal Fellowship painted in water-colours by the conductor's teenage daughter.

Trying to pluck up the courage to tell Iris that he was go-

ing to take the post at Chent whether she liked it or not, he'd
driven for what seemed like an eternity along each successive
one of the roads leading out of Yemble. Then, the car had
been a second-hand Ford; Iris's father was dead less than a
month and though she was entitled to draw on the money
he'd left her she had felt it somehow in bad taste.

The moment he saw this house, with the estate agent's
board outside offering it for sale, everything fell into place.
At nine that night he parried Iris's anger with a bunch of
flowers and a picture of the house, and next weekend they
drove up to look at it.

He was only marginally guilty about depicting the house as
something exceptional. As he'd discovered during his tour of
the district, Cornminster boasted twenty similar, and even depressing Blickham preserved a few. But he'd banked on her
unfamiliarity with the west country, and the trap closed as
expected.

—Darling, how clever of you! All these magnificent oak
beams! And leaded windows! It's like walking back into history! And it's so cheap!

While he kept silent about the drawbacks of windows that
called for lights to be switched on in daytime and the kitchen
doorway which bumped his head and the chimneys that
poured half the heat of the fire straight up into nowhere.

—The television could go in that recess but we'd have to
get a stand more in keeping with the room like an antique
chest perhaps and we can sit and watch it and listen to the
logs crackling. . . . Darling, you are sure about this job? I
mean, I wouldn't want you to take it just to please me.

Hanging up his clammy coat, Paul snorted at the memory.

—The jargon of status has rubbed off on her, all right. The
word "consultant" has a kind of magic to her ears. How soon
will I be one, how long O Lord how long? Better have something to eat before I turn in or I'll wake in the night and
have to botch up a snack in a daze. Phil Kerans thinks I'm
living out in luxury. He should have to stagger through this
room at three in the morning in pyjamas with the wind howl-
ing down that bloody chimney.

There was nothing to drink but some wine in a recorked
bottle, probably meant for cooking. Iris was a cookery snob
given to paella and soufflés which didn't quite succeed, but
half the time she couldn't be bothered and either opened cans
or suggested going out. On a registrar's salary he preferred
cans.

Carving a doorstep off a brown loaf, pricking sausages, fetching an egg from the refrigerator, he had most of his mind spare to ramble on.

—Deceived by appearances, that's my wife. With me as much as the house. Slam down the money out of Dad's—sorry: *Daddy's* estate, full of plans for a pink matched bathroom suite with shower; then when they ran the pipes and exposed the fabric, the smell of dry rot pungent as smoke. I'd rather she blamed me instead of rowing with the estate agent. Best of all herself: "Surveyor? But this is the *only* possible place for us to live while you're at Chent!"

Despite his forking it, one of the sausages burst and began to ooze obscenely out of its skin.

—Bloody hell, Mirza's right, isn't he?

He went to pour a large glass of the stale wine, hoping the beer and whisky had progressed far enough through his system not to wish a hangover on him from incautious mixing. He paused in the living-room and stared about him, remembering the awful evening when he'd brought the Pakistani home for drinks.

—Where do they acquire that art of making unwelcome visitors feel small without actually insulting them? Bred into them by their nannies. Must be. And afterwards: "Darling, I do appreciate that you have to be on good terms with your colleagues, but surely an immigrant like your friend won't be staying in England? He'll be going back to his own country?" Glossing it: "Steer clear of the wogs and butter up the bosses!"

—Keeps wondering why I don't invite the *medical superintendent* (hushed awe). Because I can't stand the bastard, is all.

He sent the egg to keep the sausages company in the pan.

—That girl tonight with her air of total disorientation ... What in hell do I really know about women? "A marriage like yours is no basis for a proper understanding"—damn Mirza for having more insight than I'll accumulate by ninety. But I do know why Iris married me and I'm lying to myself when I pretend I don't. Bright young medical student just that significant step below her on the social ladder which promised she could dictate the course of his career and see him grateful for it but not beyond hope because witness all those scholarships and ambitious parents aware of their place but pushing their boy from behind: hence, he's used to being pushed. I should have sheered off when she tried to argue me into general practice (Harley Street, a fortune from hypo-chondriacs dazzled by the chauffeured Rolls) instead of countering with persuasive statements about psychiatry the wide-open field and her first introduction to the idea of a CONSULTANT looked up to by hospital staff . . .

The burst sausage had caught on the pan and was burning. Hastily he scooped the food on to a plate and turned off the stove. He checked his next motion and addressed the air.

"God damn it, anyone else I can get away from but myself I have to live with till I die! I did go crazy from overwork af-ter two years' studying medicine and nothing can change that. I did have to waste twelve months drugged up to the eyeballs and staring at the garden and going twice a week to see that halfwitted dyed-in-the-wool Freudian bastard Schroff! And I bloody well ought to have been put in a bin like Chent so I'd remember I'm as fragile as they are!"

Curiously, hearing his own voice took the poison out of the idea. He was quite calm while he was eating his scratch meal, and when he went to bed he dozed off quickly into a deep ex-hausted sleep.

Later, though, he woke moaning from a dreamworld in which, like Alice in the woods, he stood helpless before a roomful of the commonest objects and heard cruel laughter taunting him because he could not remember any of their English names.

"Quite a poppet, this Urchin you brought in last night," Mirza said, crossing Paul's path in the entrance hall of the hospital.

"What?" For a moment Paul, preoccupied didn't get the reference; then he said, bantering to cover the effects of his disturbed night, "Oh! I might have known *you'd* want to size her up."

"Natalie told me about her during breakfast," Mirza said,

unruffled. "I thought I should look her over before this dump wipes out what vestige of animation she may have."

"What's happened to your insurance against breach of ethics?"

"It's wholly adequate, thank you. But patients are people and so are doctors—with some few possible exceptions," he concluded softly, eyes refocusing over Paul's shoulder. "Morning, Dr. Holinshed!"

"Morning," the medical superintendent said curtly. "Oh, Fidler! Come in for a word, will you?" He brushed past into his office, leaving the door wide on the assumption that Paul was instantly at his heels.

"Expecting trouble today?" Mirza inquired.

"I am now," Paul muttered, and moved towards the door.

Holinshed was a lean Yorkshireman of middle height, with hair the colour of tobacco juice receding all around his pate. Mirza's favourite allegation about him was that he had had to be forced into administration because an hour closeted with him reduced most patients to tears.

"Close the door, please, Fidler," he said now. "I have no wish that anyone but ourselves should hear what I have to say. Sit down." An abridged gesture towards the padded Victorian dining-chair placed for visitors in front of the ornate leather-topped desk.

—No doubt this room impresses outsiders: antique furniture, mock-Chippendale bookcases stuffed with textbooks, photographs of Freud, Ernest Jones, Krafft-Ebing. . . . But I think his mind is like the room, furnished with antiques.

"I had a telephone call yesterday evening, voicing rather a serious complaint about your conduct," Holinshed went on. "I don't imagine I need identify its source?"

—Oh.

But Paul was in control of himself this morning in spite of everything. He said, "What sort of complaint, sir?"

"Are you now aware of having grossly offended a distinguished local resident last evening?"

"Not that I noticed," Paul said, straight-faced.

"Then either you're singularly insensitive or I've been given a false account of what you said. The latter I find hard to credit." Holinshed leaned back, fingertips together. "Mrs Barbara Weddenhall rang me up at home to say that you'd insulted her in public and furthermore that you were drunk at the time. Any comments?"

"Well, the second point isn't true at all. And I must add, sir, that I'd hoped you knew me better than to believe it."

—Good shot. Holinshed prides himself on "how well I know my staff."

"As to the so-called 'insults': did she tell you what they were?"

Holinshed hesitated. "Actually," he admitted, "Mrs Weddenhall described them as unrepeatable."

"I think 'nonexistent' would be more precise," Paul murmured. "Have you looked over the emergency admission report from last night yet?"

"Of course not! You saw me arrive just now."

"Did Mrs Weddenhall happen to mention an offer of help which she made to Inspector Hofford of the county police?"

"I was just about to come to that. I had to reassure her that if one of our patients had escaped I would certainly have been notified. But there was, was there not, some violently disturbed person who attacked a passer-by?"

"I can hardly imagine that *you*, sir, would approve of hunting down a mentally deranged person with guns and wolfhounds! Inspector Hofford was as horrified as I was, and if I did speak sharply to Mrs Weddenhall I know I was expressing views which he and probably yourself would agree with. The alleged maniac, by the way, proved to be a girl five feet tall and weighing seventy-nine pounds who came away with me without the least resistance."

—I think I'm getting the measure of my boss: plenty of "sir" and an imitation of his own stilted diction!

Paul cheered up; the morning seemed brighter suddenly. Studying him with eyebrows drawn tightly together, Holinshed said eventually, "Did you ask Mrs Weddenhall if she had ever been criminally assaulted?"

—This will call for a little more weaseling out of.

"There were nail-marks on the injured man's face like those often found on rapists. In fact, one of the constables on the spot mentioned having seen similar ones on a man he'd helped to arrest. Since Mrs Weddenhall is a JP I did ask her—yes, I remember clearly now—if she'd had any experience of cases of rape. If I phrased my question badly, I'm sorry. But I was extremely agitated at the prospect of a posse with guns turning out to search the area."

He waited. At length Holinshed gave a grunt and reached towards his in-tray.

"Very well, Fidler. We'll say no more about it. Just bear in mind that our relations with the public are absolutely crucial, and you mustn't let your professional zeal overcome your tact. Understood?"

"Of course." Repressing the desire to grin, Paul rose.

"Thank you. That's all."

Paul entered his own office with a sigh of relief. He went to the window instead of sitting down to tackle the morning's heap of paper-work, and lit a cigarette while watching the outside working-parties disperse towards their jobs.

—One consolation about Chent: they don't keep the poor devils sitting around on their backsides in the wards all day. I wonder who broke the dam in that area. Can't have been Holinshed. The one before, the one before that?

It was hardly a fine day, but at least it was drier than yesterday. Around a yawn he stared at the gardens detail waiting for issue of their safe tools—insofar as any implement was safe. But patients weren't given anything more risky than a birch besom or a wheelbarrow unless they were comparatively stabilised.

—Hard to tell the difference between inmates on occupational therapy and the employed maintenance staff if it weren't for the former always being accompanied by nurses in white jackets. . . . Wonder if a mental hospital should be run like a medieval monastery, a totally self-sufficient community. Could be done. Except that too much enclosure of the patients runs counter to the aim of giving them back to the outside world.

The first of the morning's knocks came on his door. The visitor was Oliphant, remarkably fresh after what for him had probably been a trouble-free night's duty.

"Morning, Doc. Charge's compliments and can you make sure Dr Alsop sees Mr Charrington today? We had a hell of a job getting him out of bed and at breakfast he drew pictures all over the table with his porridge."

"Damn." Paul reached for the hanging clipboard he privately referred to as the stand-up-and-yell list. There were really no non-urgent cases in the hospital except the chronic geriatrics.

—All madmen are urgent but some are more urgent than others.

"Right. Anything else?"

"Well"—Oliphant hesitated—"Matron did say you wanted Jingler and Riley moved out of Disturbed to make up for the two discharges. You couldn't leave it a couple of days, could you?"

"I'm afraid not. It's not doing those two any good at all being among chronic patients who are worse than they are."

"That's what we thought you'd say," Oliphant muttered.

"Come off it! Granted, old Jingler is probably going to be in and out for the rest of his life, but Riley's only twenty-two and too bright to be wasted."

"He beat up his own mother, didn't he?"

"In some ways he seems to have deserved it," Paul sighed. "And they sent him here, remember, not to Rampton or Broadmoor. Never mind the arguments, though. Just get on with it. Dr Alsop will be here in about half an hour; I'll try and get him to see Charrington right away."

"Thanks," Oliphant muttered sourly, and went out.

—Maybe I'd feel more the way he does if I had to move among patients in the mass all day long . . . ?"

Paul shook his head and started on the contents of the in-tray.

The phone tinkled just as the clock clanged and clinked nine-thirty. Dumping the most routine of his case-notes—"no change no change no changes"—into their files, he picked it up.

"Natalie," the voice said. "I'm off to look round the wards. Want to call on Urchin with me, or wait till Alsop gets here?"

"Hang on." One-handed, Paul riffled the remaining documents in his tray. "Suppose I join you in Female in ten minutes, does that suit?"

"Okay."

And another knock: Nurse Davis with memos from Matron.

—Ask her how it went last night? Tactless! But it's a sunny day for one person at least. Let's see. . . . Nothing immediate, praise be. Pharmacy appropriations list: must remember to sound Alsop on this fluphenazine treatment; I think we could benefit from it. And that's that for the moment.

He pushed back his chair, suddenly eager to see Urchin again.

—That name's catching on all right. Hope she accepts it. . . . Why should I want so much to call on her with Natalie—why not wait until Alsop gets here in another few minutes? I have more work that must be done. Oh, because what I fear has happened to her: enclosure in a private universe. Anyhow, her case is a far cry from the regular rather dull admissions. Imaginary voices, delusions of persecution, pathological lethargy, all the other stock symptoms indicate that complex or not, human beings have a remarkably limited range of ways of going wrong. Like fever stemming from so many different diseases. Wonder if GP's get a bang out of rare conditions like undulant fever as a change from flu and measles. Christ, this place is doing horrible things to my sense of humour!

◆ *10* ◆

Since Chent hadn't been designed for use as a mental hospital its layout was illogical and inconvenient. The centre block, now given over to administration, the pharmacy, and quarters for the resident medical officers, was adequately compact, but the wards for the less-disturbed patients spilled over randomly into what had once been nurseries, picture galleries, gunrooms and lord knew what, while the nurses' quarters were in a range of converted stables separated from the main building by a paved yard. Only the Disturbed wing, being a later addition, was halfway functional; even so, there was no easy route from his office to the ward where he was to join Natalie unless he short-cut through the male dormitories.

And doing that wiped away the transient elation derived from outfacing Holinshed.

—Perhaps I'm not cut out for this work. Just seeing the poor devils folds me up like a clenched fist.

The dormitories were briskly busy at the moment, noisy with heel taps, raised voices and the squeaking wheels of big wicker laundry-baskets. Among the hubbub a handful of patients circulated listlessly in their nightwear, like children being punished by being sent to bed in daylight. They did view it as a punishment, he knew, but it was meant as a precaution. They were each to see a visiting consultant today, and it wasn't unknown for a patient to be so scared of these august and distant figures that he stole away from the wards and tried to kill himself.

—But what use are explanations in face of the rumours bred here? They'll think of it as punishment until the millennium arrives. . . . Experts write on the folklore of schools: kids keep alive superstitions, traditions, rituals. But lunatics invent their own.

At one window, gazing blankly out, a man one side of whose face convulsed at intervals of about ten seconds: Charrington, numbly awaiting Alsop's pleasure. He didn't respond to Paul's greeting.

—Not worth the effort, hm? What is worth the effort in surroundings like these: sloppily painted walls, patched floors, beds jammed in everywhere? If you breed rats till they're this crowded they start to kill their young. As a patient I'd misbehave until they locked me in one of the cells. Eighty square feet of privacy I'd trade for anything.

He found Natalie in the stairwell connecting the upper and lower floors of the Disturbed wing, at the end of the passage leading to the Female wards. She was talking to Matron Thoroday and Sister Wells; Paul waited till she had finished.

—Must be the "thorough" in her name Matron's trying to live up to, I suppose.

This entire hospital was a sluggish battleground between interlocking zones of influence, all the way from the grand scale of medical superintendent versus hospital secretary where the support of outside forces like the hospital group or even the Ministry could be invoked, by way of Matron's unending series of arguments on points of principle—this including such questions as what colour to repaint the drainpipes—clear to the absurd manoeuvrings which centred on the patients themselves: silent but persistent jockeying for a majority of the cases that might be milked of a paper for an important medical journal. Paul had hoped that this last, which had shocked him when he first discovered it, might be confined to teaching hospitals, but Chent suffered from it too in a muted form.

—I wish Alsop hadn't said what he did when I first arrived, about my job being an ideal launch-base for getting my name into print. At twenty-eight what do I know that's new enough to warrant being printed? A paper on this strange girl we're starting to call Urchin? I could fit one in, I suppose; I don't have to break my neck on the diploma course yet. But I'm not involved. To me patients are still all strangers, all individuals. When they become simply "cases," maybe then . . .

Matron bustled away. He moved towards Natalie and Sister Wells.

"What was all that about?"

Natalie grimaced. "It bothers Matron that we should have a patient with no clues to her identity. Hasn't she any scars? No deformities? Then how about having her fingerprints taken in case she's been arrested at some time?"

Sister Wells, a gaunt brown-haired woman whom Paul had liked since their first meeting, exposed her big horsy teeth in a sympathetic grin and led the way towards the ward where Urchin was accommodated. Falling in alongside Natalie, Paul was struck by a point he'd overlooked last night.

"I completely forgot to get in touch with Inspector Hofford!"

"I remembered just after you'd gone. Not that I had any news for him."

"What did he say about Faberdown—the salesman?"

"Still maintaining he did nothing to provoke an attack on him. Hofford was apologetic, but he said the matter would have to be taken further."

"Meaning what?"

"Sounds like a jargon phrase for making a nuisance of themselves." Natalie stopped outside one of the boxlike security cells running the whole length of the ward. "Damn. Sister, I said her door was to be left open."

"It was," the sister countered.

Paul looked around. Here, as on the men's side, those patients due for an interview with a consultant were hanging about in nightwear, and one caught his eye: a sly woman with a greasy tangle of grey hair. She put her hand to her mouth and giggled. Paul touched Natalie's arm, gesturing.

"What? Oh, Madge Phelps interfering again! I might have guessed. Convinced she's in here to spy on the others, keeps coming to me and the nurses with harrowing tales about how they misbehave. Tell her off, will you Sister?"

She jerked the cell's door open. There on the hard bed sat Urchin, tensed at the sudden intrusion.

—I've seen this cell before. HELP HELP scratched into the paint. Probably a mercy she can't read it.

Recognising Paul, Urchin got to her feet and gave him a wan smile. He returned it as warmly as he could.

—Forget the trapped-animal look. Homicidals can wear it too.

"What sort of night did she have?" he asked Natalie.

"Kirk looked in on her a couple of times, and so did I. She spent a lot of the night sitting up in bed frowning, and Kirk says she was talking to herself at one stage."

"Saying what?"

"Foreign language. I quote Kirk."

Paul rubbed his chin. "And this morning?"

"Perfectly tractable apart from having to be shown how to do absolutely everything. Oh—with one exception. She ate her porridge at breakfast, but then there was bacon and fried bread, and I gather she picked up the bacon in her fingers, smelt it, and left the table looking pale."

"I was wondering if she might be Jewish," Sister Wells put in. "She's not what you'd call an English type, is she?"

"No more a Jewish one." Paul shrugged. "Though that would account for her refusing bacon, of course. . . . I wonder. Perhaps she's vegetarian."

"Health food and nudism?" Natalie suggested quizzically.

"Picked a damned silly climate to do it in, then," Paul grunted. "Is she any the worse for her exposure, by the way?"

"Not at all. In fact she found the bedding too hot for her; she removed the coverlid and folded it on the locker."

"Feverish?"

"Nope."

"Well, I have no new ideas. You got any Natalie?"

"The more that occur to me, the more they seem stupid." Natalie glanced at the clock on the wall of the ward. "Blazes, I can't stand around here any longer. Roshman will be here any minute and he wants me to go to Birmingham with him after lunch, so it'll be a frantic morning. Let me know what Alsop says, won't you?"

"Of course."

She and Sister Wells moved away. Paul remained standing in the cell, staring at the girl and feeling a vast surge of pity for her plight. She seemed so tiny and helpless in the hospital dress of blue cotton, child-sized but even so too baggy around her waist, which she had been given. There was nothing childish, though, about the keen gaze of her large dark eyes. And, despite the ugly garments put on her, she merited Mirza's approving description of her as a poppet: there was colour in her cheeks this morning instead of the cold pallor of yesterday, and that was a transfiguration.

—Damned shame you didn't give us some name we could twist into "Elfin" instead of Urchin! More suitable by far!

"Pol?" she said suddenly.

"Arrzheen," he agreed.

Her small hand darted to her right, touching the bed, while she cocked her head at an inquiring angle. At first he didn't catch on; abruptly he realised her intention.

—She wants to know what it's called. What in the world have we stumbled into here?

"Bed," he said carefully.

"Baid!" A hesitation; then a tap on the wall.

"Wall."

"Wol!"

"Dr Fidler!" a voice interrupted from behind him. He swung around to find Nurse Foden at the door.

"Dr Alsop is here, Dr Fidler, and he says will you please join him right away."

—Damn. Well, it can't be helped. Try apologising in gestures.

He pointed at himself, at Nurse Foden, and pantomimed walking away. Urchin's face fell, but she had no words to object with; she merely sighed and resumed her seat on the edge of the bed as though resigned to letting the world do what it liked with her.

◇ *11* ◇

Dr E. Knox Alsop was a fine-looking man: over six feet, with a broad forehead, smooth dark hair and a tan meticulously maintained throughout the winter with an ultraviolet lamp. Paul considered himself fortunate to be working with him rather than, say, with Dr Roshman or any other of the hospital's regular consultants. He had an undoubted streak of vanity, which had given Mirza the excuse (if he needed any) for coining the nickname "Soppy Al," but it was chiefly confined to minor characteristics like his tan and secretiveness about what his initial E stood for. Mirza had a theory about that, too: in his view Alsop had been an exceptionally active baby before he was born, and the name was Enoch—" 'E knock-knocks!"

Nonetheless, this vanity was a foible that seldom reached the point of irritating the people he had to work with, whereas Roshman's perpetual air of harassment found expression in indecision; he would spend an hour with one of the resident MO's planning an exact course of therapy for a patient, then ring up from home the same evening with a full set of radically different second thoughts.

On the other hand, Alsop did exhibit the attitude which had enabled Mirza to coin a spare and to Paul's mind far more apt nickname for him: "Opportunity Knox." He regarded himself as inhabiting a jungle in which behind masks of civilised behaviour and conventional politeness everybody, doctor or not, was out for what he could get. No means of enhancing his reputation, status and income escaped him.

When he first cottoned on to the extent of Alsop's ambitions, Paul had been mystified as to why he was content to act as a consultant to a medium-sized provincial hospital like Chent, with its total of under three hundred beds, when the promotion ladder offered so many more rungs in big cities. The explanation had proved to be perfectly simple and absolutely typical. From correspondence in periodicals like the *British Medical Journal* he had progressed very early in his career to publishing papers, first with colleagues of greater standing, then on his own. The next step would have to be a book, and the subject he had settled on was a comparative study of the incidence of various psychoses among rural and urban populations. Chent's catchment area was eight per cent rural. Hence his presence.

Whether directly from Paul, or—as Paul suspected was more likely—after meeting Iris, he had summed up the new registrar as a go-getter like himself. Paul had done nothing to disillusion him immediately. He had listened with attention to Alsop's well-meant advice, promised to act on it . . . and then somehow let it slide. Up until about Christmas of last year Alsop had continued to prompt him, going so far as to point out letters in medical journals which called for a reply from someone—why not from Paul? And he'd likewise stressed the advantages of a registrar's post as a stepping-stone to eventual fame. Paul, slightly disheartened by the requirements of the course he'd just started on—the two-year programme for a Diploma of Psychological Medicine—had complied with one or two of the suggestions, but given up when no instant results followed, preferring to spend his free time in study.

Now, a couple of months past Christmas, Alsop appeared to be ready to write Paul off as the white hope of Chent. Paul was still helping at his once-weekly clinic in Blickham, but the references Alsop had made to letting him tackle clinic sessions on his own during the consultant's absence had remained a vague idea without plans to implement it.

—I suppose I have disappointed him. But that doesn't make him unique. My parents, my wife, even myself are in there with him.

At all events, the greeting he offered this morning was friendly enough. He waved Paul to the interview chair in the rather cheerless office.

"Chuck me that stuff from the couch, would you?" he went on. Paul passed over a small stack of files that had been dumped on the grey blanket. "How are things, young fellow?"

—Should I tell him? It's already only half a secret. But he has small sympathy for failures, and failing in marriage is about as basic as failures come.

"So-so." Paul shrugged. "The weather's been getting me down, I think. I'm coming to understand why the suicide peak starts in March."

"Thought you'd have worked that out in your teens," Alsop grunted, scanning a succession of case-notes as he talked. "Your wife still away, is she?"

"Yes."

"That's probably a contributory factor. I wouldn't go so far as that chap in Sweden who advocates promiscuity as a treatment for delinquents, but there's no doubt whatever about the therapeutic effect of regular orgasm." Alsop gave a dry chuckle. "Your friend Bakshad seems to realise that okay. I ran into him in Blickham last night with what must be his twentieth different girl since he got here."

Paul, off guard, was overwhelmed with a pang of bitterness.

—Therapeutic effects of orgasm! I've half a mind to spew the truth in his lap and see how his face changes!

But while the decision was still untaken Alsop had gone on. "You ran foul of some local bigwig, I gather—hm?"

Paul scowled. "Mrs Weddenhall, *Jay Pee!* Who told you about that—Dr Holinshed?"

"Of course."

"I thought I'd set him straight on the matter. But apparently I didn't shout loudly enough to make him listen."

"Well, there's no need to shout at me," Alsop said, glancing up. "Candidly—mind if I speak straight out?"

"Of course not," Paul muttered.

"I think you're letting things get on top of you. Bad. Mustn't do it. If you try and identify with these unfortunates all around us you're much too liable to wind up joining them. You had some psychotherapy once, didn't you?"

"A course of analysis," Paul said. And repeated his habitual cover-story: "Thought it was the simplest way of getting a patient's-eye view of psychiatry."

"Yes." Alsop nodded slowly once, and said again, "Yes. . . . Well, there's nothing to be ashamed of in feeling the strain. This isn't the easiest of hospitals to work in, despite its size. But it'd be damned silly if you let yourself crack up under the petty kind of pressure Chent can generate. So you ought to take precautions while there's time."

—Like what? Cultivate Holinshed and lick his boots a bit? Tell Iris to go to hell?

"However," Alsop went on briskly, "the schedule's too full this morning to worry about healing the physicians. Fuller than you appear to realise. I asked you to add Mrs Chancery to the roster for today, and you didn't."

Paul started. "I'm sorry! It quite slipped my mind."

"Papa Freud he say . . ." Alsop drew a large black arrow to exchange the order of two patients on the list. "You don't like the Chancery woman, I know. No more do I, but at least I remember to hide the fact. And who in the world is this 'Urchin' I see mentioned?"

"You should have the admission report on her. We brought her in last night—emergency."

Alsop riffled papers. "Not here. Holinshed must be sitting on it. Lots of gory details in it? I find that kind usually take longest to get out of your boss's clutches."

—What am I to make of cracks like that? Is it camaraderie or an assertion of superiority over Holinshed? You're fine, how am I?

Paul summed up the story as concisely as he could.

"And you find this dreadfully puzzling," Alsop commented. "I'm surprised. Female exhibitionism is rarer than male because it has more . . . ah . . . institutionalised outlets, like strip-tease dancing, but it does exist and can generally be fitted into a coherent diagnosis. I'd hypothesise an excessively restricted childhood with so much stress laid on bodily exposure that the mind just"—he pantomimed crumpling a sheet of paper—"folds up under the pressure. Did you tranquillise her on admission?"

"No, I gave her no medication at all."

"Therapeutic nihilism is an obsolete standpoint even in psychiatry, young fellow! I worked under a medical superintendent who suffered from it, but I thought he was the last surviving dinosaurian exponent of the notion. Why not?"

"Well ..." Paul fumbled for words. "Because she came quietly, I suppose you'd say."

"The fact remains, she had a mere hour or so earlier broken a man's arm with her bare hands. You say she's a tiny little thing. Well, a black widow spider isn't exactly a ferocious great monster, but I wouldn't start keeping one as a pet."

—Stuff the sarcasm, for heaven's sake!

"But how about what's happened this morning? I never heard of a case of hysterical aphasia where the patient set about getting the doctor to teach her English. Besides which, she isn't aphasic."

"All right, what's she suffering from, then?" Alsop waited with a triumphant air, expecting and receiving no answer. He sighed at length.

"I have this nasty suspicion you're convincing yourself you've run across a brand-new subspecies of mental disorder which you can write up for publication, talk about at the next congress you go to, and ultimately name after yourself."

—Sounds like a capsule version of your life story!

And a tacit admission of the truth of that followed.

"Fell into the same trap myself when I was your age or a bit younger. Remind me to dig out the case-notes sometime. They're ... well ... illuminating. Reserve judgment, young fellow, and then hang on a bit longer still. There's nothing so damaging to your opinion of your own competence as having to climb down in public from some limb you've wandered out on. Brrr!"

He acted a fit of the shivers and laughed without humour.

"Let's settle the matter, shall we? Deal with her first. Charrington's not going to cut his throat while he waits."

At first Paul was gratified by the thoroughness with which Alsop set about double-checking the results of last night's examination of Urchin, first by satisfying himself that the girl didn't understand English yet was capable of talking some language of her own, then by repeating the physical examination with a running commentary.

"Get me a urine sample, Nurse—first thing tomorrow morning, please. . . . We should have a blood sample too. Ought to type every patient who comes in and give them a card showing it on discharge. Might save lives later, case of accident. . . . Curious facial structure! Nothing Asiatic about it whatever except this very marked epicanthic fold. . . . I think you should book her an appointment for a skull X-ray, young fellow. I agree she's quite fluent in this odd language of hers—which I imagine you'll check up on, won't you?—but she could hardly have got to the middle of England on Upper Slobovian or whatever unless somebody brought her here, so injury may have caused her to revert, say to a childhood language. . . ."

—Admirably comprehensive. And yet there's a false note. I'm damned certain there's a false note.

Abruptly, with a stab of dismay, he decided he knew the nature of it.

—The bastard! He thinks I might be right in calling this an anomalous condition not in the literature; he won't admit it, but he's making damned sure he doesn't let slip the chance of reporting it before I manage to!

◇ *12* ◇

The clock was marking a quarter to two with the inevitable bang boom and *clink* as Alsop climbed into his Vanden Plas Princess R and Paul turned wearily towards the mess.

—I suppose he's right about these courses I ought to go on, but why can't the damned things crop up at a convenient time, while Iris is away? Just see her face when I say hullo darling nice to have you home I'm off tomorrow for a course and I'll be back in a fortnight. On the other hand, maybe I should try it. Declaration of independence.

He felt a stir of vague puzzlement. The proprietary attitude regarding Urchin which had come on him unbidden, because he felt his own long-standing nightmare of waking into a "wrong" world gave him special insight into her condition, had made him speak more sharply to Alsop this morning than he would normally have dared, culminating with a ten-minute argument about one of the patients due for discharge today. To his surprise, far from being annoyed Alsop had been positively cordial; for the first time in two months he had volunteered suggestions about some courses Paul might attend.

—I'll ... think about it.

Ferdie Silva was leaving the mess as he entered; neither Phil Kerans nor Natalie was present—only Mirza, distaste-fully examining a plate of stewed apples and custard which Lil had just placed before him.

"Has Natalie gone?" Paul demanded.

"I saw her go off with Rosh Hashanah, the Newish Jew Here," said Mirza, touching a spoonful of the dessert with the tip of his tongue on the last word and pulling a face. "Lil dear, lose this somewhere, would you? And give me a piece of cheese if we have any fit for human consumption. The soup is ghastly too, Paul, in case you were thinking of trying it."

"I must eat something," Paul sighed. But Mirza was quite right: the soup was half cold with patches of grease floating in it. At least the bread-rolls were today's delivery. He munched on one of them.

"Why did you want our golden-hearted Dr-rudge, any-how?" Mirza inquired, making a mouthful of the rolled r's.

"Oh, she asked to be kept informed about Urchin."

"She'll get it all on the grapevine, I imagine. I've been hearing about no one else all morning."

"Why in the world?" Paul put down his spoon, staring.

"You mean you haven't realised that no remotely identical case has arrived at Chent since the year dot or the birth of Holy Joe whichever is the earlier?" Mirza sliced his cheese with rapid elegant motions and laid it out tidily on a biscuit. "The patients know, the staff know, how is it you don't?"

"Pretty sure of the patients' diagnostic ability, aren't you?" Paul snapped.

Mirza gave him an astonished glance. "Paul, I thought a night's good sleep would have cured you of yesterday's fit of grumps! I'm sorry if I trod on your corns."

Paul controlled himself with an effort. "No, I'm the one who should say sorry. Go on with what you were saying."

"About the patients' diagnostic ability, you mean?" Reassured, Mirza reverted to his habitual mocking lightness. "Actually I have enormous faith in it. How else do you think I could get along in England?"

"If you're making a serious point, make it seriously. Otherwise shut up. I'm not in a joking mood."

"Yes, I *am* serious." Obediently Mirza put on voice and expression to match. "Bear in mind, Paul, I come from a country which is"—he raised fingers to count off the successive items—"Moslem, underdeveloped, recently ex-colonial, predominantly rural, different in just about every possible way from industrialised, citified, nominally Christian Britain. And here I am pretending to tinker with precisely that aspect of a human being which is affected most by cultural conditioning. So I was sent to an English-speaking school and an English university—so what? This is merely a late gloss on my basic orientation. I haven't been inside a mosque since I was eighteen, but the mosque is inside me. Your cracked bell up there in the tower"—a jerk of his thumb towards the ceiling—"bothers you at least partly because this is a country of Sunday morning church-bells. To me it has no cultural associations. But when that fellow in Disturbed has a bad spell and starts wailing at the top of his voice—do you know the one I mean?—I jerk like a frog's leg on a galvanic plate, because to begin with he hits the same three notes as I used to hear every sunrise during my childhood and before I can remember where I am my mind has already completed the call in anticipation: *Ya-Allah il-Allah.* . . . The muezzin was stone-blind and about ninety, but he used to climb forty feet of stairs before sunrise every day."

Reminiscently he paused, eyes focused on some faraway spot beyond the wall of the room.

—I ought to be ashamed of myself, thinking that struggling against this damned silly British class set-up is bad. How'd I make out with Mirza's problems of adjustment? Culture shock.

—*Culture shock!*

The idea was so dazzling he completely lost the thread of what Mirza was saying, and was only recalled a minute later by the Pakistani's offended question about being bored.

"Sorry, Mirza!" Paul recovered hastily. "Something just hit

me. Tell you about it in a second. Go on—this is very interesting."

"Wouldn't have thought so from the blank look on your face just now," Mirza grunted. "I was saying that in my view no patient here is *entirely* insane. Even the ones out of reach of communication probably aren't—a few of them do occasionally come back with memories of the disturbed phase, incomplete though the memories may be. Or incommunicable, which I suspect is nearer the truth. But the milder ones, suffering from things like compulsion neurosis and in here more because they get on their families' nerves than because they're overtly dangerous to themselves or society, do retain huge areas of relative sanity. Day and night they associate with their fellow patients, and though they lack the professional background required to organise their observations into the basis for a diagnosis, that doesn't prevent the sheer volume of what they see and hear from distilling into clear patterns. I've often had a patient say to me about a new admission, 'Ah, that's another of them like Mr So-and-so!' And when I looked up Mr So-and-so's case-notes, damned if they weren't right. Do you follow me?"

Paul abandoned his soup and Lil exchanged it for a plate of macaroni cheese and chipped potatoes.

"Ought to have a resident dietician," Mirza said sourly. "Do you know I've put on two inches around the waist since I came to Chent? Disgusting!"

"I see what you mean now," Paul said, having tasted this course and found it at least edible. "Once when I was a student I was told to write up a new admission to see if what I said matched the real admission report, and I was completely muddled until one of the other patients made a comment that set me on the right lines."

"But you haven't inquired what the other patients here think about Urchin? Sorry—of course: you've had a consultant riding herd on you all morning. You haven't had time."

"Tell me what you've been hearing, anyway."

"Know Miss Browhart? Schoolteacher, keeps her skirt pinned together between her legs because of 'those dirty boys?' "

"And they're behind every bush and around every corner. Yes, I know her."

"She buttonholed me this morning and told me about Urchin in confidential tones. 'Poor thing'—I quote—'she's not crazy, she's just terrified.' " Mirza pulled cigarettes from his pocket. "Mind if I smoke while you're eating?"

"Go ahead." Paul hesitated. "Do you agree with her?"

"Trying to make me commit myself about a patient I haven't even examined? But I heard the same sort of thing from Sister Wells. 'Never had one like her before,' she told me. 'She's not stupid—in fact she's very bright—and I can't work out why she has to be shown everything, even which way round to put her dress on.' " Mirza clicked his lighter. "And I furthermore understand she's been getting people to tell her the English names for all the things in the ward."

"Correct. She did that with me this morning."

"To coin a phrase, this strikes me as anomalous. What do you think?"

"Let's hear your view first. I'm busy eating."

"How can you stuff down so much of that slop . . . All right, though I think this is simple cunning on your part." Mirza frowned. "I'll lay a bet that Alsop has been trying to convince you she's suffering from fairly conventional symptoms of hysteria: exhibitionism, hysterical amnesia and all that jazz. While at the same time being perfectly aware that she's way off the beam."

"I wish to God," Paul said with sudden passion, "that I had your gift for predicting people's behaviour."

"It's not a gift. It's a means of intellectualising all the things people in this country take for granted and I've had to learn because they're foreign to me."

"What do you think about culture shock?" Paul demanded.

"What? Oh, you mean this condition that results from being dumped in the middle of China or somewhere and not even being able to read the signposts." Mirza tapped ash from his cigarette. "Well, I suppose a lot of my Pakistani friends in this country are suffering a mild form of it—after being used to a wealthy family at home, they come here, live like pigs in a slum district, can't be bothered to wash the windows let alone paper their rooms, don't try and make any friends among the local people but just sweat out the course of study or whatever they came here for and go home with a sigh of relief." He paused. "Was that question about anything, incidentally?"

"About Urchin," Paul said reluctantly.

—It seemed like a paralysing fit of insight when the idea hit me. Spoken aloud it just seems silly.

"I see. You're thinking of her as being—let's see—like the

illiterate dependants of some of the immigrants I know, haled off to Britain by better-educated relatives without a word of any language but their own. So what was she doing in the woods without clothing? Had some irate husband taken her out after a row and dumped her to teach her a lesson?"

"I wouldn't make guesses as elaborate as that," Paul said, amused. "But at least it may give me a line of attack."

"More power to your elbow. But if you suggest it to Soppy Al, make sure he thinks it's his inspiration, not yours. He is rather intolerant of other people's bright ideas, isn't he?" Mirza glanced at his watch. "Damn, I promised myself ten minutes' reading after lunch and now I must run. . . . What are you going to do about Urchin, anyway?"

"Oh, a string of things Alsop asked for: urinalysis, skull X-ray—which reminds me, I must book an appointment at Blickham General. And one or two wrinkles I dreamed up myself. By the way, do you happen to know a really good non-verbal intelligence test?"

"No such animal, in my view. But you could ask Barrie Tumbelow."

Paul snapped his fingers. He had met Tumbelow the last time the latter came to Chent to grade the congenitals— the imbeciles and morons who ought to have been in an institution of their own rather than an asylum, but who had had to be shuffled off here for lack of other facilities.

"Thanks, I should have thought of that myself."

"He might be able to advise you, I suppose. I do feel it's typical of Holy Joe to rely on a pediatrician with a hobby instead of a proper child psychologist, though. If we— Never mind! My prejudices are showing. See you later."

Left alone, Paul mechanically absorbed rather than ate his stewed apples, mind elsewhere.

—Not crazy, just terrified? No, it's too pat, when one of the commonest kinds of mental disorder consists mainly in groundless terror. And yet there's something so rational about Urchin. . . . Granted, paranoids are rational, with knobs on, but paranoia's psychotic and nobody seems to think she's worse than a hysteric. . . . If she really wants to learn English, we'll have to teach her. Without words, there's nothing to be done whatever.

❖ *13* ❖

Trouble with Urchin started the following day.

Following his talk with Mirza, work kept Paul late in his office. With conscious rectitude he stopped at the Needle in Haystack only to buy a couple of quarts of beer, then went straight home to study over his evening meal.

The nagging sensation that in some way he owed more to Urchin than to his other patients because she was suffering a real equivalent to his imaginary fears kept coming between him and his textbooks until in exasperation he made a firm resolve not to think of her again before, at the earliest, he had the lab reports and X-rays as a basis to work from.

Sticking to that decision, he spent most of next morning reviewing his case-load and obtaining from the ward sisters and charge nurses comments on the chemotherapy he'd been prescribing for the patients. He would have got on well but for two major interruptions. The minor ones never stopped and he was adjusted to them.

First there appeared a rather saddening new admission: an old woman referred from Blickham General where she had been being treated for a broken right hip. The long stay in hospital, as all too often happened, had wasted what little remained of her independence; day by day her personality had degraded until after postponing discharge to the latest possible moment Blickham General diagnosed irreversible senile dementia and contacted Chent.

It was like the delivery of a package, not a human being: a sticklike frame swathed in blankets, toothless face blank with infantile preoccupations. She had fouled herself on the journey and stank of faeces.

—Selfish, but I feel glad that women live longer than men. I can expect to be decently dead before I reach that stage.

Almost two-thirds of Chent's inmates were women, and the proportion among chronic geriatric cases was higher still. Small wonder, Paul had sometimes thought, that the ancients

called hysteria after the womb if throughout history women
had been twice as likely to go mad as men.

The second interruption began by way of a phone call.

"Dr Fidler?" He recognised Sister Wells's voice. "Trouble
in the ward, I'm afraid, involving this girl Urchin."

One second of stupefaction. Then: "I'm on my way!"

—Don't tell me she's broken someone else's arm!

He found Nurse Kirk and Sister Wells in the female
dormitory, the former standing aggressively over sly-faced
Madge Phelps, who was clutching a hair-brush with a gaudy
floral back, while Urchin sat on an empty, tidy bed occasionally touching an angry red mark on her cheek.

"What happened?" Paul demanded.

Sister Wells thrust a lock of stray hair back under her cap.
"Madge says she caught . . . uh . . . Urchin trying to steal her
hair-brush, whereupon she hit her with it. I've been trying to
verify this, but it's not exactly easy."

—Among the other things lunatics make: their own version of truth.

Paul frowned. "What are they doing here anyway?"

Nurse Kirk spoke up. "Madge wouldn't go out this morning—said she was suspicious of Urchin. So we left her in her
nightwear to be seen to later. And there isn't much point in
trying to get Urchin out of the ward, is there—not understanding what people say to her?"

"She's been keeping up this learning-English act," the sister
amplified. "I'm afraid it's been annoying the other patients
rather, being followed around and pestered for the names of
perfectly ordinary objects."

—*Act?*

But Paul let that pass without comment.

"Madge took an interest in her over breakfast and my
guess is that not finding anyone else left to talk to Urchin
started trying to get the names of Madge's belongings. But
not even the nurses touch Madge's stuff without asking, or
they're likely to lose a handful of hair. A smack with the
brush I'd call getting off lightly!"

"Dirty thief!" Madge said loudly. "Ought to be locked up
in her cell all day and all night and we could look through
the peephole and laugh at her."

Urchin got down off the bed. Dejectedly she walked back
to her cell and shut the door behind her.

"She understood that all right, apparently," Sister Wells
said in surprise.

—Did she? No, I think it was just a case of giving up against hopeless odds.

Before Paul could speak again, however, there was a call from the far door.

"Sister! Sister—Hello, what's going on?"

—Matron in all her gory, as Mirza puts it.

Having heard the story, Matron Thoroday rounded on Paul. "Sedation, don't you think, Doctor? Can't have this sort of thing wasting the valuable time of my nurses."

"No," Paul said.

Matron blinked. "I beg your pardon?"

"I said no. I don't propose to prescribe any medication for Urchin until I'm satisfied she's suffering from a disorder which requires it."

The matron was marginally too well-mannered to snort, but she implied it. "Sister, how do you feel about it?"

"Stick needles in her," Madge said. "Lots of needles. Lots and *lots* of needles!"

"Be quiet," Matron ordered briskly, and Madge looked frightened. "Sister, you were saying . . . ?"

"Well, she isn't really being much trouble," Sister Wells murmured.

"A moment ago you were saying she was pestering the nurses and patients. Make your mind up, Wells!"

—There's something I detest about blotting out patients who make a nuisance of themselves.

The realisation came to Paul accompanied by a faint aura of surprise. Perhaps it was Mirza's remark of yesterday about the churchly associations of the cracked bell in the clock-tower, bringing back an admonition which once he had thought of frequently but not for many years: *suffer fools gladly*.

—Though there are fools and fools . . . No, nuisance is one thing, and we tolerate it in those who are nominally sane. Violence, hurting: that's of a different order, and when our skills are exhausted there's no alternative. We call the pharmacy and . . . But why should we resent being bothered by those who are trying to communicate with us, and to communicate terrible things, at that? Even if we leave them no other means of expression except their own filth!

He said sharply, "Please don't argue, Matron. In my judgment Urchin needs neither sedation nor any other immediate attention."

"I feel you may be overlooking something, *Doctor*. This

Urchin—and what a ridiculous name that is, by the way!—
this young woman definitely broke a man's arm. I don't want
that to happen in the hospital, and I'm sure you agree with
me." Matron Thoroday wasn't used to being talked back to;
the words lacked her normal forthrightness.

"On the contrary," Paul returned, "I think *you're* overlooking the fact that she was the one who got hit, and you're
talking as if she did the hitting. Has Madge Phelps done this
kind of thing before, Nurse?" he added, turning.

"She goes for anybody who tries to touch her property,"
Nurse Kirk said.

"Whose patient is she?"

"Dr Roshman's."

"Is he prescribing anything for her at the moment?"

"She's on Largactil, but he has just reduced the daily dosage."

"Put her back on the former dosage for the rest of today,
and if Dr Roshman inquires why, refer him to me, will you?"

—Unanswerable question: am I doing this to spite Matron,
or is it the right thing in view of Roshman's vacillating
habits? It's true he changes his mind more often in a week
than Alsop does in a year, so I'll just have to pray that his
first guess was the right one.

Matron's cheeks were turning scarlet, but he tactfully kept
his eyes averted, addressing Nurse Kirk.

—The way I'm going on, they're liable to start accusing me
of favouritism among the patients. One further point. *One*.

"Apart from trying to get them to teach her English, has
Urchin been annoying the other patients?"

"Well, yes," was the reply, to Paul's dismay. "She watches
them."

"What's so bad about that?"

"I mean she stares at them and tries to copy what they're
doing."

"Because she doesn't know what to do herself?"

"I suppose so. But I'm not surprised they find it a bit irritating." The nurse hesitated. "Then, of course, they didn't like
the way she behaved in the washroom this morning."

"How?"

"She took off all her clothes and positively scrubbed her
private parts. And it shocked the others. We have several patients who've been brought up to always use a separate face-
towel, and seeing her wipe her whole body with her face-
cloth upset them dreadfully."

Paul made a mental note to follow up that hint. Obsession with the cleanliness of the sexual parts could indicate the nature of the underlying disorder.

—If there is one. I think my good resolution is going to hell. Too many enigmas for my peace of mind.

"I'd have thought there was a fairly simple solution," he said aloud. "Let her have a shower, or a tub."

"But we don't normally do that in the mornings before breakfast," Matron said with an air of restrained triumph. "I imagine the other patients would regard this as a special treat, wouldn't they, Sister?"

"I'm afraid they might," Sister Wells admitted.

"Sometimes people get my goat," Paul said, his patience running out. "A person who's exceptionally clean gets called dirty by those around her. This is ridiculous—in the strict sense, it's *crazy*. Just make your minds up which will cause less trouble, having her wash all over in public or having her sent for a shower in private, and then let her get on with it. Now, if that's all, I have work to do, and so have you!"

◆ *14* ◆

"This is Holinshed," the phone muttered. "Come down to my office, will you?"

—Blast the man. As if I didn't have my hands full! My turn for duty again tonight, and the Operating Committee tomorrow, and I'm drowning in a sea of papers.

But Paul remembered to put on his politest face as he tapped at Holinshed's door.

"Ah, Fidler! Sit down. You know Inspector Hofford, I believe."

Raincoat unbelted and dragging on the floor either side of his chair, the policeman nodded his greeting.

"Sorry to bother you, Doctor," he said. "It's about this girl Urchin, of course. Mr Faberdown won't let the matter rest. I've been trying to work out some means of passing it off lightly, with the help of Dr Holinshed here. But . . ."

"Are you going to prefer charges against the girl?"

"I don't see much alternative," Hofford sighed.

Holinshed broke in, his voice brittle. "Inspector Hofford is prepared to co-operate in every possible way, but apparently it's largely up to us. As I understand it, the tidiest course is to certify the girl unfit to plead."

"Except," Hofford murmured, "that when we spoke before, Doctor, you gave me the impression you thought she might have been . . . ah . . . temporarily upset by attempted rape, rather than mentally deranged, in which case the whole affair takes on a different complexion."

"Is Faberdown sticking to his story?" Paul asked.

"Like a leech, sir," Hofford grunted. "And I gather you haven't yet found an interpreter to tell us the girl's side of it, so she's in no position to contradict him, is she?"

Paul turned over the alternatives in his mind.

—Well, it would certainly be cruel to put her on show in a public court, which is what I suppose it would come to. But there's something so dreadfully final about the piece of paper which sets it down in black and white: so-and-so is clinically insane. It revolts me. Mirza is right. Even the worst of our patients remains a little bit sane.

"Inspector, is this very urgent?" he inquired.

"Of course we'd like to clear the whole business up as quickly as we can, but . . . well, no, not what you'd call urgent. Mr Faberdown is still in the hospital himself and certainly won't be out until after the weekend, and I take it the girl will remain here."

Holinshed coughed gently. "You sound worried, Fidler. May I know the reason?"

"Frankly, sir, I wouldn't be prepared to certify her unfit. I honestly don't think anyone could."

"But I gather from Matron that she's been behaving in a hr'm!—disorderly manner in the ward today."

—What was I thinking earlier about lunatics making their own version of truth? Why specify lunatics?

"The way it was reported to me, sir, she was in fact attacked by another patient, and the nurse stated she made no attempt to retaliate. Matron insisted that I sedate her, but I refused."

—Oh-oh. I think I just went a step too far.

A frigid light gleamed in Holinshed's eyes. "If I follow you correctly, you're implying that she's a miserable victim of circumstances and the salesman despite his denials is the one who should be arraigned in court. Now this," he continued, raising a hand to forestall Paul's indignant interruption, "Strikes me as a highly speculative standpoint. Where are the traces of this attempted rape? I didn't find them in the admission report. And in any case, according to Inspector Hofford, this leads to enormous complications."

"Well, yes," the latter agreed. "To take the worst aspect of the problem, she's presumably an alien, and once we try to establish what a foreigner is doing wandering around a Shropshire wood without clothes, let alone identification, we get mixed up with the immigration authorities, the Home Office, and lord knows who."

"Have you checked with Missing Persons?"

"That's one of the reasons I called here today. I'd like to arrange for a photograph of her."

"Well, she's going to Blickham General tomorrow for a head X-ray. They have an arrangement with a local photographer; I can probably organise it through them."

"I'd be much obliged," Hofford said, and made to rise. "I think that's as far as we can take matters today then, Dr Holinshed," he added.

"Just a moment," Holinshed put in, eyes on Paul. "Does Dr Alsop share your view that the girl is actually normal, Fidler?"

"That's not what I've been saying," Paul snapped. "But it was drummed into me during training that one should never mistake the result of different customs or some physical handicap for true mental disorder."

"And what . . . ah . . . physical handicap applies to this girl?"

"Matron told you about the rumpus involving her. But apparently she neglected to mention that she's trying to get the patients and nurses to teach her English."

"Seriously?" Hofford brightened. "Well, that's some consolation. Of course, you don't learn a language in a day, but if she's making the effort we may eventually get her side of the story. Oh, by the way, while I think of it! Have you found out what the language is that she *can* speak?"

"If I get time today," Paul said with a meaning glare at Holinshed, "I shall try and make a tape of her talking, and send it to the philology department at the university with a sample of some peculiar writing she did for us. Someone's bound to recognise it."

"Bound to?" Holinshed echoed. "And suppose she's fabricated an imaginary language?"

Paul retained self-control with an effort. "According to a friend of mine who lectures in languages, it's next to impossible to invent a wholly new one. Something shows through—sentence structure, or the roots of the words. Proof that she's talking an invented form of some natural language would be the evidence we need to show that she's mentally disturbed."

—Thought so; you'd missed that.

Holinshed gave him a suspicious glance: *are you having me on?* But his tone was cordial as he gave his blessing to the idea.

—Tomorrow you'll be convinced it was your own suggestion in the first place.

"If that's all, then, Inspector . . . ?" the medical superintendent added.

"Yes, thank you, sir."

—If I ever get good at hospital politics, I think I shall start to hate myself.

Paul dropped into his chair and picked up the phone. He dialled.

"Stores," a voice said.

"Dr Fidler here. We have a tape-recorder, don't we?"

"Yes, sir. But Dr Rudge has it at the moment. She's making up a programme of music for the Saturday dance."

"Well, she's gone to Birmingham with Dr Roshman. So would you have it sent up here, please?"

—Saturday? Blazes: tomorrow. And my duty, too. The ghastly parody of a festive occasion. Still, it's at least a gesture towards normality.

He dialled again, this time the office in Urchin's ward, and gave instructions for her to be brought up in ten minutes.

During that time he made cursory preparations for the monthly meeting of the Operating Committee, due the next day. The committee was a half-arsed body including senior and junior medical staff, admin staff, and a representative from the committee in charge of the entire local hospital group. With the departure of Holinshed they would probably get around to rationalising the running of Chent and put it under a proper medical advisory committee. Until that time, however, Holinshed—like all the medical superintendents Paul had ever come across—preferred to retain his personal power despite being constrained to pay lip-service to modern organisational methods.

—I swear the reason he holds these meetings on Saturdays is to keep them short. Everybody's always eager to get away.

Then the door was opening and there was the tape-recorder, but no tape, because they'd taken off the one on which Natalie was compiling music for the dance, so he had to send for one, and then Urchin was being brought in and another slab of work was destined to be held over for this evening.

—I shall never get my DPM at this rate. . . . Oh well: I shall just have to sit up late tomorrow night, cramming facts into my brain against the bell in the clock-tower.

He forced a smile and waved Urchin to a chair.

"All right, Nurse, no need for you to hang around," he told the girl who had escorted Urchin up from the ward. And added with a trace of bitterness as the door closed, knowing the question would receive no answer, "I wish to God I could tell, Urchin—are you crazy or not?"

❖ *15* ❖

She gave a hesitant sweet smile and murmured, "Pol!" He grinned back.

—Done something to herself since I saw her earlier. Looks even more attractive despite the baggy cotton dress. Oh yes: not so baggy. Got a belt from somewhere. That'll annoy Matron. Visions of strangulation and hanging herself in the toilet . . . Better start with a sample of her writing, I guess.

Opening a notepad, he pantomimed the action with a ballpen. She gave a curious little twitch of her head which, since it was different from the quasi-Balkan negative she had used before, presumably implied "yes."

Taking the pen, she inscribed, rather than wrote, a series of symbols. He had meant to watch the movement of her hand, but somehow his gaze got delayed on the way and he found he was studying her face instead. She had the child's habit of

putting her tongue-tip between her teeth when she was concentrating.

She showed him the paper, and he realised with a start that
she had written FEMALF WAAD.

—Not bad for a person wholly unused to our alphabet, I
suppose. Indicates a good visual memory. But not what I
wanted.

He took the notepad, balled up the sheet she had used, and
attempted to imitate the spiky symbols she had produced on
the evening of her arrival. At first she looked bewildered; after a few seconds, though, she gave a peal of laughter and
reached for the pen again.

This time she worked more quickly. The result was a table
of twenty-five symbols arranged in a square. She pulled her
chair around so that she could sit up to the desk with him
and point at each in turn with the pen.

"Beh!" she said, naming the first. "Veh. Peh. Feh. Weh."
The pen flicked along the top line.

—Hang on, young lady. You're not supposed to be
teaching me your alphabet, which for all I know you made
up in your spare time. But I ought to know what sounds attach to the letters, I guess.

With a sigh, because this involved further expenditure of
precious time, he wrote transliterations for each sound she uttered. Studying them, he frowned. There were two or three
cases where he had had to approximate; the sound didn't occur in English. In particular there was a harsh aspirate akin
to the Swedish "tj" which he couldn't even imitate. Yet . . .

—Odder than ever. No vowels. Nonetheless it's a more logical grouping than the ordinary alphabet: that series at the
top, for instance, voiced and unvoiced plosives with their as-
pirated forms alongside . . . If you did invent this, you're certainly not stupid.

He made to tear the sheet off so that he could send it to
the university's philology department, but she checked him
with a hurt expression.

—Damnation. You thought you were here for a language
lesson, didn't you? How can I explain that I simply haven't
the time?

He pointed to all the papers stacked in his in-tray, and
pantomimed removing them, dealing with them and sending
them away. She watched with her usual triple reaction: in-
comprehension, understanding and amusement. Eventually
she interrupted him by catching at his hand to save him re-

peating the whole routine, and for a moment her cool small fingers linked with his.

With a sinking feeling Paul recognised the predicament he had drifted into.

—Oh hell.... You like me and you trust me. I owe it to you to help you more than this.

So, resignedly, he invested more irreplaceable time in what could too easily prove to be pandering to a lunatic's fantasy. In exchange for the table of symbols she had given him he wrote out the alphabet and added where possible the values from hers, then pronounced the vowels for her.

In return she demonstrated that her system was a syllabary, not an alphabet, provided with a series of dot-and-dash modifiers like Hebrew. To conclude, she wrote two brief words at the foot of the page: her own name, and his.

—Enough! Enough!

Paul set aside the notepad, to her dismay, and started the tape-recorder. Picking up the microphone, he said, "I'm going to try and get a sample of her own language from a patient here at Chent whom we've nicknamed Urchin. There may be one or two false starts since she doesn't speak any English."

He played back what he'd said. The sound of his voice emanating from the machine didn't appear to surprise her. Add one to the list of inconsistencies she displayed: she could have missed tape-recorders far more easily than cars in the modern world.

He aimed the microphone at her.

"Wol," she said, pointing at the wall. "Flaw-er. Wind-daw. Daw-er. Cil-ling...."

He withdrew the mike with a sigh. As well as a good visual memory she clearly had a keen facility for auditory learning, but while it was reassuring to know she was progressing with her study of English it didn't help much. Wiping the tape, he considered ways of explaining what he wanted.

But he didn't have to. She figured it out almost at once and said something rapid in her own tongue. He smiled broadly and restarted the machine.

This time he taped about two minutes of totally unrecognisable speech. It had a certain rhythmical quality, but he had no way of telling whether that was because she was reciting a bit of poetry, as anyone might do at a loss what else to say on a recording, or whether it was characteristic of the language generally. Anyhow, it should suffice for the experts to begin on. He shut the recorder off.

She caught his hand and gave him a pleading look.

—Why can't I be as quick to work out your meaning as you are to deduce <u>mine</u>? Hmmm ... I get it, I think. You want to hear a voice, even if it's your own, say something you understand.

He replayed the brief passage and discovered he was right. She put both hands together between her knees and squeezed, lips trembling in echo of herself. At the end she blinked, and a tear ran down her cheek.

—Oh, lord. Why doesn't somebody come and rescue you from Chent? I don't care what you were doing out in the woods the other night; you don't *look* crazy.

And yet ...

In imagination he heard the sound of a human arm-bone snapping. He winced and recovered his professional detachment. Mechanically, very conscious of her large dark eyes on him, he rang for a nurse to escort her back to the ward.

When he put down the receiver she touched the notepad questioningly. He waved her to go ahead. Taking the pen, she started to sketch. He recognised the drawing before it was complete: a map of the world, with a triangle and a lozenge for the Americas, a sprawling Eurasian land-mass, a bulging-pear version of Africa and Australasia jammed into the bottom corner more to show she knew it belonged than in any attempt at accurate location.

—This girl is a hell of a lot brighter than I am. It just never occured to me to show her an atlas and get her to point out her homeland on it.

He jumped up and crossed to the shelf of reference books at the far side of the office. Surely there must be a map of some sort among them. At random he selected a tome on *Climatic and Other Environmental Factors in the Aetiology of Disease*. The frontispiece obligingly proved to be a world map.

He showed it to her, and she pushed aside her crude sketch with an exclamation of delight. Her finger stabbed down on the British Isles.

—So she knows where she is, at any rate. How about where she comes from?

Convinced that scores of questions were about to be answered at a single blow, he tapped his own chest, then the map, hoping she would see the connection Paul-England. Then he pointed at her. She obediently imitated him, but her finger landed on the same spot as his: the west of England.

Paul sighed. This girl's intelligence seemed to operate by fits and starts. He made wiping gestures to convey a wrong response and once more pointed at her.

The same thing happened, accompanied this time by an expression of infinite sadness.

He shrugged and gave up. But the recognition of her intelligence, even though it was patchy, reminded him that he wanted to give her some non-verbal tests. Waiting for the nurse to come and fetch her, he put through a call to Barrie Tumbelow as Mirza had recommended.

Tumbelow was at his Friday afternoon clinic and couldn't be reached. Paul left a message for him to ring back, and cradled the phone just as the nurse arrived.

Unwilling to leave, Urchin rose reluctantly to her feet. She seemed trying to make her mind up about something. Paul gestured for the nurse to stand back, wondering what was coming now.

Abruptly Urchin touched the notepad with a questioning tilt of her head. Paul snapped his fingers, and exclaimed aloud, "Of course you can!"

He handed her the pad and a pen, and she clasped his hand with gratitude before turning docilely to the nurse and following her away.

◆ *16* ◆

Half past nine clang-clinked from the clock-tower as Paul dumped his overnight bag on a spare chair at the side of the committee-room. Holinshed's secretary, a stiff-mannered fortyish woman named Miss Laxham—about whom Mirza had once posed the question of what it was she lacked and concluded that it was gonads—was distributing duplicated copies of the minutes of the previous month's meeting; they exchanged a cool good morning.

Paul leafed through the documents laid before his place. Relieved, he saw that the agenda was straightforward and the meeting would be a short one. He pushed it aside and unfolded his copy of the local weekly paper. Published on Fridays, it had been waiting for him when he got home yesterday, but he hadn't bothered to read it. Only this morning, gulping down a hasty breakfast, had he wondered whether the affair of Urchin and Faberdown was reported in it.

—Nothing on the front page. Good. But it might be on the middle spread. . . . Oh my God. Here it is by the shovelful.

He flapped the paper over centre to fold it back and read with a sinking heart: MADWOMAN ATTACKS SALESMAN NEAR YEMBLE. About ten inches of it, with a blurred photo of the copse where it happened, a quote from Mrs Weddenhall in which she appealed irrelevantly to people to keep their children from talking to strange men, and a statement that Dr Holinshed of Chent Hospital had no comment to make.

—At least they left me out of it by name. I'm just "a psychiatrist from Chent."

He glanced up as another committee-member entered: Dr Jewell, a local GP who served as medical consultant for the hospital.

"Morning, Fidler," he grunted as he settled his portly body into a chair. "See you're reading up on our local sensation. What do you think of the editorial comment, hm?"

Paul turned back to the preceding page, dismayed. What he found there was worse yet.

"While no one can fail to sympathise with the plight of the mentally afflicted . . . The complexity of the human mind is such that its breakdown defeats the best efforts of psychologists. . . . Our primary duty is to society. . . . We must act in full knowledge of the fact that the Beast in Man can and all too often does break loose. . . ."

—So what do they want us to do? Keep the inmates in chains on dirty straw? Wait till it's a member of your family who goes crazy. Though maybe you'd just pretend it hadn't happened. After all, when I myself . . .

"Morning!" And here was Holinshed, with Matron Thoroday, Ferdie Silva, Nurse Foden on behalf of the nursing staff, Mr Chapcheek from the Hospital Group—about whom Mirza had a very Mirzan theory regarding which of his cheeks were chapped and why—and finally the hospital secretary, Pratt-Rhys, a greying man who had clawed his way up the promotional ladder in lay admin posts through sheer determination and was never tired of reminding his colleagues that he had left school at sixteen and had no university degree.

"Dr Roshman sends his apologies," Holinshed announced. "But everyone else appears to be here ... ? Yes! Let's get straight down to business, then. Ready, Miss Laxham?"

She poised her pencil and Holinshed rattled his copy of the minutes.

"Minutes of the meeting of Chent Hospital Operating Committee held on blah-blah, present the following blah-blah. Dr Bakshad deputising for Dr Silva indisposed, apologies from Mr Chapcheek unavoidably detained until after start of business, Item One the minutes of the previous meeting were read by the chairman and agreed by all present as a true and correct record. ..."

Letting the drone of words pass him by, Paul recalled Mirza's comment on that meeting, which he had attended because Ferdie Silva was laid up with a temperature of a hundred.

"Why not draft a set of permanent all-purpose minutes for that committee, like a perpetual calendar? Think of the time it would save—especially time spent listening to Holinshed!"

He hid the smile which the idea brought to his lips. Holinshed didn't approve of people smiling while he was talking.

His own situation on this committee, as indeed at the hospital, was anomalous. In a larger hospital he would have been working under a senior registrar. Chent, with its average of less than three hundred patients, was torn between Holinshed's desire to have it treated as a "large" hospital and the determination of the Hospital Group to regard it as a "small" one. The staff structure exhibited the consequences.

In passing, Paul remembered suddenly a phrase from a letter Iris had received, years ago, from an official at the Ministry. During their engagement, as though having second thoughts after learning how determined he was to work in mental hospitals rather than go into general practice, she had written to inquire about prospects for promotion and salary if he stuck to his plan.

"This Ministry," the official told her frostily, "does not lay down a rigid staffing pattern or establishment of ranks for individual hospitals."

—You can say that again!

His discovery of the letter had precipitated a row that almost terminated the engagement.

—Suppose it had broken up? Would I be here now?

As always, his imagination conjured up a painful vision of being resident here in conventional fashion, having to lie awake night after night listening to that maddening cracked bell overhead, until exhaustion drove him to a fatal error, a patient killed himself, censure followed from the General Medical Council . . .

With an effort Paul dragged his mind back to the things that had attracted him about his post. In particular, the psychiatric registrar here enjoyed a large measure of independence compared to his opposite number in a hospital with more patients, because there was a gap in the ladder above him. What he had failed to reckon with was the way in which the extra responsibilities piled on top of his routine work, thus slashing the time he had expected to devote to study.

—When did I last have a clear weekend? Beginning of December, I think, when Iris insisted on doing the Christmas shopping. . . . Oh, come off it. Suppose I were at Blickham General: I could easily be working a twenty-hour day, with premature labours, survivors from car accidents, scalded children, drunks with their heads cut open . . .

There would be a chance to catch up with his textbooks tonight, at least; he'd jammed three of them into his overnight bag. He'd have to look in at the patients' dance, but he could get away with an hour of that, possibly less, and retreat to the staff sitting-room for peace and quiet.

He sneaked a glance at the clock on the wall. They were down to the halfway mark on the agenda and it wasn't quite ten o'clock yet. Marvellous: and an even shorter session than usual, and he hadn't been called on to utter a word.

"Thank you," Holinshed murmured as yet another item on the agenda was rubber-stamped. "That brings us to number ten, any other business. Has anybody . . . ?"

"I think we should discuss the item which appears in this week's local paper," Dr Jewell said firmly. "Dr Fidler, you have a copy of it. Perhaps you'd show the chairman?"

Dismayed, Paul pushed his copy of the paper towards Holinshed. There was a frigid pause.

At length Holinshed said, "Are you certain that will serve any useful purpose?"

"It's aroused a lot of public concern," Jewell countered. "Several of my patients have raised the matter with me. A mental hospital is an awkward neighbour at the best of times, but when something like this happens the situation is aggravated."

Paul edged forward on his chair. "Dr. Jewell, you're talking as though one of our patients had escaped! The way to look at it, surely, is to remember it's just as well it happened near here, so that there were people on the spot capable of coping with the problem."

—I think I just earned a smidgin of approval from Holy Joe!

"I'm afraid you aren't quite with me," Jewell said. "What I'm referring to is not the event itself but the way it was handled. I don't wish to bring personalities into this, just to remind everyone that relations between Chent and the public aren't improved by discounting the legitimate fears of lay people regarding lunatics."

The words burst from Paul's lips before he could check them: "Has Mrs Weddenhall been getting at you?"

"Dr Fidler, please!" Holinshed muttered.

"I don't know what you mean by 'getting at me,'" Jewell retorted. "But she's taken a good deal of interest in all this, and as a JP and a prominent local figure she'd bound to influence public opinion."

Somehow, without realising, Paul was on his feet. "Then let me tell you something which she didn't! What your precious Mrs Weddenhall was proposing to do was to hunt this maniac down with wolf-hounds and a posse armed with shotguns! And the—the *maniac* turned out to be a half-pint girl who wouldn't come up to the shoulder of the man she's supposed to have attacked. Do you want me to send for her so that you can see for yourself?"

"I hardly think that will be necessary," Holinshed declared in a forceful tone. Paul sat down again, shaking as much from embarrassment at his own uncharacteristic outburst as from the anger that had prompted it.

"My apologies, Dr Jewell," Holinshed continued. "But I'm compelled to agree with Fidler—though not with the way he expressed himself. The matter does not fall within the purview of this committee and I propose to rule further discussion out of order. And if that's all, I think we should adjourn right away."

The door of the hall was open. Still trembling. Paul walked towards it for a breath of fresh air.

—Christ, there are times when I want to get to hell out of this place and forget I ever saw it!

He lit a cigarette with unsteady hands, eyes fixed on one of the big white Daimler ambulances which was parked across the driveway, rear doors open. People moved towards it. For a second he didn't recognise who was among them, his mind being too full of other things. Suddenly it penetrated. He checked his watch: not quite twenty to eleven, and he'd made the appointment at Blickham General himself for eleven sharp. He swung on his heel, catching sight of Ferdie Silva making for the stairs.

"Ferdie! Do me a favour? Are you going to be in for lunch?"

The plump Guianese nodded.

"It's my duty. Stand in for me till I get back, will you?" The duty tour ran from noon until noon, though this was seldom a nuisance except at weekends.

"Provided you're not too long about it," Silva consented doubtfully.

"No, two o'clock should be the latest." Feverishly Paul thrust his overnight bag through the window of the porter's office. "Look after this for me, would you? Thanks a million, Ferdie—do the same for you sometime."

And he dashed out of the door just in time to flag down the ambulance taking Urchin for her head to be X-rayed.

◆ *17* ◆

This ambulance, he noted with relief as he squeezed in alongside the male nurse occupying the passengers' section of the bench seat in the cab, was not one of the security vehicles used for transporting the badly disturbed cases, but what he'd heard one of the drivers refer to as a "walking wounded bus"—its stretcher-racks convertible into ordinary seating or else capable of being folded back to make room for wheelchairs.

He twisted around in his place and peered through the glass separating the cab from the rear compartment. The security vehicles had such glass, too—more of it, indeed, if you thought only in terms of area—but theirs was reinforced with wire until what it brought to Paul's mind was the back of

Mrs Weddenhall's Bentley, caged for the transport of her enormous dogs.

The moment he showed his face, Urchin made as though to jump from her seat. She was dragged back by the nurse beside her, a girl called Woodside, pretty, but much too tall to be popular with the men—easily matching Paul's five feet eleven. She had a reputation for treating patients roughly. He scowled at her.

There was only one other patient in the back, a harmlessly silly man called Doublingale. Paul decided he should have ridden there rather than in front—the nurse beside him had extremely sharp hip-bones—but it was too late to change his mind now.

The trip was slower than usual owing to the Saturday morning shopping traffic in Blickham. Paul kept sneaking glances over his shoulder, noting Urchin's reaction to her surroundings. These were hardly attractive: the fringe of red-brick houses that turned the nearer side of Yemble into a dormitory for the larger town was itself dull, and beyond it lay bleak towers of council apartments served by another parallel road. It gave way shortly to small untidy factories, a scrapyard, the cattle-market and some railway goods sidings.

To Urchin, however, the view was apparently something to be absorbed without criticism. Only at one point did she display anything but intent interest: when they halted for a red light outside a butcher's shop just before reaching their destination. For a long moment she gazed in seeming disbelief, then swallowed hard and shut her eyes until they moved off.

—Of course. The episode with the bacon. Hmmm.... Not just vegetarian, but actually revolted by the sight of meat. Which brings me back to this notion of culture shock. But what the hell kind of culture?

He'd sent the tape and sample of writing to the university, but there was no telling when he would receive a verdict from the experts.

The young houseman in charge of the morning's X-ray schedule at Blickham General was very apologetic about the three emergencies from a car-crash who had shot his appointments to hell, but by the sound of it all three might be suffering from skull fractures, so Paul was undisposed to complain. He glanced around the outpatients' waiting-room, chilly and depressing, and abruptly snapped his fingers as he recalled what Hofford had said about photographs of Urchin.

"That's all right," he exclaimed. "In fact, it suits me very well. I'll bring her back later, shall I?"

"Suit yourself, but try not to be longer than thirty minutes." The houseman looked lingeringly at Urchin, huddled in a child's woollen overcoat. "Nothing serious, I hope?"

"It's hard to say. The poor kid doesn't speak English."

"As a result of something? I see. Pity! Dreadfully young to go off her rocker, isn't she?"

—Are you? Aren't you?

The problem buzzed maddeningly in Paul's brain like a trapped fly as he led Urchin across the entrance yard of the hospital, very conscious of the eyes of the driver in the ambulance which had brought them. The photographer's shop he had mentioned to Hofford was virtually opposite, and the driver watched them all the way.

Portrait photos mounted on thread jumped as he pushed open the door. Behind the counter, a suave young man framed by a black velvet curtain looked up.

"Good morning, sir, Harvey Samuels at your service, what can I do for you?"

His tone was weary, as though he was tired of doing anything for anyone.

"You do passport photos while you wait?" Paul asked.

"Yes, sir. Fleeing the country, are you?" An insincere smile. "Never mind me, sir, just my little joke, you know. Is it for yourself or the young lady?"

"For her."

"Three for ten and six, that all right? Come this way, please," he added to Urchin, raising a flap of the counter.

"I'll have to come with her, I'm afraid," Paul said. "She doesn't understand English."

Surprise fleeted across Samuels's face. "The pictures are for a British passport, are they, sir? I'm afraid I wouldn't know if they're suitable for any other country."

"They're not for a passport at all. I just want some pictures in a hurry."

Samuels shrugged and pushed back the curtain. Encouraging Urchin with a smile, Paul accompanied the photographer into a cramped little room dominated by floodlights and a group of three cameras aimed at a plain metal stool. On the wall behind the stool a white sunburst was painted to give portraits a sort of halo effect.

"Get her to sit down, please," Samuels said, switching on his lights.

"Don't go to a lot of trouble," Paul warned. "A good plain likeness is all I need."

"Making the young lady plain is probably beyond even my abilities, sir," Samuels answered as though it were a stock compliment.

Paul attempted to lead Urchin to the stool, but she baulked and clung to his hand, wide eyes staring at the cameras.

—Don't let me down now, Urchin! You weren't put off by the tape-recorder, so why should this bother you?

He gave her shoulder a reassuring pat, and she timorously yielded. But the hard fear remained on her face. Since Samuels took the injunction about a simple likeness literally, it was captured on the plate.

—I hope her friends or family or whatever recognise her with that ghastly expression!

Relieved that the job was over, she stood as close to the door as possible while he was paying for the pictures and arranging to pick them up before returning to Chent.

—Did she expect to be shot, or something?

But she surprised him for the latest of many times when he opened the door to go out. Catching his arm, she pointed at one of the pictures on display, then at her own face. She suddenly turned down her mouth and narrowed her eyes in a parody of the expression she had worn in the studio. It lasted only a second, and was wiped away in a peal of laughter.

—In other words: I must have looked hideous!

Grinning, he escorted her back to the hospital. A car drove by as they left the shop; absently he put his arm on her shoulder to prevent her walking in front of it. Equally absently he forgot to take it off until they were crossing the hospital yard and he realised the ambulance driver was still at the wheel of his vehicle.

—That's how to start gossip. Mustn't do it.

But the impulse was hard to resist, nonetheless. Urchin was so childlike in many ways that all his paternal instincts were aroused.

—If only Iris . . . But we've been through that, and I don't feel ready for a replay of the argument yet.

The houseman was just coming in search of them when they arrived, and led them straight to the X-ray room. A nurse entered Urchin's particulars on a form, made a quick check of her hair for metal clips or anything that might show on the plate, and opened the inner door with its red radiation-danger sign.

Over Urchin's shoulder Paul had one clear view of the equipment: a couch, a chair, various supports for legs and arms requiring examination, and the blunt-snouted machine itself.

Then Urchin had spun around.

"Hey, where do you think you're going?" the nurse said, making to seize her arm. Fast as a striking snake the arm was out of reach, and back again, fingers straight in a jab to the inside of the nurse's elbow. She screamed and dropped the papers she was clutching.

Paul, petrified with astonishment, put up a hand as though to ward Urchin off, saying stupidly, "Now just a second . . . !"

But he was in her way, and that was enough. She slammed him off balance with the point of her shoulder, hurling her tiny body upwards like a pouncing cheetah and driving at the vulnerable base of his sternum. He doubed up, all the wind knocked out of him, and she was past him, out of the room, and gone.

◆ *18* ◆

"Patient exhibited unaccountable fear of the X-ray equipment," Paul wrote with careful legibility. "It was judged inadvisable to make a second attempt at securing plates of her skull, as her violent reaction—"

He stopped, set down the pen, and lit a cigarette, wondering about the rest of the sentence he was entering in his report. Absently his left hand wandered to the pit of his stomach where Urchin had charged into him with such deadly effect.

—No matter how carefully I phrase it, anybody is going to get the impression she's really dangerous. What was the bit in the paper about the Beast in Man breaking loose?

He shuddered gently at the narrowness of the margin by which he had escaped real trouble. If Urchin had taken to her heels and got lost in the crowded town, there would have been no end to it: police, a search, a major local scandal and demands for an official inquiry. . . .

She'd let him off lightly, by going no further than the hospital yard and waiting passively until he staggered out after her. She had resisted being taken indoors again, but she'd climbed peaceably back into the ambulance and ridden alongside him with no more trouble.

Nonetheless, the matter couldn't be allowed to slide. The nurse she had attacked was very ill; the blow had ruptured the vein on the inside of her elbow, resulting in a horrible-looking haemorrhage, and the poor girl had fainted from pain. So Urchin was in her cell with the door locked, and he had taken advantage of the trust she still reposed in him to pour a heroic dose of tranquilliser down her. At last report she was asleep.

—God's name, what did her mind conjure up from an innocent X-ray machine? A mad scientist's gadgetry out of a horror picture?

But the moral was clear. He'd seen and felt for himself what she was capable of. Faberdown couldn't have stood a chance against her; with her skills she could have broken not just his arm, but his neck.

—Which, I suppose, is evidence for a fundamental personality disturbance. Even if she is a little shrimp, the average girl isn't so scared of her fellow human beings that she trains as a killing fighter.

The idea was still a trifle frightening. It was one thing to see the hero of a TV thriller or a movie bashing the villains in a struggle choreographed as formally as a ballet. It was something else entirely to find himself face to face with a lethal weapon in the shape of a slender, attractive girl.

—And there's half the trouble, if you'd only confess it. Hasn't living with Iris taught me not to judge by appearances? If Urchin had come in with a typical slack face, slopped around careless of how she looked instead of trying to be clean and neat, and shown apathy instead of lively interest in what goes on around her, I'd have shoved her to the back of my mind and got on with my work.

Determinedly he picked up the pen and poised it to continue his report. The phrase on which he had paused, however—"her violent reaction"—seized his imagination by the scruff and dragged it off down one of the familiar, fearful alternative world lines which so often haunted him.

—Demanding of the ambulance driver which way she went: "I didn't see her, Doc, I was lighting a cigarette." Wandering crazily around the streets and mistaking other people for Urchin, a child in a similar coat, a woman with a similar head of hair. Informing the police, having to face Hofford, having to face Holinshed: "This is an unforgivable breach of your professional responsibility which I shall be compelled to report to higher authority." Explaining to Iris when she gets back why I'm facing probable dismissal . . .

The pen he was holding cracked with a noise like a dry stick. He stared at it stupidly. The vision obsessing him had been so agonising that he had closed both hands into fists; his palms and face were moist with sweat. Angrily, he hurled the broken pen into the wastebasket and took up another.

—But it was almost more real than this desk, this office with its windows darkening towards sunset! As if I, this consciousness looking out of my eyes at such innocuous surroundings, were not the real Paul Fidler; as if, at some inconceivable angle to this actual world, the real "I" were trapped in some disastrous chain of events and crying out so fiercely that this brain which till so recently we shared thinks with his thoughts instead of mine!

Hand shaking, he drove himself to complete the report: ". . . proved that she had been trained in unarmed combat. She did not resist being brought back to Chent; however, I judged it advisable to sedate her, and . . ."

—Bloody hell. Now I've used "advisable" twice in three lines.

He hated the atmosphere of the hospital at weekends. The sense of purpose which the daily activity of the staff normally lent to the place was exchanged for one of vacuous futility. The coming and going at Saturday lunchtime—mostly going—awakened in the patients a fresh awareness of being confined, and resentment stank in his nostrils. Living out, he escaped the worst impact, but on a duty day it struck him all the harder for not being accustomed to it. To compound his depression, the food provided for the staff was worse than ever at weekends, because the real cooking was done beforehand and the meals were a succession of warmed-up leftovers.

—At least I can study for a few hours before I turn in.

He pushed open the door of the sitting-room, not expecting

to find anyone else here. Given the chance, the resident staff quit the premises and stayed away till the last permissible moment. To his surprise, Natalie was sipping a cup of tea in a chair facing the door. She looked tired.

"Hullo!" he said. "Of course, you're looking after the dance tonight, aren't you?"

"Bloody farce," she said morosely. "Like the worst village hops plus one extra horror—canned music instead of a proper band, which can at least be relied on to liven the proceedings by getting drunk. Well, I let myself in for the job, so I can't complain."

"How's the tea today?" Paul asked, tinkling the hand-bell.

"Above average. Probably they didn't tell the girl that they use stale leaves on Saturdays. . . . I hear Urchin was in trouble today, incidentally."

"I'm afraid so," he acknowledged; then, when she continued to regard him with a speculative expression but did not speak, he added, "What do you want me to do—show you my bruise?"

"Sorry. I didn't mean to stare." She drained her cup and set it aside. "It's just that you looked somehow . . . annoyed?"

"Should I not be?"

"But who with?" she countered. "Getting annoyed with mental patients is a waste of time, and in any case I don't think it's Urchin you're upset about."

"Who, then?" Paul snapped.

"Yourself. You've been going a bit by appearances in her case, haven't you? The episode this morning must have been a considerable let-down."

"Is this meant to be advice or sympathy?"

"Sympathy," Natalie said, unruffled by Paul's obvious irritation. "But there's advice coming, if you don't mind. Gossip positively pours in while we're getting ready for a patients' dance, you know, and this had better come from me rather than from Holinshed. Is it true you were seen in Blickham with your arm around Urchin?"

"God's name!"

"Paul, simmer down. This is a segregated institution and like every other of its kind it's positively obsessed with sex. I know without being told that it was a bit of fatherly reassurance for this girl who seems totally disoriented. But if there's going to be any more of it you'd better leave it to—well, to me."

"Who told you this?"

"Like I said, gossip goes the rounds while we're making ready for a dance."

"Well, it might be better if you didn't listen to so much of it!" Paul barked, and strode out of the room.

He was half inclined to skip dinner, since it meant sharing the otherwise empty dining-room with Natalie, but he came to the conclusion that that was ridiculous. There had been no call to shout at her, and he ought to apologise.

As it turned out, she had ordered dinner early to get back and supervise the start of the dance. She was on the point of leaving when he arrived, and he had to compress the planned apology into a few hasty words. She accepted it anyhow, pleasantly enough.

Eating his solitary meal, he thought about Natalie's comment that the hospital was obsessed by sex. It was no exaggeration; the mere fact that expression of physical love was impossible because there was nowhere that patients could find privacy made sexuality not just the greatest single root cause of the inmates' disorders apart from senility, but far and away the richest source of rumour and scandal.

Gloomily he wondered, as he had done the other evening at the Needle in Haystack, whether any other of the hospital gossip concerned himself and if so what it said.

—Dance. Christmas dance, the only time Iris has ever been further into this building than Holinshed's office. Did they see deeply enough into her personality to guess or half-guess my problems? The zest seemed to go out of it when I realised she was going to go on refusing to have children, and that seemed to suit her okay, so ... But a psychiatrist of all people should know that out of sight doesn't mean out of mind. Do something about that, maybe ... ?

He toyed with the idea, remembering Mirza's suggestion which had so disturbed him. Then he tried to push it aside, but everything conspired to prevent him: in particular, the spectacle of the female patients assembled for this ghastly parody of merrymaking.

Most of the time, shut away from men, they neglected their appearance, but a dance was always preceded by a flurry of titivating, of changing into a dress set aside for "best" and so seldom worn it had survived the disintegration of the rest of what they had when they arrived and the issue of ugly standard replacements, and of making up. Even the most withdrawn cases dabbed on a bit of powder and smeared lipstick inaccurately across their mouths.

The result was ghoulish, especially in the case of someone like Mrs Chancery, who at sixty-five was still convinced she was a flapper capable of laying men low in swathes with one deadly flash of her kohl-rimmed eyes.

The dances were held in the large female sitting-room, decorated for the occasion with a few paper streamers and some jars of early flowers. The idea was to make the women feel they were the "hostesses" at the party. A table covered in white cloth served as a bar for tea, coffee and soft drinks.

When Paul arrived, the male patients had barely started to trickle in, but the tape-recorder was already blasting out music and two or three couples were on the floor. Young Riley was showing off, partnered by Nurse Woodside, whose smile was glassy and self-conscious. At present the music was recent pop; later, to placate the older patients, it would go over to sentimental ballads with lots of strings, and at the end they would probably abandon dancing, as usual, for a singsong accompanied at the piano by Lieberman the overambitious locksmith.

—How seriously do they take it all?

The question crossed his mind as he exchanged greetings with patients on his way to collect an orange squash at the bar. The lordly patronising of Holinshed, who would drop in later and "show the flag"; the fact that the nurses were in mufti instead of starched aprons; the presence of a handful of visitors from outside, either friends of the staff, relatives of patients, or dogooders undertaking a charitable act—none of this added up to festivity!

—Who do we think we're kidding?

Abruptly the thought evaporated. Through a gap in a group of women patients around the far door of the room he had suddenly caught sight of an all-too-familiar figure peering at the dancers.

—God damn, has Lieberman been up to his tricks again? Urchin's supposed to be shut in her cell!

◆ *19* ◆

The tune blaring from the recorder ended. Nurse Woodside, casting around for a way of avoiding another dance with Riley, scanned the assembly and at once spotted Urchin. A hard expression deformed her attractive face, and she made to march in the girl's direction.

"Nurse!" Paul hissed. He caught up with her in a few long strides.

"What . . . ? Oh, it's you, Doctor." Nurse Woodside shook back her nape-long blonde hair; she was certainly very pretty tonight, in a black dress with fine red stripes which minimised her Junoesque bulk. "I thought that girl Urchin was supposed to be locked in!"

"She is. But we mustn't kick up a public fuss. Ask around, will you, and see if anybody admits having let her out?"

He was uncomfortably aware of Riley's gaze fixed on him as he spoke. When the nurse moved to comply, Riley called out, demanding another dance; the sharpness of her refusal annoyed him, and he stamped ostentatiously towards the bar.

—I hope he's not building up to a scene later.

Paul had considerable sympathy for young Riley. He came from the sort of background calculated to act as a forcing-bed for homosexuality, being the only child of an overprotective slut of a mother who regarded her son's girl-friends as a threat to her hold over him. The strain, against which he had fought with tenacity Paul rather admired, had ultimately driven him to beat his mother up and wreck her flat, whereupon he had been committed to Chent—quite correctly, because by then he was really deranged. But he was improving now his mother was out of his way, and Paul had high hopes for his early release.

Nonetheless, he did have a terrible temper.

A fresh influx of male patients followed, under the discreet supervision of Oliphant in a blue suit and red tie. Several of them, to cover their nervousness—they were much shyer than teenagers when it came to asking for a partner—made a production of greeting Paul, and it was with difficulty that he extricated himself to hear Nurse Woodside's report.

"Doctor, she must have got out by herself. No one admits to unlocking her door, and I don't see how one of the other patients could have done it."

"Better go and inspect the cell, then," sighed Paul.

The empty female dormitory had a peculiarly awful air tonight, like a ship which the passengers had abandoned in a panic: on the beds a confusion of clothing, on the lockers makeup kits, vanity mirrors, hair-brushes, all as if their owners had dematerialised in the act of using them.

Like the doors of all the other cells, Urchin's was fitted with a somewhat old-fashioned lock, but it was sunk in the wood, not screwed to the surface, and the keyhole on the inner side was blanked off with a solid metal plate. The paint was so chipped by the battering of desperate patients it was impossible to tell if it had been tampered with. Paul shrugged.

"Well, however she got out we can hardly drag her back. After her performance in Blickham this morning I wouldn't care to try it, anyway. We'll just have to keep a careful eye on her until the dance breaks up. She's heavily tranquillised, so she's unlikely to cause trouble."

That was true; nonetheless he returned to the dance with a tremor of apprehension. Urchin was in the same place as before. By now, however, Riley had spotted her too, and—sensibly enough, since she was more attractive than any of the women around her—was vainly trying to get her to dance with him. The bystanders were sniggering at his lack of success, and this was making him irritated.

—Poor devil. Apart from the nurses, who is there of his own age to partner him? Most of the young girls here are congenitals, too stupid to manage their own feet.

With a final scowl Riley gave up the attempt, caught sight of Nurse Woodside and approached her again. She would rather have declined, but a pleading glance from Paul persuaded her and she took Riley's hand, sighing.

Some while later Paul concluded that Urchin was only interested in watching and could safely be left to her own devices. He wandered around the floor to the tape-recorder table, and there, after a dismal shuffle in company with one of the older male patients, Natalie joined him.

"Thanks for sticking it out, Paul," she murmured. "Give it another half-hour and I think it'll be okay. Twenty couples dancing seems to be the break-even point; after that they unwind and actually enjoy it."

"Anyone else coming? Mirza, maybe?"

"Not after the Christmas dance, and I'm glad."

"How do you mean?"

"There was almost a free fight over who should have the next dance with him. Weren't you there?"

"Er . . . no. Iris talked me into leaving early."

Natalie nodded. "Mirza's too damned handsome, that's the trouble. And a wonderful dancer into the bargain. . . . But Holinshed's promised to drop in. Should be here any minute."

A man came up and diffidently asked her for the next dance. Excusing herself to Paul, she moved away.

For some time after that he just stood, lacking the willpower to do as he knew he ought to and dance with two or three of the women. Holinshed arrived and duly showed the flag, as he always called it, chatting with elaborate condescension to the staff but too remote for the patients even to address him. Paul was watching him from the far end of the room when Sister Wells came up to him, gawky in a dress patterned with blue roses.

"There's a phone-call for you, Dr Fidler. It's your wife. Would you like to take it in the ward office?"

—Iris? What can she want on a Saturday night?

Puzzled, he walked into the office, shut the door to exclude the booming music, and picked up the receiver.

"Iris?" he said neutrally.

"What on earth are you doing there?" the distant voice said. "I've been calling and calling you at home! What's all that noise I can hear?"

"We've got a patients' dance on."

"Oh. Well, I want you to come and rescue me."

"What? Where are you?"

"Freezing to death on Blickham Station!"

"Well . . . ah . . . can't you get a taxi home?"

"Don't take me for one of your patients, will you?" Iris countered acidly. "If I could get in when I got home there might be some point in using a cab. But I left Bertie and Meg's in rather a hurry and I forgot my door-key."

A sinking feeling developed in Paul's stomach.

—I suppose I could; Natalie would cover for me, though I hate the idea of asking. I could run into Blickham, drop her at home and come back, all within the space of forty minutes. But . . . Damn it, I just don't *want* to very much.

"Paul, are you there?" Iris demanded shrilly.

"Yes, of course. . . . Well, it's a bit awkward, you see. I'm on duty tonight."

"All by yourself?" The words were charged with sarcasm. "Big deal! Anybody would think you were one of the patients, the way they keep you in."

—Oh my God. She can't possibly have found out about . . . ? No, it's just a cheap gibe. But am I going to do it, or not?

"If you'd let me know you were coming—"

"I didn't know myself until four o'clock!"

—There's a terrible blankness in my mind. I can think words but I can't utter them. What I want to say is . . .

The door of the office slammed open and there was Sister Wells, gasping.

"Doctor, *quickly!*"

"What?" Paul covered the phone.

"It's Riley. There's going to be trouble."

"Right away!" He added, "Darling, there's an emergency. Hang on, I'll be back in a moment."

"Never mind," Iris rasped. "I suppose I can break a window and climb in!"

"I'm sorry, but I *must* dash."

He dropped the receiver on the table, as if he expected to continue the conversation, but the click of the connection being cut followed him out of the office.

—Now there'll be a row and she'll make out it's my fault but if she'd let me know when she was coming home I could have arranged to swap duties with someone and . . .

But all his private concerns evaporated the moment he entered the room where the dance was being held. The scene was as fixed as a photograph. Everyone had drawn back around the walls, cowering, except the two figures in the centre of the floor: Nurse Woodside and Riley. The girl's face was as white as chalk.

—Small wonder.

For Riley had taken a bottle from the bar, smashed its end, and now held the jagged neck poised like a knife.

Movement resumed. Natalie switched off the tape-recorder. Nurse Woodside attempted to back away, but a threatening wave of the bottle froze her again. Oliphant and another male nurse sidled past the jabbering patients, trying to get out

of Riley's field of vision and tackle him from behind. But he
was aware of this, and as they moved so did he, following the
rim of a circle with the miserable nurse at its centre. Seeming
hypnotised, she turned with him, always facing him.

"What happened?" Paul whispered to Sister Wells, gnawing
her knuckles beside him.

"I think he tried to kiss her and she wouldn't let him," Sister Wells muttered. "So then he shouted something about
making her, and went to get that bottle, and that was when I
fetched you."

Paul's eyes darted swiftly over the room. "Has Dr Holinshed gone?"

"A moment ago. I sent someone after him, but I think it
was too late."

—So it's up to me.

The thought was chilling; it seemed to congeal the progress
of time. At an immense distance he heard Riley's voice,
wheedling: "Make your mind up, Woodsy dear—are you going to do it, or shall I make sure no one ever wants to kiss
you again?"

Paul took a deep breath, gestured to Oliphant to come
forward with him, and strode out to the middle of the floor
with a sense of fatalistic resignation. "Riley!" he snapped, and
was infinitely relieved that his words didn't come out thin and
squeaky. "That's enough! Put that bottle down—and sweep
up the mess you've made!" he added, inspiration coming
from the crunch of glass underfoot.

As though the interruption had broken a spell, Nurse
Woodside rolled her eyes up in their sockets until the whites
showed and slid fainting to the floor.

"Scared of us, aren't you?" Riley taunted, and spun to
confront Paul, the bright sharp glass weaving in his hand.
"Scared silly of us lunatics! You make us bow and scrape and
order us about, and all the time you're pissing yourselves with
fright in case we stop cringing. Come on then, let's have you!
Where's Lord Godalmightly Holinshed gone?"

—Have to rush him. Nothing else for it. Do I have to be
first? Come on, somebody. Anybody? No, it must be me. . . .

Beyond Riley he saw Natalie inch cautiously forward. He
felt a pang of shame at standing still himself and his feet
moved involuntarily. Taking advantage of the distraction of
Riley's attention, Oliphant made a lumbering grab for the
bottle. He was too slow. Riley dodged, jabbed—and there
was a red mark on Oliphant's knuckles, dripping.

Paul exclaimed and charged Riley. He missed the hold he was aiming for, on the right arm, and knew at once it was a mistake to have come within reach. Desperately he clawed at the younger man's clothes. His left hand got a purchase on the sleeve of his jacket above the elbow, but Riley had too much leverage; the grip lasted a heartbeat and was lost and the round horrible end of the broken bottle like the rasping sucker of a leech loomed vast as a tunnel before Paul's eyes. He had an instant to prepare himself for pain, and thought with curious detachment of being blind.

—So this is the moment when the other Paul Fidler and I become one: the moment when the vision of the disastrous future moves from my imagination into the real world. I've always known it had to come, some day, somehow.

He let his eyelids roll down in a last childish flicker of hope that if he couldn't see the broken bottle it would go away.

Astonishingly the pain never came. Instead there was a smashing sound—the bottle on the floor. Then a thud—Riley keeling over. And a scream—Riley, snatching his right hand with his left.

Paul blinked. Everyone was suddenly there: Oliphant, Natalie, Sister Wells. Paul had eyes for none of them. He could only see, standing over the prostrate Riley, the small determined figure of Urchin, who had done ... *something* ... so that he was still alive.

◆ *20* ◆

After which there were all the loose ends to tidy up.

In the vain hope of minimising the sensation, they tried to continue the dance after Riley had been sedated and taken to a security cell, but the idea was absurd. The gloating gossip that spread among the patients nauseated Paul. Eventually, still shaking with remembered terror, he ordered them bedded down. But that was a long job, involving extra issues of tranquillisers for the most excitable.

Perhaps the saddest part of it was that Lieberman missed his chance to show off by leading the traditional sentimental singsong by way of finale. He sat at the side of the room, face long as a fiddle, and resisted all attempts to move him until two of the male nurses carried him bodily away.

On reviving, Nurse Woodside was violently sick in the middle of the floor, to the hysterical amusement of the patients. But Paul only heard about that. At the time he was examining Riley and trying to figure out what on earth Urchin had done to him. The right arm which had seemed to give him such agony was unmarked bar scratches where he had flailed it about among the crumbs of glass on the floor. It was almost by chance that he spotted a small oblong bruise beside the shoulder-blade, exactly the right size to have been caused by Urchin's fingertips.

Awkwardly he reached behind his own back to poke at the corresponding area and located the site of a sensitive nerve.

—Christ, where did she get her knowledge of anatomy? Half an inch and she'd have hit bone, harmlessly!

But as it was, the shock had jolted Riley's arm straight and opened his fingers.

—And saved my sight, if not my life. But how can I express my thanks?

With or without words, he needed to try; when he left Riley, however, he found that Urchin had gone meekly back to her cell, which was now securely locked. Peering through the peep-hole he saw she was in bed with the light out, and gave up his intention of disturbing her.

He sat with Natalie in the staff sitting-room for a while, drinking a late cup of tea and carrying on a desultory conversation from which an annoying point kept distracting him: only the other day he had ordered Riley transferred from the Disturbed wing against Oliphant's wishes, and now here was Oliphant with his fingers bandaged because of Riley. The cut was shallow, but that hardly signified.

When Natalie left to go to bed, he opened one of his textbooks and sat staring at its pages. Time and a great many cigarettes wore away, and his mind refused to absorb the words.

He had never before in his life been so close to being killed. But simple death was not so terrifying. Earlier today he had had that curious notion about another, somehow more real, version of Paul Fidler diverging from a moment of crisis down another and more disastrous life-line, so that what was to the *alter ego* real experience provoked these recurrent vivid imaginings. Paul Fidler in a world where he had died was inconceivable to Paul Fidler still alive and breathing.

But Paul Fidler blinded, moaning through a red mask of blood . . .

He had put up his hands before his face without realising, to reassure himself that he could see them. With a shudder he forced his churning mind back to the here and now and once more stared at the open book on his lap.

—No good. Suppose I'd insisted on Urchin being shut in her cell again; nobody else could have stopped Riley. Suppose Natalie hadn't thanked me for staying at the dance up to what she called the break-even point, and I'd slipped away early as I'd at first intended: who would have had to tackle Riley then—Natalie herself, one of the nurses? Would Urchin have done the same for somebody else?

Those questions were too remote to conjure up equally clear visions; they didn't involve him so personally. Nonetheless they possessed a dull, nagging power to distract him, and the book remained open at the same page, unread.

The clanging and chinking of the clock at midnight was the last straw. "Oh, God *damn!*" he exploded, and slammed the book on a nearby table.

"What the—? Paul! You look terrible!"

Mirza must have been on the landing opposite, about to enter his own room. Startled by the noise, he had put his head around the door of this one.

"We had some trouble during the dance," Paul explained apologetically. "Riley went for me with a broken bottle."

"*What?* No wonder you're pale! Hang on, let's see what we can do about that."

Mirza picked up the two empty teacups and disappeared. There was a sound of splashing from the direction of his room; then he was back, the cups freshly rinsed and dripping.

"This'll set you up," he murmured, and handed Paul three fingers of whisky.

"I didn't know you drank," Paul said irrelevantly, accepting the liquor with eager gratitude.

"I was raised not to touch alcohol, of course, but I was also taught to think for myself, and what I think is that you need a drink. Sit down and tell Uncle Mirza the whole story."

By fits and starts Paul complied. Mirza listened intently. At the end of the recital he jumped to his feet.

"It was the clock, I suppose, that made you swear so loudly before I came in?"

Paul nodded.

"Well, lying awake listening to it is about the worst possible treatment for you tonight. This your bag here? Go on—take it and go home."

"But—"

"I'm on duty, not you. As of this moment. Shift yourself before I change my mind about being public-spirited!"

—Thank God for Mirza. Though I'm not sure sending me home to an argument with Iris is any better than lying awake at the hospital. . . .

The lights were out along the street now; an economy-minded council switched them off at midnight. He dipped his headlamps as they swerved across the frontage of the house. All the windows were dark.

—Put it off till morning if she's asleep? Lie down in the living-room on the couch?

He crept up to the door. How had she got in? No sign of a broken window. Perhaps he'd forgotten to bolt the kitchen door; he'd left in a hurry this morning.

He was just hanging up his coat when the lights snapped on and there she was on the stairs in gossamer-thin shortie pyjamas.

"Well!" she said. "What happened to this night duty you were telling me about?"

Dazzled after the darkness outside, Paul blinked at her. Somehow during her absence he had kept a mental picture of her only with make-up on; encountering her with her face cleansed for sleep, a trifle shiny with some sort of nourishing cream, was like meeting a stranger by the same name.

He said, "I told Mirza you'd come home, so he volunteered to stand in for me."

"Who?" She came the rest of the way down the stairs, huddling her arms around her body as if to screen it from his gaze.

—What did Mirza call her: "lovely but unsociable"? I don't know that "lovely" is the word. Pretty, yes . . . I suppose.

Belatedly he answered her question. "My friend from Pakistan that you were so rude to when I brought him here."

She stopped dead. She might have been on her way to give

him a kiss, not wanting to make a grand issue of what had happened earlier, but that settled the matter.

"If I'd known this was the sort of welcome home I was going to get I wouldn't have bothered to come! I was stranded at the station for nearly a bloody hour, and then when I did get hold of you you wouldn't come and pick me up, you wouldn't even finish talking to me before you ran away to see to one of your precious lunatics—"

"You got in all right, didn't you?" Paul snapped. "I suppose when you looked again you found you did have your key!"

"No, I did not! The taxi-driver went around the house with me and we found the kitchen door unbolted. Anybody could have walked in and looted the house!"

—My heart's not in this. I haven't got the head of steam up for a proper row.

Paul turned aside and dropped into a chair. "Sorry to disappoint you," he said. "I'm not in the mood for a bust-up. I was just damned nearly carved up by a madman with a broken bottle."

"What?"

"You heard me. He was threatening one of the nurses. That's why I had to run away from the phone, and why I'm damned if I'm going to apologise for not coming to fetch you from the station."

"Are you serious?" she said in a thin voice.

"Of course not. I'm tremendously amused. It positively made the evening for me and I don't know why I'm not shrieking with laughter!"

"Darling, how was I to know?" Iris said after a pause. She advanced on him uncertainly, eyes scanning his averted face. "Goodness, it must have been awful. . . . Look . . . ah . . . Bertie Parsons gave me a bottle of vodka. Would you like some?"

—I don't know what I'd like. Except out. Stop the world I want to get off.

Exhausted, he sat without stirring except to light a cigarette, while she scampered up to the bedroom for a robe, then produced the vodka and mixed drinks for them both.

"Who was it?"

"A young fellow called Riley. I thought he was on the mend because he hadn't given any trouble lately. I was wrong."

"What started it?" She came over and put the glass into his

hand, then fetched a cushion from the settle opposite and squatted down at his feet, turning to poke the fire; she must have lit it on coming in.

"He tried to kiss one of the nurses. Woodside. You met her at the Christmas dance—pretty, but very big, as tall as I am."

She set down the poker and rested her arm on his knee. Her blue eyes turned up to his face, large and liquid. "It would have been nasty, wouldn't it?"

"Nasty!" He gave a short laugh. "Ever *seen* a man who's had a bottle ground in his face?"

"Tell me exactly what happened," she insisted, and began to caress the inside of his leg.

—Where's the affection come from all of a sudden? You haven't behaved like this in nearly a year!

Mechanically, as he recounted the story, he pieced together the reason, and damned the training which gave him insight for that.

—It excites you, doesn't it? Starts the little juices running! Thinking about Riley threatening Nurse Woodside to make her kiss him: that gets the breath rasping in your throat. I can hear it.

He gulped the last of his drink and roughly thrust his hand down the neck of her robe, groping for her nipple with the tips of his fingers. The contact made her stiffen and shiver. He flicked the butt of his cigarette into the fire and slid forward off the chair.

"Paul ..." she said, the words muffled by a tress of hair that his movement had drawn across her mouth.

"Shut up," he said, his lips against her neck. "You've been away for over two weeks, and I came within inches of never seeing you again and I want to celebrate."

"But I ..."

Yet, even as her mouth breathed reluctance, her hands were tearing at his clothes.

—Christ. Married four years, nearly five, and I find this out the night I'm bloody nearly killed.

That was the last thought before he gave himself up to the plunging and churning of her body under his.

◆ *21* ◆

On Sunday Paul drove Iris to Ludlow in chilly spring sunshine, and they had a good dinner in Cornminster before going home. The other Paul Fidler kept his distance; thoughts of death and blindness had no place in a countryside hesitantly emerging from winter lethargy, showing new green on the trees and shy flowers under the hedgerows.

But once Paul was at work again on Monday, his *alter ego* crept back at the edge of awareness. By force of will he reduced his accumulated work to manageable proportions, and only then did he allow himself to consider the problem weighing on his conscience: what he might do for Urchin to balance the debt he now owed.

He reached for a notepad and began to map out what he was already thinking of under the somewhat grandiose title of "Project Urchin." Instantly the telephone rang.

With a mutter of annoyance he picked it up.

"Barrie Tumbelow here," said the distant voice. "I gather you've been trying to reach me. I did call up on Saturday morning, but apparently you'd just gone out."

—Of course. When I dashed off to Blickham I completely forgot about the message I left asking him to contact me.

"I need some advice," Paul said. "We have a patient here who speaks absolutely no English, and I want to measure her IQ."

There was a moment of silence. "You do realise," Tumbelow said at last, "that this isn't my speciality? I can claim to know a good deal about measuring infantile intelligence because that's part of my ... ah ... basic armoury, but ... You do mean an adult patient?"

"Yes."

Tumbelow click-clicked his tongue against his teeth. "Well ... Ah-hah! I think you may have come to the right shop after all. I picked up a preprint at a congress I went to recently about IQ testing of deaf-and-dumb adults. That ought to include some suitable non-verbal material for you. Hang on. . . . Yes, here we are. This was a project to correlate the *g* coefficient of several different testing methods wholly exclusive of any verbal content. Does that sound like what you're after?"

"Absolutely ideal," Paul agreed.

"I'll let you have the loan of it, then," Tumbelow promised, and rang off.

Pleased, Paul reverted to what he had been doing when he was interrupted.

Obviously, the first step was to list everything he knew about Urchin in the order in which the facts occurred to him, like an amateur detective in a mystery novel collecting clues. Ultimately, perhaps, a pattern would emerge, but at this stage he felt baffled.

—She took the tape-recorder in her stride, but she was scared of the photographer's cameras. And what in the world frightened her so badly about the X-ray machine?

He ploughed on until he had filled three sheets of the notepad, then went back to the beginning and entered against each item action he might take to answer the implied questions. The phone rang a second time while he was busy with this, and he picked it up, sighing.

"Dr Fidler? Oh, my name's Shoemaker. You sent us a tape and a sample of writing by one of your patients."

"Oh, yes!" Paul sat up straight. "Have you identified the language for me?"

"I . . . uh . . . I'm afraid not. But I judged from the tone of your covering letter that you were in a hurry for the information, so I thought I'd better let you have a progress report. The matter sort of fell into my lap, you see, because I happened to be here on Saturday morning when it arrived. I took the sample of writing home with me—easier to deal with than the tape, naturally, because there are so many thousands of different spoken languages—and I went all the way through Diringer's book *The Alphabet*, which is pretty much the standard work, and I drew a complete blank."

"Are you certain?"

"Well, I suppose it might be something that Diringer missed, but that seems most unlikely to me. There's a slight resemblance to runic in the form of the letters, but the vowel-determinants given alongside certainly don't belong to a runic system."

"How extraordinary!" Paul said.

"Yes—yes, it is." Shoemaker hesitated. "Don't take my word for gospel, though. There are still a lot of other lines I can try: I'll play the tape over to everyone I can corner during the next few days, and I'm making a transcription of it in Bell Phonetic which I'll send down to London. But while I was doing that it suddenly struck me: if this is material from a mental patient, could it possibly be an invented language?"

"That occurred to me too," Paul said. Out of the corner of his eye he saw the door open, and waved impatiently at the intruder to wait. "But I thought it was next to impossible to devise an imaginary language."

"Quite right. It's almost bound to bear traces of the inventor's ... uh ... linguistic preconceptions. There was the case of a girl in France at the end of last century who claimed to be in telepathic communication with Martians, and hoaxed people right and left until a philologist showed that she was talking not 'Martian' but a crude variant of her native French. Nonetheless, I'd be grateful if you could make absolutely certain we're not wasting time on something she's made up from whole cloth."

Paul promised to do his best and cradled the phone. Turning, he saw that the visitor he had so casually made to wait was Dr Alsop.

"I'm dreadfully sorry!" he exclaimed.

Alsop waved the apology aside. "It sounded important—but what was it all about, anyway?"

Paul explained his plan for "Project Urchin" and handed Alsop the notepad on which he had made his preliminary list.

"Very thorough," the consultant approved in a cordial tone. "There are some things here, of course, which puzzle me, but I assume that's because I haven't been told about them yet. What have X-ray machines got to do with the case?"

"Thanks for reminding me. I missed one thing." Paul reclaimed the notepad and wrote in: *Knowledge of anatomy, karate or other unarmed combat.* Meantime, he described the near-disaster at Blickham General and the events of Saturday night.

"Sounds like a useful person to have on your side," Alsop murmured. "Question is, how do you persuade her to stay there without being able to talk to her?"

"She seems to be trying to learn English."

"Seriously, or as a way of gaining attention for herself?"

"Seriously, as far as I can tell."

"Now that *is* interesting. . . . May I just see that list again? Thanks." Alsop ran his eye down all three pages of it. "You've certainly gone into great detail. What do you expect to get out of it—a paper, a series?"

—A healed girl.

But Paul didn't voice that. He said merely, "It's too early to guess, isn't it?"

"Very wise. Well, you can rely on me for any advice I can give. I've been hoping you'd settle to something ambitious instead of loafing along with your routine work, and I'm very pleased."

Paul chose his next words carefully. "What I really would appreciate is some backing. If there's any difficulty about my asking for special facilities, for instance. Dr Holinshed and I—"

"Don't say another word," Alsop smiled. "It wouldn't be good for inter-staff relations. But you can count on me."

He slapped both thighs with his open palms. "Well, we'd better get on, hadn't we? There's a full roster of patients at the clinic today, and I daren't be late. Which reminds me: I have to go up to London next weekend, and I'd rather like to stop over on Monday and see my publisher about this book I'm doing. Would you mind taking next week's clinic for me?"

—Breakthrough!

Throughout the morning's series of interviews with patients Alsop continued to eye Paul with curiosity. However, it was not until the door had closed behind the last of those on the stand-up-and-yell list that he leaned over confidentially and spoke what was on his mind.

"You haven't said anything about it, young fellow, but I've reached a conclusion. Your wife's back. Am I right?"

For a moment Paul was taken aback. Then he managed a sickly grin, while Alsop chortled appreciation of his own insight.

Alsop had another appointment before proceeding to the clinic, and asked Paul to drive into Blickham and join him later. Pleased with the good impression he'd made today, Paul returned to his office and continued with his routine tasks, free from thoughts of the disasters that might have been.

Until the phone rang, and Holinshed's voice ground in his ear like icebergs crashing in a stormy sea.

"Fidler? Come down to my office right away!"

◆ *22* ◆

Paul closed the door briskly behind him and sat down without being asked. Holinshed scowled disapproval of the act and adopted his familiar headmasterly pose with elbows on chairarms, fingertips together.

"I am informed, Fidler, that you have been guilty of what one can only term a number of gross errors of professional judgment during the past few days. It's very seldom that I have cause twice within a week to rebuke a member of my staff, particularly one who holds a position of responsibility. One is prepared or this kind of mistake among the very junior staff who are as yet lacking in experience, but in people such as yourself one looks for a degree of caution and foresight."

Paul stared at him incredulously.

—Maybe Iris was right after all. Maybe I don't belong in this line of business. Not when the psychiatrists sometimes seem madder than their patients!

He said, completely forgetting the technique for dealing with Holinshed which he had been so pleased to master at their last interview, "What *are* you talking about?"

"I don't like your manner, Fidler," Holinshed snapped.

"And I don't like your accusations. Substantiate them or apologise."

The words hung in the air like smoke. Paul felt anger turn slowly sour in his belly until it was transmuted into alarm at his own outburst.

"Are you denying"—Holinshed was practically whispering—"that you gave instructions for the transfer of Riley from the Disturbed wing, thus directly setting in motion the train of events that climaxed in one of my nurses nearly being killed?"

—Oh my God. How am I going to get out of this one? Hang on: "Your wife's back." Therapeutic value of orgasm. Mostly double-talk but it'll sound convincing.

"Are you familiar with the background of Riley's case?"

"What? Fidler, I make it my business to acquaint myself with the history of every patient committed to Chent!"

"Then you can't have overlooked the element of extreme homosexual tension which contributes so much to his condition. He's making valiant efforts to achieve normality, but at his age he's still a virgin, simply because his inability to establish a stable relationship with a girl is resulting in impotence. Keeping him under maximum security is going to compound his problems by preventing even casual contact with women. I stand by my decision to transfer him, I'd do it again tomorrow if the occasion arose, and what is more I risked my own life on Saturday night in support of this belief. Were you not told about that?"

"What would you have had the nurse do—stand necking with him in the middle of the dance-floor?"

"Do you think I want to make things worse for him by encouraging him to imagine that one of the nurses finds him irresistible? But she rebuffed him as fiercely as if he was liable to rape her. He's incapable of that, as far as we can tell. What he needs is acknowledgment of his masculinity from other people to reassure him that he's not queer. Dr Alsop has brought to my attention some work by a man in Sweden on the relationship between sexuality and delinquency, and there appears to be some relevant material there."

Gradually Paul had been working back towards self-control. He wound up the last statement in exactly the stuffy tone calculated to impress Holinshed, and knew he had recouped most of the lost ground. Everything now depended on what the other "professional errors" might be.

—He's never going to like me. But by God I think I might make him scared of me before I leave this disgusting hole!

"The fact remains," Holinshed said, with marginally less conviction than before, "a patients' dance is hardly a proper proving ground for your theories about Riley, and more than Blickham General is for your theories about the girl you've decided to call Urchin. A nurse there was actually injured!"

"It was on Dr Alsop's recommendation that I took her for the X-ray. I took every precaution I could think of, including having the photographs made which Inspector Hofford asked for, since it occurred to me that to undergo a strange but innocuous experience would predispose her to submit quietly to the X-ray."

"Instead of which she proved not merely unco-operative but downright dangerous!"

"On the other hand, on Saturday evening she was both co-operative and courageous." Paul glanced at his watch, but kept talking to stop Holinshed breaking in. "I have to join Dr. Alsop at his clinic this afternoon, but I can spare a few minutes to outline the project which we've been mapping out this morning. We propose to conduct an exhaustive analysis of Urchin's behaviour, with a view to reconciling the obvious inconsistencies into . . ."

When he came out, he was shaking. He was late for lunch and had to gobble his food to avoid being overdue at the clinic. Nonetheless he was triumphant. Not one further word had been breathed about his "errors."

However, talking wasn't enough. He was under no illusions about the price he'd paid for facing Holinshed down. So far, Holinshed's dislike had been on principle; he liked his juniors to be subservient, and had even less affection for Mirza than for Paul.

All that was changed. Within the past half-hour Paul had staked his claim in the arena of hospital politics, and the side he had chosen to come down on was his own.

At the cost of probable indigestion, he reached the clinic five minutes early, gloomily preoccupied.

Alsop was refreshing his memory with the notes of last week's session; glancing up on Paul's entry, he exclaimed, "Hullo! What's happened to your sunny disposition since I left you?"

"To be candid," Paul said wryly, "Dr Holinshed has."

"Need I have asked? Tell me the worst, then."

He heard Paul out with a judicious air. "You're going to have to watch yourself," he opined. "Cede a little ground in Riley's case, for example, because being dead right all the time is a sure way to aggravate the situation. Tactics, young fellow, with the emphasis on the *tact*. Your overall strategy, though, is sound, and if you stick to it you'll make him wish he'd never opened his mouth to you. Okay?"

Without waiting for a reply, he went on, "There's one thing I should have thought of this morning, incidentally, which didn't strike me until I was driving out of the gate. After Urchin attacked the nurse here, how was it she was allowed to join the other patients at the dance? I'd have expected her to be safely shut away."

A chilly sensation, like a cold wet hand, passed down Paul's spine.

—What does my life hang on? A hair, a thread, a strand of cobweb?

"Do you know, that went completely out of my mind? I must have suppressed it. She *was* supposed to be locked in her cell, and we couldn't discover how she got out."

"Papa Freud he say," Alsop grunted, "don't let a lucky outcome make you overlook potentially significant facts." He chuckled unexpectedly. "And don't let it lead you down blind alleys like to one which this moment occurs to me."

"What?"

"Well, to what profession would you assign a rather attractive young woman who is (*a*) skilled in unarmed combat and (*b*) able to pick an unpickable lock? According to what I learn from television and the cinema, she ought to be a secret agent, oughtn't she? Come on, time's wasting. Get the nurse to show the first customer in."

♦ *23* ♦

Across the room the TV set uttered murmuring noises and the greyish light of its screen played on Iris's face. Practice had taught Paul to shut out its distractions while he was working. Shoulders hunched, he leaned on the gate-legged oak table and consolidated Urchin's dossier with the latest crop of improbable observations.

Following up every last one of those anomalies would take months; each seemed to point to a separate conclusion, and logic said that all bar one would be dead-ends. Urchin's blood, for example, was group AB—already the least common of the major groups—and rhesus negative into the bargain, suggesting that her genetic endowment was quite as odd as he'd expected on seeing that her face united the Asiatic trait of the epicanthic fold with features otherwise wholly European.

But there was no known connection between the two.

He was so preoccupied that when Iris abruptly spoke he at

first mistook the words for a line of dialogue from the television. Realising the error, he turned.

"I'm sorry?"

"I said the programmes are terrible tonight." Iris shrugged. And, after a pause: "What are you doing? Something for the diploma course?"

"No. Notes on the patient who was found wandering in the woods on the road near Yemble."

—Lying by omission: is that going to trap me one day? I judge somehow it would be offensive to Iris if I told her this is the same woman patient who saved me from Ridley's attack. I'm building such a stock of semi-secrets. . . .

"I think it's a disgrace, the way they keep piling extra work on you," Iris said.

"This is something I volunteered for."

"Goodness, haven't you got enough on your plate with the diploma course?"

"This is equally useful in a different way. It's a project I've started with the help of Dr Alsop, my consultant."

—Magic word.

"Oh!" Interest sparked. "I remember you saying he'd been after you to write a paper. Is this . . . ?"

"Quite likely."

—If I ever make enough sense of it.

"Is there something special about this patient?"

"Well, it's a bit technical, I'm afraid."

"You're always telling me that," Iris pouted. "In fact sometimes I get the feeling you're refusing to talk to me about your work. Maybe I haven't had the training to understand all the fine points, but I'm not so stupid that you have to shut me out of that half of your life."

—I have been here before. Oh, never mind: it was a hell of a good homecoming. Let's keep the mood as long as we can.

Oversimplifying to the point of irrelevance, he did his best to explain until Iris yawned pointedly and he broke off to suggest going to bed, whereupon she rose and gave him a warm smile.

"I like hearing you talk about your work," she said. "I don't pretend to follow everything, but it sounds very impressive!"

Paul hid his bitter reaction to the words.

—Incantations. That's all it is to you, and to how many other people? A set of magical phrases which will conjure the

evil spirits out of the bodies of the possessed. But there's no
magic about it. It's more ... carpentry. Rule-of-thumb stuff.
Taking the broken bits of a person and sticking them back all
anyhow, provided they're stuck tight.

But he didn't want to explain that; it was twenty to
midnight. He let her words stand at face value and approached her with a smile, putting both arms around her and
nuzzling her neck.

She eased herself free with an arch whisper: "Just let me
slip into the bathroom for a moment, darling!"

And suddenly, bright as lightning:—My God! The night of
the dance, when thanks to Mirza I came home. The first
time, the absolutely first time ever, when "the bathroom"
didn't intervene!

He clenched his fists as a wild exultation grew in him. At
the far back of his mind a rational voice seemed to argue
that the odds were enormously against it, but that was
drowned by the thunder of blood in his ears.

—If only, if only ... Christ, I hope it's true. I hope it's
twins.

And, drunk on the imagined triumph, he ran up the stairs
after Iris two at a time.

At the beginning of thier marriage, he had been as willing
as Iris to avoid parenthood. Her father had still been alive,
and although she could expect to inherit most of his money,
and had some already which her grandparents had left her,
this didn't justify bringing up children on a new doctor's salary. It made excellent sense to delay until he achieved, say,
registrar status.

Gradually, however, he had grown suspicious of the way
Iris declined to discuss their eventual children, concluded that
she had a psychic block against motherhood, and awkwardly
tried to suggest that talking about it might be therapeutic.
That was a mistake. It led to the first and worst of a series of
screaming matches in which she accused him of treating her
as a resident patient instead of a wife. Once or twice he was
tempted to wonder if she, like him, was hiding a breakdown
experienced before they met each other, but he abandoned
the idea.

No: she was simply unwilling to face the hard work and
inconvenience imposed by children on their parents.

If she had been afraid of childbirth itself, Paul would have
been perfectly content to adopt children; his training had

convinced him that a personality is moulded more by influence than chromosomes. But this didn't appeal to Iris any more than bearing her own. At last he was compelled to recognise the truth which Mirza with his usual insight had expressed as "wanting to boss you around." A tactful understatement.

In effect, he was Iris's compensation for not having children. Through managing his career she was transmuting the urge that should have been channeled towards rearing a child.

Curiously, that discovery—belated because he was reluctant to admit the implied slight to his self-esteem—was reassuring. Thanks to it, he genuinely could regard her as a resident patient with a problem to be cured. But for all his hinting, probing, teasing, he had made no dent in the barrier of her refusal.

Now chance might have succeeded where scheming had failed. Honest appraisal predicted that the result would be shock, dismay, tears; optimism argued that he could persuade Iris to accept a *fait accompli* even if he hadn't been able to bring her to a conscious positive decision.

That reminded him of Mirza's charming definition of an unwanted pregnancy: a *fétus accompli*.

With luck, he'd got one. But he said nothing whatever about it to Iris.

—Christ. What sort of a gap in my personality has been mortared up by the idea of being a father? Suddenly I feel like Superman. Pile the work on me and I come back for more; heap the papers in my tray and I go through them like a whirlwind; show me a tough textbook and the facts and theories slam straight into my subconscious; challenge me with a difficult patient and I don't waste time worrying and second-guessing myself, I go to the root of the matter and nine times out of ten get it right on the first shot. Soppy Al is jubilant and even Holinshed is turning polite on me!

Yet—and this in its way was a silent admission that he didn't really expect the mood of elation to survive the transition from wishful thinking to an argument on practical terms—he kept putting off and putting off the discussion he realised he must have with Iris, just as he had postponed confessing to her about his nervous breakdown until it was too late to mention it at all.

◆ *24* ◆

The phone rang.

"Inspector Hofford for you, Doctor," the operator said. "One moment."

—Oh lord. Is this the end of the rearguard struggle I've been putting up, staving off a definite decision about Urchin? No, I won't sign the paper saying she's insane. I don't care how certain the experts are that her language doesn't exist; she's a hell of a sight better balanced than half the people I have to deal with on the staff of this bin! Somebody else can certify her. I won't.

Paul's reflex anger almost prevented him from hearing what Hofford said when he came on the line; he was convinced he would be told the opposite.

"Morning, Doctor. You were right about Faberdown!"

"I . . . *what?* Oh, marvellous! How do you know?"

"He's a bit too fond of his liquor, and last night he made the mistake of drinking in the local which my Constable Edwards uses. He'll make a detective yet, that chap. Faberdown was holding forth about how much commission he'd lost through his broken arm, and somebody asked how it happened, and he . . . well . . . started grumbling about the girl who'd done it to him. Said she looked so tiny and harmless and he thought he could easily hold on to her, so he decided to have a go."

Paul hung excitedly on every word.

"So Edwards sorted him out when the pub shut. Not exactly routine procedure, but saves a lot of trouble. He cornered Faberdown and told him if he didn't let the whole thing drop he'd be the one on a charge and not the girl. And this morning I've had a visit from him, all shifty-eyed and embarrassed. He wants to let things slide, because it's 'not fair on this poor girl who's a bit off her head.' "

"Will you thank Edwards for me, very much indeed?"

—Blessed are they who expect the worst, for they shall get it!

Humming, Paul cradled the phone. He was almost alarmed at the reversal of mood which had come over him since the day of Urchin's arrival, when even such a slight change as the movement of the sitting-room furniture wound him up to irrational panic. Now, by contrast, he could half-believe he had tapped some magical force that made things turn out right, even events he could have no control over like this careless admission of Faberdown's.

The door of his office trembled to a ferocious bang, and one of the deputy porters entered, swinging a large cardboard package by its string.

"Morning, Doc. Parcel just arrived for you!"

A glance at the name of the dispatching firm showed that it was what he had been expecting: a kit of standard intelligence tests including most of those described in the article Tumbelow had loaned him.

He opened it up. Surrounded by a welter of torn tissue paper, he studied the instructions and found them clear and concise. He was already familiar with many of the tests from the receiving end, and although he hadn't administered any since he finished training he anticipated no problems.

—Hell of a well-matched battery, this! Correlative tables, weighting factors, lists of common anomalous deviations . . . Yes, we can go places with this lot. When?

He frowned over his day's timetable.

—Suppose I start at one-thirty. This lot, plus a man-drawing test, will take about an hour; that means postponing the two o'clock appointment to half past, and then . . .

He made some rapid changes to the schedule, notified the appropriate departments, and asked the stores to send him up a stopwatch to time the tests with. Then he arranged for Urchin to be brought to his office at one-thirty sharp.

After gulping down his lunch, he roped in Nurse Davis, willingly enough, to time the tests for him. She was quick on the uptake, and he completed his briefing of her comfortably ahead of time.

Offering her a cigarette—he wanted one himself because his nerves were unaccountably jangling—he asked her on impulse, "Nurse, this girl Urchin has been here for some time now. What do you make of her?"

Nurse Davis's dimples deepened enormously. "That's a queer one, Doctor. But queer in the wrong way."

"How do you mean?"

"The peculiar things she does are kind of consistent, get me?"

Paul hesitated. "Do you think she's actually insane?"

"That's a funny kind of question!"

"So give me a funny answer," Paul snapped.

"I don't have any answers, Doctor. But . . . All right, I'll go out on a limb. She strikes me as acting foreign. Not crazy—foreign."

A tap on the door, and Nurse Foden delivered Urchin at the very moment the clock above chimed and clinked the half-hour.

Paul studied the mysterious girl as she settled in a chair facing him across the table he had pulled out to use for the tests, warily as ever.

—Wary, yes. But not terrified any more. Must have made up her mind she isn't going to be tortured. . . . So Nurse Davis thinks she "acts foreign." I wish to God I knew what kind of foreign!

He had finally received a next-to-definite opinion from the philologists he had consulted about her language. They said they could find nobody who recognised it; the spoken form bore some relationship to the Finno-Ugrian language family, as the written form did to runic, but none of them would commit himself by giving it a name. In short, they had been as helpful as Dr Jewell when, in his capacity as the hospital's medical consultant, he made some vague remark about the epicanthic fold being a feature of Mongoloid idiocy.

—Mongoloids tend to be sickly and die young. This girl's very much alive, and I don't have to test her IQ to tell that she isn't an idiot.

"Good afternoon, Paul," she said with elaborately precise diction. The exaggerated vowel-deformations that had marked her first attempts to pronounce English had given way to an almost accentless mirror of those around her.

"Good afternoon," he returned.

"What we do today?" A thrusting forward of her tongue between her lips, as though stoppering the escape route of the words, and a correction. "Sorry. What *will* we do today?"

—Apparently it's not enough for her to get her meaning across. She insists on doing it idiomatically.

"Very good," he approved. But it was bound to be a waste of time giving a verbal description of what he planned. She would catch on through simple example. Nonetheless he spoke as he set out and demonstrated the first test: a form-board designed for bright primary children and retarded adolescents.

"When I say 'start' you put *these* in the holes."

She went through the easy ones so quickly it wasn't worth worrying about the timing. He moved ahead to the more complex versions, based on the combination of tangram-like pieces of multicoloured card to match assorted geometrical figures—squares, stars and crosses. Silent at the side of the room, Nurse Davis noted the times on a printed form which had been included in the package.

He had been expecting Urchin to show the first signs of difficulty when it came to the colour-reversal sequence, involving the reconstruction of previously accomplished figures with the contrasting colours exchanged. But she caught on to the idea so quickly that Nurse Davis almost missed clicking the stopwatch.

—Lord! I don't have to check the instructions to know that she's over the limits of measurement on *all* those!

He turned to withdraw the next test from the box: a Passalong test, sophisticated cousin of a well-known children's puzzle, in which the order of sliding squares had to be reversed within a time limit. When he glanced back he found that Urchin had taken several of the scraps of card belonging to the previous tests and grouped them, tangram-fashion, into an amusing sketch of a man and a woman standing together.

Seeing he was ready to proceed, she swept them aside with a chuckle and leaned forward to examine the Passalong. When he thought he had made it clear what was wanted, he told her to start.

She stared at it without making a move, long enough for him to grow worried lest he had failed to convey the purpose of it. Just as he was about to call it off and try a fresh run, she shot out her hand and completed the task with swift, economical motions. As far as he could tell, she had figured out the optimum series of moves and then carried them out with no false starts.

—She's going to rate over 150. Could be a lot higher.

Next he tried a sequence-touching test: tapping coloured cards in the same order as the examiner had done. At first there were only four, but more were added. When he had exhausted the seven supplied with the kit, Paul included on impulse two more belonging to another test. Urchin went through the entire nine with matter-of-fact briskness and not a single error.

—I'm not even within shouting distance of her abilities!

Sighing, he turned to the last tests he had on hand. If none of these presented her any difficulty, he'd have to send for a battery of advanced adult tests and sort out the ones least dependent on the use of words.

The concluding group consisted of pattern recognitions: simple matching to begin with, then tests for awareness of topological identity, including inversions, mirror-images and deformations, then some really tough ones—both odd-man-out and group-completion involving points of resemblance so subtle Paul felt himself baffled by them, and finally a series dependent on analogies rather than actual identity.

Here at long last there were a couple which she didn't get right, but they were in the hardest section of all, and she did the correct thing by skipping them when they failed to strike her at once, so that she completed the remainder within the time limit.

—She's enjoying this. Look how her eyes are sparkling.

Well ... That left one simple test, too subjective for his own taste but vouched for by experts as adequately correlated with g. He gave her a large sheet of white paper and a pencil, established that she knew what the word "draw" meant, and told her to draw a man.

Rising, he went over to the window and beckoned Nurse Davis to show him her timings. He ran down them, comparing each with the highest score in the tables supplied, and eventually shook his head.

"Something wrong, Doctor?" the nurse ventured.

"I wish there was!" Paul blurted. "Then I'd feel happier about her being in Chent!"

"She's done very well, hasn't she?"

Paul gave a sour grin. "She's over the limit on almost all these tests, which means she'd place about a hundred and eighty on the scale. And this is meaningless. I remember one of my professors saying that IQ tests were defensible up to about a hundred and twenty, debatable up to a hundred and fifty, and laughable anywhere above that because the subject is probably brighter than the man who invented the test. Time must be just about up, hm?"

Nurse Davis turned back towards Urchin and looked over her shoulder. After a second she began to giggle.

"You ought to be flattered, Doctor! It's good enough to be framed!"

Paul stared at what Urchin had done. Nurse Davis was right. He was looking at one of the most masterly pencil portraits he had ever seen, and the subject was himself.

◆ 25 ◆

A hawthorn hedge visible from the window of the staff sitting-room had put on white blossom as thick as a snowstorm. Gazing at it, Paul reviewed the progress he had made in dealing with his twin problems: Urchin, and Iris.

Having obtained concrete proof of Urchin's intelligence, he had been left on the horns of a dilemma. Her behaviour continued apparently rational, with no further outbreaks like the attack on the nurse at Blickham General—nothing, in fact, but a slight disagreement with a newly arrived nurse who tried to force her to eat a stew with meat in it against Paul's instructions that she should be allowed a vegetarian diet. This suggested that Nurse Davis's description of her as "foreign" was the correct one.

On the other hand, she was becoming so fluent in English that Paul was inclined to wonder whether she was really learning it for the first time. There were two alternatives: she might be relearning something temporarily lost through hysterical amnesia, or she might all along have been pretending not to understand. The last possibility was the least likely. Shoemaker had been dogmatic about the difficulty of constructing an imaginary language which would baffle a trained philologist. However, she rated as a genius in every test he had been able to apply; perhaps someone of such outstanding intellect could devise and stick to an invented language.

A showdown with Iris could not be put off much longer. Faced with its inevitability, Paul had begun to feel less and less certain of persuading her to accept the pregnancy. He needed some sort of reassurance of his own abilities, and sought it in an early resolution of the mystery of Urchin. She was now in command of a vocabulary which ought to have let her answer inquiries about her origins, even if only in the most general terms. He had worked up gradually to some direct questions, growing more and more irritated with her evasions, and today he was virtually certain she had lied to him when she claimed not to know the right words to phrase her answers.

On the verge of accusing her, he had suddenly recovered his professional control and realised that if she was lying to him this must be due to a disturbance of the personality. He would be very ashamed of himself if he lost his temper with a patient for something that the patient couldn't help. Which of the staff at Chent should know better than Paul Fidler, ex-madman, what that helplessness was like?

Having dismissed her, he found himself in the grip of another of his visions of disaster narrowly avoided: this time, a fantasy in which Urchin lost her trust in him because he had shouted at her, refused further co-operation and ultimately retreated into such apathy that there was no hope of her ever leaving Chent. It upset him so much that he abandoned his work and came to collect his tea and biscuits ahead of time.

There was no urgency about Urchin's case. He sensed that. A point might be reached at which she felt sufficiently confident of her ability to express her meaning and began to talk freely, but no one—probably not even she herself—could forecast when it would arrive. By contrast, the embryo in Iris's womb was growing inexorably in accordance with biological laws, and he could name to the week, if not to the day, the very latest moment when he would have to face the issue.

Knowing that, he still could not concentrate on preparing for it. His mind remained dominated by Urchin, as he saw her during his daily rounds of the hospital. Sister Wells had given her a portfolio with a broken handle from the cupboard where the unclaimed effects of deceased patients were stored; she had mended it neatly with a braided cord, and now carried it everywhere. It contained the objects she had accumulated to help her find her bearings: notepad and pencil, a child's picture dictionary, a cheap atlas in limp covers, a drawing-book which he had bought for her when, on impulse, he adopted Nurse Davis's suggestion and took the portrait she had made of him into Blickham to have it framed. It now hung on the wall of his office; when she'd seen it there for the first time, Urchin had hugged him in delight at the compliment.

A couple of times he had asked to inspect the contents of the bag, but even the atlas, which fascinated her so much she had annotated almost every page in her curious spiky private writing, did not afford a lever with which to pry open her defences. A request to point out her home still produced the same response as at first: she indicated the vicinity of Chent.

—Could she have been raised in total isolation, Kaspar Hauser fashion, by some lunatic genius who taught her a language he, not she, had invented . . . ? No, it's absurd; she'd be so agoraphobic. But it makes as much sense as the other possibilities!

Radio was relayed throughout the hospital during the patients' daytime rest-periods, and there was a TV set in each of the sitting-rooms—fitted with locked switches so the staff could control the choice of programmes. Paul regarded this as overprotective, but it wasn't a matter on which he wanted to start an argument. He had observed Urchin's reaction to both. Music puzzled her, whether the broadcast was of a symphony concert or the top twenty pops, but she listened to the spoken word with avidity. Television was especially useful, it seemed; when the commentary matched words written on the screen—sales slogans in commercials, sports results given both verbally and visually, and so forth—that supplied her with a sound-to-spelling key. Yet she always appeared dismayed at what the screen reported, as thought the entire world contributed to some universal, horrifying fantasy.

The last evening when he was on duty, Paul had been making a quiet tour of the wards when he came on a group of female patients watching a current affairs programme. The ragbag of subjects included a controversial new play, a row over the government's defence policy, and the escape of a notorious criminal from jail.

A little apart from the others, Urchin stood—she was too short to sit and watch except in the front row of chairs, and long-term patients claimed those as of right. Unnoticed in shadow, Paul studied her, hopeful for a clue to her condition.

The excerpt from the play, and the interview with the author which followed, were meaningless to her, but when she recognised familiar words she repeated them to herself. That seemed sensible.

The subject switched to defence policy, and there were newsreels from Viet-Nam: troops burning a village of thatched huts, helicopters hunting a fleeing man across a rice-paddy until a well-aimed shot brought him down, refugees leading their children along a muddy road. These affected her deeply; she bit down on her lower lip.

But there was little to enlighten him here, Paul decided. Most averagely sensitive people might be equally upset. He was on the point of slipping away when the final item came on.

At first Urchin appeared not to understand it, but when the meaning seeped through—a sketch showed the route the escaped prisoner had taken, and pictures of spiked walls and guarded gates told their own story—she was so overcome she had to turn away. Turning, she saw Paul staring at her, and for a moment her eyes locked with his.

They were full of tears.

"Hullo, Paul!" Mirza exclaimed, jingling the hand-bell; although weeks had gone by, no electrician had appeared to resite the push of the electric one. "You're not exactly a bundle of joy today, are you? How's Iris?"

"Oh—she's fine, thanks."

"Glad to hear it." Mirza paused while Lil brought him his tea, then continued: "Well, whatever it is that's getting you down, it can't be the woman who's the next closest to your heart. Urchin's making remarkable progress, isn't she?"

"Yes and no. . . ." Paul shrugged. "Certainly she's coming along better than I have any right to expect."

"So what's the big depression for? Holy Joe been at you again?"

"Not that either." Paul gave a wan smile. "The truth is, I suppose, I'm fundamentally unused to things going right for me. Holinshed's got off my back, Alsop is delighted with what I'm doing, my work is under control for a change—so I ought to be overjoyed. But the more things go right, the worse it's likely to be if they go wrong, isn't it?"

"It's about the most pessimistic philosophy I've ever heard of," Mirza murmured, stirring his tea with a gentle tinkling of his spoon.

Paul hesitated. For a moment it was on the tip of his tongue to take Mirza into his confidence and ask his advice about Iris. He had no one else to turn to, and he could be sure of the Pakistani's sympathy. But in another moment this room would be full of people, and he dared not risk them picking up even the tail-end of his oppressive secret.

He compromised. "Time for a drink before dinner, Mirza? We've got out of the habit since Iris came home."

"I'd like to," Mirza nodded. "But not before dinner, I'm afraid. I shall be working late. Afterwards?"

Paul tossed a mental coin. Evenings at home alone with Iris were becoming a torment, because every time he glanced at her he found himself seeking signs of her condition. He was convinced that her period was overdue, but she hadn't mentioned the fact, and he still hadn't found a way to raise it himself. On the other hand, no matter how much he wanted to talk to Mirza, there would be a row if he announced he was going out on his own.

"Why don't you bring Iris down to the Needle about nine?" Mirza said, while he was still debating.

"Well . . ."

"You could run into me by chance. And I don't think a little frigid politeness would be bad for her. How about it?"

—Better than sitting at home like last night, I guess.

"Yes, okay. About nine."

Iris welcomed the suggestion of going out for a drink, probably—Paul suspected—because it distracted her from her own anxieties. Even before Mirza "ran into them by chance," however, she had lapsed into apathy, answering Paul in monosyllables.

Once the Pakistani had joined them, Paul studied her narrowly, expecting a recurrence of the behaviour she had exhibited when he had invited Mirza home. Tonight, though, she seemed to lack the energy for it, and he realised with some surprise that it couldn't have been the automatic, conditioned process he had assumed. It required conscious control and a lot of effort.

—In which case . . . A defence mechanism. Habits equal stability/security the existence of people who behave differently, regardless of colour which is only an extra outward sign, is a threat to the personality. The way *we* do things is the "right" way. The purpose of freezing out the alien is to avoid being exposed on future occasions to more reminders that "right" is an arbitrary term. In its most advanced form this is culture shock: where the victim is so outnumbered by people following different customs and unspoken assumptions that privacy equates to effective insanity. But that means . . .

Paul exclaimed and snapped his fingers. Mirza broke off in

the middle of a story he was telling, to which Iris was not even pretending to listen, and blinked in surprise.

"Sorry," Paul said. "But thanks very much, Mirza. You've just given me a brilliant idea."

◆ *26* ◆

A tap came on the door of Paul's office. Without turning, he called an invitation to enter.

The visitor was Mirza, carrying a bulky package which he dumped with a bang on the corner of the desk. "For you," he announced.

"What?"

"I saw it in the porter's room just now and offered to bring it up for you. Wish I hadn't. It's heavy." Mirza perched on the window-sill, both long legs at full stretch.

"Very kind of you," Paul said. He laid down his pen, offered Mirza a cigarette from a packet on the desk, and absently lit one himself while scrutinising the parcel. His name was on the label all right, but the address originally written beneath was that of the hospital where he had worked before coming here; someone had scored it through and substituted Chent's.

"No trouble," Mirza said. "As a matter of fact, I suddenly remembered a few minutes ago that I wanted to ask how your brilliant idea turned out."

"Which idea?"

"The one that hit you in the Needle the other night."

"Oh!" Paul leaned back in his chair and gave a short laugh. "It didn't work too well in practice, I'm afraid."

"Was it something to do with Urchin?"

"Tell me something, Mirza: do you read minds, or do you simply listen at keyholes?"

"I take it that's a way of complimenting me on my omniscience. But it's not a very clever guess. You've been thinking about practically nothing else for weeks."

Paul tapped the first ash from his cigarette. "Yes, I'm

afraid that's true. . . . Well, if you really want to hear about it . . . ?"

"You said I gave you the idea. I'm naturally interested in the fate of my offspring."

—He could have chosen another metaphor than that.

Paul hid his desire to wince. He said, "All it amounts to is this. Although Urchin now seems to understand and even speak English pretty fluently, she's been refusing to talk about herself. She may be genuinely unable to—she may be amnesiac, in other words—or she may be so scared of saying the wrong thing that she's afraid to, because being not only in a strange country but shut up among lunatics she has no guide to what's right and acceptable. I thought I'd try and put her in a more familiar context and get her mind running on wherever it is she comes from."

"Sounds reasonable," Mirza opined. "How did you set about it?"

"She made a tape for me when she first came here—just a couple of minutes talking in her own language—and the philology department at the university sent it back when they gave up trying to identify it. So I hid the recorder and switched the tape on without her noticing. It shook her so much I thought I was getting somewhere, but she realised what I'd done almost at once, and she was so angry at being tricked she clammed up worse than ever. Then I've tried to get her to draw scenes from the place she comes from, and sing me a song that she likes—obviously the music she hears on the radio isn't the kind she's used to—but I've drawn a blank so far. Still, not to worry; it's early days yet."

Mirza stretched forward to drop ash into the wastebasket. "*Nil carborundum*—that's the spirit. I wish you luck, anyhow. She seems like a nice person, and it would be a pity to have her stuck in Chent for the rest of her life. . . . By the way, aren't you going to open this?" he added, tapping the parcel.

Paul gave him a suspicious glance. "It's not some sort of surprise package you've made up, is it?"

"Cross my heart," Mirza grinned. "It's just my 'satiable curiosity, I'm afraid."

"Oh, very well."

Shrugging, Paul slashed the string and peeled back the outer wrapping of paper and corrugated board. Inside that was a wooden box.

"No wonder it was heavy," Mirza commented.

The lid of the box was tied, not nailed, and came away easily. Underneath, almost buried in a welter of wood-shavings and still more corrugated board, was a clock.

—What in the world . . . ?

He lifted it out. It stood a foot and a half high. The dial was set in a kind of pedestal of polished brown wood with brass pillars at each corner. That much was ordinary; the rest was a gigantic sick joke. For above the pedestal stood a shiny brass figure of Father Time, naked skull grinning under a draped hood, one bony hand clutching an hour-glass, the other a scythe. Removal of the clock from its packing had triggered off the last energy stored in its spring, and as he turned it upright the scythe began to wag back and forth in rhythm with its ticking.

A line of fine writing was engraved across the base of the statuette: *In the midst of life we are in death.*

"Why, that's fabulous!" Mirza exclaimed, darting forward to examine it more closely. "I wish I knew people who sent me presents like this."

"You're welcome to it," Paul muttered. "I think it's hideous."

"Oh, come now!" Mirza said. The scythe had stopped its wagging and he was touching it with a fingertip as though testing the sharpness of the blade. "Grotesque, yes, but rather splendid nonetheless. Who's it from?"

"I have no idea."

Mirza picked up the box and rummaged among the shavings." Maybe there's a note. Yes, here we are. And the key for it, too."

He handed Paul a single sheet of pale pink notepaper, folded once. It bore a short message which he read with dismay.

"When I spotted this it reminded me of you, and of the fact that I never did give you a token of my appreciation. I hope it reaches you safely. I did phone the hospital the other day but they wouldn't tell me where you were. Regards—Maurice."

—Oh, no. Oh, *no!*

"Goes for eight days, it says on the dial," Mirza reported with satisfaction, closing the glass of the clock after winding it. The scythe resumed its lunatic wagging.

"Shut up," Paul said.

Taken aback, Mirza hesitated. "I'm sorry," he said at length. "I thought it was a bit of a giggle. What's wrong?"

Paul stabbed his cigarette into an ashtray. "It's from somebody I hoped never to hear of again—a man called Maurice Dawkins. He was one of my first patients. Used to attend a group-therapy session I ran. Classic manic-depressive, prognosis ... well ... uncertain. He developed a fantastic transference and fixated on me so severely it became a bloody nuisance."

"Queer?"

"As the proverbial nutmeg. But with such a load of guilt about it he couldn't fall for anybody who might reciprocate—only for people with whom there was no chance of them joining in."

"Poor devil," Mirza said sincerely. "What happened eventually?"

"I got him off my back the first couple of times, and he showed good response to treatment. We got his cycle flattened out, and in fact we heard nothing about him for over three months. Then there was some crisis in his business—he's a partner in a firm of antique dealers—and his fixation took charge again. The first sign we had of it was when he sent me a present out of the blue. Like this. Only the first time it was a mirror."

He made a helpless gesture. "Then there were phone-calls, and then he camped out on my doorstep one evening and I found him when I got home from taking Iris to the theatre. We got him straightened out, same as before, and there was an interlude of calm, and then God damn if the same pattern didn't repeat."

"What did he send you the second time?"

"It's not bloody funny!" Paul rasped.

"No. Sorry." Mirza looked down at his fingertips. "Are you expecting him to chase you all the way to Chent? Surely your old hospital would have more sense than to tell him where you've gone."

Paul hesitated. "The trouble is," he said finally, "he knows some friends of Iris's. He could trace me if he wanted to."

—But that isn't all he knows. Damn the man. Damn him.

"If you don't mind," he went on, "I'd better find out who's in charge of his case now and warn him." He reached for the phone.

"It sounds like a bind," Mirza said sympathetically, and went out.

Waiting for his call to London to go through, Paul lit another cigarette with shaking fingers. The hideous clock

mocked him with its grinning skull; he stared at it but did not
see it. His mind was obsessed with one of the worst visions of
impending disaster that had ever struck him.

—What in hell made me think that confessing my secret to
Maurice was a good idea? Comfort, reassurance: "It could
happen to anyone, it even happened to me." And the trouble
I had to go to, keeping him away from Iris for fear he should
let the truth slip. If she were to find out now ... I can hear
her telling me that the reason she won't have my children is
because of their tainted heredity. It was a breakdown from
overwork, not a psychosis, but she wouldn't want to be told
the difference. I should have been honest five years ago. I've
dug my own grave.... No. I haven't dug anyone a grave.
You don't put aborted foetuses in graves. You just throw
them away.

He sat imagining this dreadful prospect for fully ten
minutes after speaking to the former colleague who had
taken over Maurice's case, until he realised with a shock that
Urchin was due for her daily session shortly and he was in no
state to cope with her. Guiltily, he did something which he
had last been compelled to do when Iris left for her visit to
the Parsonses and he was worried that she might stay away
for good.

He went down to the dispensary and stood for a while contemplating the tranquilliser shelf. The pharmacist was busy
on his weekly stock-taking at the other end of the room. At
length he settled for something comparatively innocuous: a
few Librium capsules in their ugly green-and-black gelatine
shells. Much practice during his breakdown had enabled him
to swallow them without water, and he took one immediately.

Waiting for the accompanying bubble of air to come back,
he stared at the ranked boxes, jars and packets.

—A cupboardful of miracles, this! Powdered sleep, tablet
sleep, liquid sleep; energy in pills, in vials, in disposable sy-
ringes; drugs to suppress hunger and stimulate appetite, to relieve pain and to cause convulsions ... Will the day come
when a descendant of mine stands in a dispensary and selects
a tablet labelled *Instant Sanity, adult schizoid female Cau-
casian 40–50 kilograms*? Christ, I hope not. Because—

The anticipated burp arrived. Since he had momentarily
forgotten that was why he was standing here, it erupted with
maximum noise, and the pharmacist turned his head and
grinned. Sheepishly Paul moved away.

—Because long before we get to the Instant Sanity pill dreadful things will have happened to us. Drugs to keep the masses happy, like opium in last-century China and the British hashish monopoly in India; drugs for political conformism ("AntiKommi for those left-wing twinges"), for sexual conformism ("Straighten up and fly right with Ortho-Hetero twice a day"), for petty criminals, for deviates, for anyone you don't like. Pills for bosses to give their workers, pills for wives to give their husbands . . .

But that idea abruptly switched the fantasy from waking nightmare to a sore subject in real life, and he determinedly shut the matter to the back of his mind as he returned to his office.

The clock, which Mirza had thoughtfully adjusted to the right time, showed that Urchin was due any moment. He snatched it up and dumped it on a shelf behind him, where he at least didn't have to look at it, though thanks to Mirza its gentle ticking would last a week or more now. As he sat down, an alarming idea occurred to him and he twisted to watch the minute-hand reach the half-hour mark.

—If it chimes as well, I think I shall throw it out of the window.

But he was spared that; only the clock overhead in the tower sounded.

And here was Urchin being delivered by Nurse Woodside, and he hadn't the vaguest idea what he was going to do today.

When he had worked through the preliminary chat—mainly answers to Urchin's inevitable questions about words she'd run across lately but couldn't fathom the meaning of—he still had no fresh ideas, so he merely reviewed some of his earlier ones. She still would not connect herself with any country in the atlas bar Britain; she still would not draw a picture of any scene except familiar views of the hospital and its grounds; she still declined to sing him any song apart from mimicking the sounds of a current pop hit which she must have heard *ad nauseam* on the radio.

Dispirited, Paul contemplated her, at a loss for any other inspiration.

—It's not that I haven't learned a great deal about you, Urchin. I have a stack of paper nearly an inch thick listing what I know. Trouble is, what I've found out doesn't hang together. You refuse to eat or even touch meat, but how the hell do you reconcile adament vegetarianism with breaking

Faberdown's arm? I know pacifists who manage the reverse
of that and preach non-violence over steak and potatoes, and
it doesn't seem nearly so incongruous. And if you are amnesiac and can't, rather than won't, talk about your background, why hasn't it affected the rest of your mind? If your
auditory memory is so good you can imitate the garbled
sounds of a pop song practically as exactly as a tape-recorder, and your knowledge of English is already incredible,
then . . .

She was looking past him at the clock with an air of vague
disquiet.

—Urchin, Urchin, what *am* I going to do about you?
Look: either you're a sane foreigner, in which case it serves
no purpose to pretend you don't know what I'm talking
about, or else you've invented a fantasy life in a private
world. And if that's the truth, with your intellect you damned
well ought to have made a better job of it! You ought to welcome my willingness to string along with the gag; you should
have ingenious answers ready for questions on any subject.
Blazes, even Maurice used to do better than this when he was
in his manic phase. He'd elaborate huge fantasies on the basis
of what the real world offered, and be as eager to have other
people join in the game as a child making a pirate ship from
an upturned table.

For a moment his eyes met hers. Uncomfortable, perhaps
realising she had disappointed him, she could not face his
gaze but looked past him again.

—So . . . what next? Association test? Inadequate vocabulary. No, I'm afraid it's a matter either of sheer patience or
breaking down her resistance with drugs. And frankly I don't
know where to start.

He sat for a while longer in silence, reviewing the possibilities that modern chemotherapy offered, and concluded at last
that he wasn't going to get anywhere today. Since there was
other work to be done, he roused himself and stood up.

She didn't react to his moving. Bewildered, he stared at
her. Her eyes were open, glazed, and her mouth was a little
open too.

"Urchin?" he said idiotically.

She said something in her own language, but no part of her
body except her lips stirred. Alarmed, he stepped to her side
and was about to touch her when a great light dawned. He
followed the direction of her gaze, and saw that a bright

—Has she got the distinction, or . . . ?

Paul cogitated. "How about . . . let's see . . . Nurse Woodside?"

"She's a *little* crazy."

He was inclined to be amused at that; you could make out an excellent case for Urchin being right. He took a deep breath and advanced the interrogation another key step.

"Why are you here, Urchin?"

"Because you— No, you're not sure. Because *somebody* believes I'm crazy too."

—Interesting!

"Why do they think that, Urchin?"

"Because I have to learn English. Because I don't know about many things, this kind of clothes, knife-and-forks, tell the time with clocks like that." She pointed past him at the statuette of Time, and the gesture turned into a groping motion as though she was trying to pick words out of the air. "Everything is so different!"

The last word peaked on a cry of despair. He waited for her to calm down; then he set about putting the remark into context.

"Where's your home, Urchin?"

She looked momentarily blank. "Here!"

—Funny. Wouldn't think "home" was a difficult concept. The patients talk all the time about the homes they've left, or hope to go back to. . . .

"Where did you live before you came here?"

A hesitation. "Not . . . not far away."

"What did you call your home?"

That produced an incomprehensible sound, apparently a word of her own language. Paul sighed and made one last attempt.

"The first time I saw you, in the woods: where had you come from then?"

"There!"

Paul made a resigned note consisting in the single word *Topsy.*

—I'spect I just growed!

"What do you find so different, Urchin?" he pursued.

"People are different—look different, dress different. Different-*ly*. The way they talk the way they do things. Everything everything."

"And you're here because you find everything is different."

"No!" She jerked upright as though annoyed at his lack of

perception. "Is because—*it's* because you think me different."

Paul cocked an eyebrow. This was a nutshell analysis of the status of the insane implying considerable insight on Urchin's part. Before he could frame his next question, however, she burst out in a way that suggested weeks of pent-up frustration about to let go.

"I was so frightened you would think me crazy because I don't know all that!"

"But you said I didn't think you were crazy," he murmured.

"Not!"

"Then why should 'somebody' think you are?"

"Because I can't explain what I am."

Paul hardly dared draw the breath to utter the next question; he sensed he was on the verge of a breakthrough. "What are you, then?"

"I—" An enormous painful swallow; her whole body was racked with conflicting tensions. "I can't tell you," she said finally.

"Why not?"

"They made me not to tell."

"Who are *they?*"

Another phrase in her own language. A repetition produced no clearer answer. He tried an oblique approach.

"Are 'they' telling you not to talk to me now?" he suggested, thinking of paranoiac voices.

"No. They *told* me not to."

"Long ago?"

"Yes . . . no . . . long for me, long ago for me."

"Can they reach you here at Chent? Can they talk to you now, or can you talk to them?"

"No." The word quavered between pale lips, and she linked her fingers and worked them nervously back and forth.

"Then if they can't reach you, they can't hurt you, can they? So you can answer my question."

Silence. Inwardly seething, Paul preserved an expression of calm while he cast about for yet another argument.

—So near and yet . . . In the woods where I first found her: talks as if she sprang from the ground! What was it she said to me then? I can hear it in memory, I think. *Ti-*something?

Aloud, he said on the spur of the moment, "Urchin, what does *triake-no* mean?"

Faintly she answered, "Like you would say, "how do you do?" Except it means—it means exactly 'who are you?' "

Paul jolted upright. "Is that what you say when you meet somebody, where you come from? Instead of 'hello?' "

"Yes, when you meet somebody, ask who you are."

"Arrzheen! *Tiriak-no?* Tell me! Tell me in English—*tiriak-no?*"

"Visitor," Urchin said. No voice carried the word, only a hiss of breath. "Person from other . . ."

"Other . . . what?"

"Other time!"

Paul was shaking so much he could hardly hold his pen; his clothes were clammy with tension-induced sweat. But by force of will he overcame the excitement of his triumph and inscribed on his memo pad his final note for the day.

And in a fit of uncontrollable exuberance he added to it six exclamation marks.

◆ *28* ◆

For once the visions that his imagination conjured up to distract him from his work for the rest of the afternoon were not of disaster but of impending achievement. He wanted to share his good news with somebody, but there was no one available: Alsop could not be reached, Natalie had gone to Birmingham again with Roshman, and Mirza was away at an interview for another post he'd applied for.

This last, which Paul hadn't heard about, brought him back to earth with a jolt.

—The so-and-so! He never told me he was thinking of moving on. Chent without Mirza would be intolerable. But I can hardly wish a good friend bad luck, can I?

Short of Holinshed, that meant Iris would be the first person he could tell about his breakthrough. At first the idea was unattractive; bit by bit, though, he began to warm to it.

—She won't understand the full implications, of course, but I can make it clear enough to impress her, and . . . Yes, I can suggest going out to dinner to celebrate (I think I have enough cash in my pocket) and talk about how much it'll mean to my career to publish an account of Urchin's case and then I can work the conversation around from professional advancement to the subject of starting our family!

It all seemed so straightforward in the heat of the moment that he hummed a cheerful tune as he rushed through the rest of the work awaiting him. Counterpointing the thoughts in the forefront of his mind, phrases and sentences occurred to him which would be useful in the paper he was now definitely going to prepare.

—The influence of changing environment on the content of the dreams and waking fantasies of psychiatric patients has become a subject of great concern in recent years. Since the archetypal symbol of charging horses was first found to have been supplanted by the image of a thundering steam locomotive . . .

—Fear of spiritual failure, particularly the compensatory phenomenon which induced weak personalities to conclude that if they could have no other claim to notoriety they might at least be selected by God for exceptionally harsh punishment, has been dethroned as the primary constituent of mental disorder by elements related to sexuality. However . . .

—The following remarkable case involving systematised delusions of otherworldly origins elaborated by a patient of outstanding intellect, whom we shall refer to as "U," suggests that elements derived from still other features of our changing society may well enter into our . . .

He was half minded to set about drafting a preamble there and then, and got as far as rolling a sheet of paper into his typewriter before realising that for all he knew the fragmentary admission he had secured today from Urchin might be strenuously denied tomorrow. He shrugged and got to his feet. A better way of using his time would be to tackle Iris while he still had his excitement to buoy him up.

A quarter of a mile before he reached home, however, the engine of his car spluttered and died. With a wrenching sense of his own stupidity he recalled that this morning, on the way to work, he had noted the low reading of the fuel gauge, but neglected to stop and fill up because he was late. Tonight he had been so wrought up he hadn't glanced at the instrument board.

Cursing, he rolled to the side of the road and got out. He could do one of two things: walk home and collect the two-gallon can which ought to be in the car but wasn't, because the other morning he'd found there was no dry kindling to start the living-room fire with and he'd had to pour petrol on the hearth before he could make it burn; or walk back to the filling station in Yemble and borrow a can from there, which would mean driving back to collect the ten shillings deposit and wasting extra time.

It would be quicker to go home.

Of course, it would undermine the impact he hoped to make on Iris if he started by admitting he'd run out of petrol. Best of all would be if he could sneak around the back of the house without her noticing, collect the can from the kitchen, and slip away again, returning noisily with the car in another ten minutes.

—Lord, I wish I wasn't built the way I am! Running out of juice can happen to anybody, but I have to take it as an insult to my ego and I'm reduced to creeping around by back doors and hoping my wife won't notice. This isn't how I thought marriage would be. I expected to be able to share everything, even the big disheartening problems, spread their load and make them easier to carry.

Nonetheless, shamefacedly, he put his plan into effect. When he quietly entered the gate, he was relieved to see Iris's silhouette on one of the leaded windows; she was talking on the phone. He heard a peal of laughter as he passed.

—Keep at it. I never thought I'd be glad that you can't enjoy a phone-call if it lasts less than twenty minutes.

The kitchen door was unbolted. He tiptoed inside and found the can of petrol where he had left it. Just as he was about to pick it up, Iris's voice came to him clearly.

"How do you spell that? . . . S–W–E . . . Swerd. Good, thanks a million."

It was exactly as though someone had opened the top of his head and poured ice-water into his brain. The world froze.

—Oh my God. No, it can't be true. Not Swerd. Not that slick bastard with so many rich patients the law daren't touch him!

Like a man in a dream he forgot what he was in the house for, forgot about returning to the car and making his triumphant official entry armed with his good news and the suggestion they go out to dinner. He walked to the door of the kitchen and flung it open.

At the phone Iris exclaimed in alarm, spun on the stool

where she sat to make long calls, and dropped a pencil tap-tap on the tiled floor. Her face went milky pale.

"Paul!" she whispered. "Goodness, you gave me a fright!" And, with a creditable attempt at recovery, continued to the phone: "No, it's okay, Bertie. It's just Paul coming in. Thanks very much—see you."

She put down the hand-set and made to tear a sheet from the memo pad on the telephone table. Paul strode across the room and clamped his fingers on her wrist.

"Paul! What's the matter? Stop it, you're hurting me!"

Teeth so tightly together the strain on his jaw muscles made his ears sing, Paul roughly forced apart her grip on the paper. Crying out, she let go and retreated a couple of paces.

"Paul, what's wrong?" she whimpered.

"You damned well know what's wrong!" he snapped. Stomach knotted in anger, voice thick with anguish, he shook the incriminating note at her. She had copied down the name "N. J. Swerd" and a telephone number.

"It's ... it's nothing! It's a friend of Bertie's! He rang up just now and—"

"Liar," Paul said. "Dirty, rotten, stinking, *silly* liar. Do you think I don't know who Newton Swerd is? Christ, he's a standing bloody joke in every medical school in Britain, the dean of the Harley Street abortionists, five hundred guineas and no questions asked!"

Her mask of prevarication crumpled. She began to edge away from him as though to avoid a physical attack; when she had managed to get the high back of a black oak chair between them she halted, teeth chattering.

"How the hell did you think you could keep that sort of secret, living in the same house as a doctor? Did you imagine I wouldn't realise you were pregnant?"

—This isn't the way I wanted to start talking about my child. I wanted it to be a happy thing. How did I come to tie myself to this selfish, bossy, greedy woman Iris?

Staring at her, his anger too cold to blur his eyes with tears, he read on her face that indeed she had hoped to deceive him until the job was done. She was trembling so much she had to cling to the chair for support.

He waited. After another minute she regained enough self-possession to speak coherently.

"What the hell do you mean by sneaking in and spying on me?"

"Spying on you!"

—Where do women like her learn such effrontery? Raised to it, I suppose. Taught it in the nursery by starched nannies, the hands slapped when the lesson isn't properly absorbed!

"God damn it, Iris, I want to be a father! Can't you get that through your head? I *want* children! It's *natural* to want children! Marriage is *about* children!"

"It's easy enough for a man to say that! Men don't have to produce the babies!"

"If you're that scared of childbearing you need treatment!"

"Don't I get it from you every day of the bloody week? This isn't a home—it's an asylum! You can't take off your professional hat long enough to behave like a normal husband!"

"How in hell is a normal husband supposed to behave when his wife goes behind his back to her dirty-minded friends begging the name of an abortionist?"

"What the hell makes you so sure it's your child I want to get rid of?"

Uttered in a near-scream, the words filled the air like choking smoke. Behind the screen of their echo, Iris realised what she had said. First her hands clamped on the chair-back so tightly all the blood faded, leaving the skin dry and stark as parchment; then she began to shake in terror, her jaw moving up and down so that her white teeth tapped and tapped at the brilliant red of her lower lip, the only remaining trace of colour in her whole face being the lipstick and mascara that she wore. Her eyelids had dropped like curtains to shut out the fearful world.

At last the dam broke and the tears came. Blinded, she stumbled towards the stairs, while Paul stood stupidly in the middle of the floor, folding and refolding the sheet of paper with Swerd's name on it as though his hands had taken on independent life.

"But I don't care," he heard himself say, and then when she showed no sign of having heard, repeated in a shout: "I don't care, you silly woman. I *just . . . don't . . . care!*"

◆ *29* ◆

Overhead there was a soft heavy plumping noise: Iris throwing herself on the bed, her usual refuge from a row. Paul stood with one hand on the banister rail, feeling the rage drain from him and leave nothing behind but a hollow emptiness.

Shaking, he took out a cigarette, and realised when he had finally got it to his lips why the job had been so difficult: he was still holding the scrap of paper on which Iris had written Swerd's number. With conscious theatricality he rolled it into a taper and thrust it at the embers of the fire. It caught. He raised the flame of his cigarette and let the rest of the note fall among the ashes.

—What can I do if she persists? It's not in my nature to make threats and carry them out. I could say that if she goes ahead I'll report the matter to the GMC and the police, and where would it get me? What weight will Paul Fidler's word carry against the famous Newton Swerd and his two tame psychiatrists certifying that the child would "permanently impair the health of the mother?"

He drew on the cigarette with quick ragged puffs.

—It'd be grounds for divorce. . . . But I don't *want* to be divorced. If someone asked why not, when Iris can behave like this, I wouldn't be able to explain, but it's somewhere in the fact that I don't want to have to start all over again at that adolescent business of picking up and making a good impression on and wearing down the resistance of . . .

At that point his thinking became too incoherent to form words. He waited, mind blank; eyes fixed on the fire, until the cigarette burned his fingers; then he turned and began to walk upstairs, movements sluggish from a vast invisible load.

Iris was lying on the bed, face buried in the pillow, moaning softly. He sat down beside her and tried to take her hand, but she jerked it away from him.

He stayed where he was. In a little while, as he'd expected, she quietened and stole a glance at him which she hoped he wouldn't notice.

"Iris?"

"Leave me alone, damn you."

—So that next time we have an argument you can use my going to charge me with heartlessness? No thank you.

Alarmed at his own cynicism Paul said, "Iris, please!"

"Oh, shut up," she muttered.

"You must try and understand! Look, we went over this when we first got married, didn't we? It made sense then to put off having a family. But I'm not a struggling new doctor any longer—I'm holding a pretty responsible post, and even if it's not overpaid it does carry a reasonable salary. We aren't compelled to delay our family now."

"All you can think of, isn't it?" Iris whimpered. "How much is it going to cost, can we afford it?"

Stonily Paul said, "I never made it a secret that I want children."

"You didn't try and make me like the idea, did you? You just kept your mouth shut until I was caught by surprise and now you're spying on me and threatening me and I could kill you, I really could."

The venom in her tone startled him. He lost the thread of what he had been about to say. While he was silent she swung her legs to the floor and reached for a cigarette from the bedside table.

"Look, darling," he ventured at last, "if you're really so terrified of having your own children, we could do what we thought of doing before, and adopt . . . ? I mean, could we sort of make a bargain? We could apply to an adoption society right away, and I'm sure I could make the . . . uh . . . the arrangements you want without your having to go to Swerd, who charges the earth."

The words almost choked him, but he was so desperate for compromise that he spoke them regardless.

"Thank you for that, anyhow," she muttered.

"For what?"

"For not saying that if I don't like the messing painful business of having children I must be out of my mind. Christ, what kind of an ivory tower do you psychiatrists live in, with your glib generalisations? None of my women friends like having kids! Why don't you stop making these wild statements about what's 'normal' and go and ask some women how they actually feel?"

"You're not going to take your selfish pampered glamour-girl friends as a fair cross-section of the human race!"

"What makes them more selfish than men, for God's sake? They're not asking any more than the same advantage men are born with!"

"If you want to make excuses, surely you can do better than that."

"What?"

"If it was just the bearing of children that you couldn't face you wouldn't be so anxious to avoid talking about adoption, would you? What you're trying to get away from is the ordinary adult responsibility of looking after children, bringing them up, educating them!"

"With the mess I've made of my life, why should you want me to?"

"What sort of a mess?"

"You heard what I said downstairs."

"About the child not being mine? For God's sake, woman, I haven't got your obsession with biological parenthood!"

" 'Biological parenthood!' " she echoed in mockery of him.

"Raising children is being their father in the only way that counts! I don't give a damn whose the children are, yours or ours or neither."

She stubbed her cigarette. "So you don't even want to know who else's it might be?"

"What for? So I could go and ... and horsewhip him, or something?"

"Don't make me laugh. You'd never do anything like that in a million years. You're too spineless."

He jolted to his feet, fists folding over with a faint clapping sound. She cringed away as though expecting to be punched.

"A nice juicy divorce case," he said after a pause. "Is that what you want? To keep up with your smart friends, I suppose! Which wife has Bertie Parsons got to now—his third, isn't it? I suppose you're a nobody in your circle unless you're divorced or queer or sleeping with your grandmother!"

"Paul, I—"

"Move!"

"What—?"

He dragged the arm on which she was leaning away from the pillows, turned them over and retrieved his pyjamas from underneath. Seizing his overnight bag, he tossed into it slippers, razor, toilet gear.

"What are you doing?" Iris cried.

"Going to spend the night at the hospital. The company there may be mostly insane, but at least they haven't got your particular kind of nastiness." He slammed the lid of the case.

"But you . . ."

In the doorway he glanced back at her, baring his teeth in a skeletal parody of a grin.

"I'm sorry if I've proved a disappointment to you, Iris. But there are some things you should have reckoned with before marrying me. I'm not scared out of my wits by the idea of children, and I don't take kindly to being used as a child-surrogate, which is what you've been trying to make of me, and it doesn't take a hysterical row or the threat of a lunatic with a broken bottle to work me up to the pitch where I want to make love. I think if you had to marry a doctor you should have picked on someone like Swerd. He must be a pretty cold fish to make such a success of his line of business."

Her face was absolutely white as she reached for the bedside clock and hurled it at him. He pulled the door to, and heard it shatter into ringing fragments of glass and metal on the other side.

—So that's that.

And yet somehow he could not accept what his intellect told him: that this was final. It had grown to seem a part of being married, as far as he and Iris were concerned, that mortal insults should be tacitly ignored the morning after.

—Maybe she'll realise what she's done; maybe she'll decide that she wants to patch it up after all. . . . I'm bound to be asked what I'm doing at the hospital. Whose duty is it? I hope to God it's Mirza's. I could confess the truth to him, and just possibly to Natalie, I think, but Ferdie and Phil are the next thing to strangers, so . . .

He was out of the house, out of the gate, before he realised with a shock he had forgotten to collect the can of petrol. He hesitated. Without tilting back his head he looked up at the bedroom window. Iris was there, watching.

—If I go back in now, it'll start all over again. No, this has to look serious no matter how willing I am to climb down if she gives the least sign of relenting.

Dismally he trudged off along the road. When he came to the car, he locked the case inside and continued to the Yemble garage to collect a gallon in one of their cans. The dying impulse of his anger sustained him as he retraced his steps,

poured the petrol into the tank, and drove back to return the
can and buy another couple of gallons for safety's sake.

Waiting for the attendant to bring him change, he debated
with himself: give in, or . . . ?

—It's no bloody use. She was right to say I'm spineless. I
haven't the heart to make the final break. If she forces me
into it, say by sneaking away to Swerd while my back is
turned, then I can probably go through with it. But I seem to
prefer to let things drift on as they are rather than face the
prospect of starting afresh.

When he drove out of the filling station he turned home-
ward instead of towards the hospital, and within another few
minutes was in sight of the house. The instant he rounded the
last bend, however, he jammed on his brakes, pulses in his
temples hammering so fiercely he thought he might faint.

A taxi was drawing away from the house. Through its rear
window he could see the bright blonde outline of Iris's head.
Beside her on the seat were piled the three cases she always
travelled with, and she was drumming on the topmost with
the tips of her fingers.

She didn't notice him.

Later it occurred to him that he could have driven after
the taxi, overtaken it, forced her to stop and come back. Instead he sat numbly until it had disappeared, saying to
himself over and over, "You fool—you fool—you fool!"

◆ *30* ◆

There was a nearly full bottle of cooking sherry in the
kitchen cupboard. It might be enough to get drunk on. He
poured it splashing into a glass, gulped, poured again.

A tap at the door, and when he went to answer, a tearful
Iris ready to throw her arms around him and whisper close to
his ear, "Darling, it's no good, I can't go through with it, I
love you and if it's a boy we'll call it Derek and if it's a
girl . . ."

Nothing. No one. Wind in the chimney-top.

The phone rang, and when he picked it up he heard Iris's voice tremulously saying, "Darling, I miss you and I'm so ashamed of what I've done—will you take me back so that we can start again?"

The small neat modern form of the two-tone telephone, out of place against oaken beams and whitewashed plaster; on the memo pad beside it, the indentations of the note Iris had made, pressing heavily with a ballpoint pen.

A letter dropped through the door; opened, it ran, "Dear Paul, I want to marry Gellert because it's his child, not yours, and the threat of the abortionist was just to let me see your face, my solicitors will be in touch with you."

The glass was empty again. He refilled it.

"Well, you can't say I didn't warn you," Mirza sighed. "Why didn't you do as I suggested? You could have found out how much she wanted to keep you, and if she didn't care enough to mend her ways you'd have saved months of mental anguish."

And again; the level of the bottle was down to half.

"This is a serious matter," Holinshed told him frigidly. "One must inevitably judge the competence and social adjustment of psychiatric staff by the success with which they conduct their personal relationships. It has come as a shock to me to learn, from reliable sources, that your wife is in London flaunting an affair with a notorious . . . ah . . . playboy. Gossip is already circulating among the patients. I cannot put up with this kind of thing. Your employment at Chent will terminate directly we find a suitable replacement."

A car pulled up noisily outside. He dashed to the window. But it was merely someone who had lost his way and was turning around in a gateway opposite.

"Still hoping your wife might come back to you?" Maurice Dawkins gave the unpleasant high giggle which he only affected during his peak manic phase, when he acquired enough false courage to regard his swish mannerisms as funny. "But I told her about you going around the bend, and she was absolutely fascinated—kept ringing up for more and more details. Of course, I hadn't got them all, so I made some up. She's beside herself, my dear. Who wouldn't be, finding they'd been married for years to a lunatic without realising?"

"Of course," Oliphant said, "you're a doctor and I'm only a deputy charge nurse. But doesn't the fact that you've been in a bin yourself make you a bit too eager to side with the loonies? We're the ones who have to clear up the mess when you make mistakes, you know. Seen this scar where Riley cut my hand at the dance? Dr Jewell says I'll have it the rest of my life."

"It's a delicate matter, Dr Fidler," Matron Thoroday murmured, "but it's one which I must bring to the attention of Dr Holinshed. My belief is that because the disorder for which you were certified bore so much resemblance to Urchin's condition you're supporting her against my nurses, and this is making their position intolerable."

"But I wasn't certified! I just had a breakdown from overwork!"

The cry of despair echoed away into the empty house. There was no one to hear it but himself.

"As you know, I tend to judge my colleagues objectively," Alsop said. "I'm impatient with failures; either a man has what it takes, or he hasn't, and I prefer the former. There are few more fundamental failures than letting a marriage go smash—and don't offer excuses. You decided to marry the woman, presumably when you were in full possession of your faculties and over the age of discretion. If it weren't for the exceptional success you're making of Urchin's case, I'd—"

—No. More like . . .

"What persuaded you to be taken in by this farrago of rubbish?" Alsop demanded coldly. "I wouldn't expect a first-year student to be hoodwinked the way you've been! I gather your colleague Bakshad told you that a marriage like yours was no basis for a proper understanding of women. You should have taken the comment seriously. You made a miserably bad choice of a wife, but that's of no concern to me—I'm keeping this on a professional level. And my view is that you've allowed your head to be turned by a clever trickster, because she's young and appealingly helpless and rather pretty. These notes of yours are worthless. They're the most spectacular example of self-deception I've ever seen from a supposedly responsible psychiatrist!"

Back and forth, back and forth, Paul paced with the glass in his hand, feeling the alcohol gradually numb the nerves of his fingers and toes. On every tenth or twelfth circuit, he detoured into the kitchen where he had left the bottle of sherry on the table with the cork out. It was almost empty now.

—No, no, no, that's all I've got left. If that's taken away from me I'm finished, done for, dead.

"I fooled you, I fooled you! My name isn't Urchin, it's plain Aggie Jones and I come from Wrexham and Mam and Da wouldn't let me leave home and live on my own so I wanted to hide for a few months where they'd never think to look for me—"

—No!

Paul took a deep breath. The first violent shock of Iris's departure had faded, leaving his mind clear, if a little askew from its usual course.

—I can't be wrong about Urchin. It all fits: the language no one can identify, the peculiar cast of her face which resembles no known racial type, the fact that she had to be taught how to speak English, wear our kind of clothes, use a knife and fork . . . Wait a moment.

He closed his eyes and rocked gently back and forth on his heels.

—In what sense do I mean "it all fits?" That what she claimed today is true? No, I can't possibly mean that. I'd be a laughing-stock. Lord, I am getting drunk. I thought this wine was so vile I couldn't choke it down sufficiently fast, but my head's swimming and the room is beginning to go round.

He had to open his eyes again, to escape the illusion that the whole earth was surging up and down beneath his feet.

—Got to hang on to Urchin's case. Letters in *BMJ*, signed Alsop consultant Fidler psychiatric registrar Chent. Notes of work in progress: new elements in the fantasies of female hysterics with special reference to. Final paper: I am indebted to my colleagues—no, *former* colleagues at Chent for. By then: "So you're Fidler, are you? Been reading your stuff in *BMJ*. Thought the eventual paper was a model of its kind. By the way, there's post due to fall vacant at Nuthouse shortly. Won't be advertised until next week, but if you're considering moving on . . ."

But the forced attempt to envisage good things happening failed. The nagging suspicion remained that if he had been so deceived and cheated by Iris, why not by Urchin too?

—Cure her, discharge her, look after her while she finds her feet in the strange outside world, make sure her medical supervision ceases to be my responsibility, be able to approach her as a pretty girl instead of a case-history.

That was no good either. For one thing, the optimism he was preaching to himself was so pale and unreal beside the previsions of disaster his subconscious kept spawning, unbidden. For another . . .

—Cure her? How the hell, when she acts more rationally than Iris does? She's the one who needs therapy, the wife scared witless by the idea of performing her natural functions as a woman! I should have come straight out and told her so, instead of beating around the bush and waiting for "nature to take its course." She's unnautral, that's the long and the short of it. Wait till doomsday, she won't change.

The sherry bottle was empty. Ten minutes till the pubs closed. Time to drive to the Needle and get some more liquor.

—In this state? Well, if I'm very careful . . .

But instead he opened cupboards, looked in drawers, hunted the house high and low, until in the bathroom medicine cabinet he found the bottle labelled "Alcohol 100%, for medicinal purposes only."

—Not much different from vodka, I suppose. . . . Suppose it were surgical spirit denatured with methanol, that poisons, blinds and ultimately kills: what would I do?

He couldn't answer that question. But mixed with orange juice and chilled with a cube of ice it made a passable drink.

—As to Urchin, I was all set this evening to start drafting the paper about her. I must have been crazy. I'm not even going to tell Alsop that I've made a breakthrough, just in case I'm being overeager. They'll look at me, judging by appearances, and maybe with luck they'll say, "Paul's bearing up well, isn't he? His wife left him, you know, but then she was always rather a cold-hearted bitch and treated him disgracefully." And only I will know that it's success with Urchin's case that sustains me, until I'm sure beyond a shadow of doubt that it's all coming right, and then I'll . . .

He realised with a stab of dismay that he was addressing himself aloud, because his mind was so foggy it needed that crutch to guide its thoughts forward. When he prevented himself from forming the words with his lips, the terrors rushed in on him again.

—Alsop will . . . Holinshed will . . . Iris will . . .

Angry, he made to pour another of the fierce cocktails he'd concocted with the raw spirit, but put his glass down an inch this side of the table-top. It smashed on the floor. Kicking it aside, he seized a replacement and filled it to halfway.

—Iris *won't* complain about having to clean up behind me. That's a consolation, isn't it?

Spilling a little from the can, he added orange juice and

sipped. The fierceness stung his palate; gasping, he put in more juice.

—This time it's not a question of being obsessed by the things that might have gone wrong but I somehow escaped. The hopes and fears of all the years are met in me tonight. Got to face facts, Paul. Lost, one marriage, finder please don't inform Dr. Paul Fidler.

"You out there," he said mildly. "All those other Paul Fidlers—are you listening? Years you've plagued me with your damnable sorrows, making me worry till I was sick about the things that didn't happen to me but happened to you—understand me? Failed your scholarship exams, got thrown out of medical school, never picked your way back to sanity after the breakdown but spent the rest of your life in the bin, got turned down by Iris when she broke off the engagement— lucky bastard, you! Well, how do you like it the other way around for a change? I'm in the cart this time, I'm thinking the dismal thoughts, and I hope to God you rot with them."

Swaying, one hand clutching the glass as if it were a torch casting light to guide him, the other poised to fend off furniture, the banister rail, the bedroom door, when each in turn threatened to come around and hit him in the face, he made his way to the bedroom and turned down the covers. Tugging aside the pillow, he realised that he had taken away his pyjamas. The overnight bag was still in the car, forgotten.

—Never mind. Who's to care? Damned silly clothes we men wear nowadays, this tie keeps trying to strangle me, doesn't want me to take it off, no wonder I'm pulling on the wrong end, oh, *damn* the thing.

He pitched forward on to the bed. Around him the house stood empty except for the hordes and hordes of other Paul Fidlers, trapped in the dead ends of disaster, mourning silently that not even this last one of their infinite number was to escape into freedom.

• *31* •

—It's the density of the events you see, coming on me thickly like a hail of midgets and a rainstorm. This and that I could cope with one at a time but I have only two pairs of hands to catch them as they go past. It's the difficulty of chess where you can't move to take the other player's piece because you'd expose yourself to check. I sit on the black square and fume at the people going past me on the white ones.

He grew aware that Urchin had stopped talking a long time ago and now sat, statue-still, watching the elsewhere vision she had been describing. Hypnotised, she would not care if he neglected to put another question yet awhile. She would not even react to the sound of the desk-drawer sliding if he eased it open and took out another pill from the stock he kept there.

—Which of them? Careful, bad to put myself to sleep by accident . . . oh no, I took the sleeping-tablets home, didn't I? Sleep at home, almost overdid it this morning woke up late and had to come in without breakfast. But shaved. Mum's the word, keep it from showing outwardly, mum's the wife but I wonder if she's had the abortion already, bloody half-shaped human thing gone ground with garbage to the sewers of London. No wife no mum no bloody good. God damn look at the time on the clock, get on with the work chop-chop, get ahead chopped off *ouch*. Settles it. Tranquilliser.

He swallowed the pill. Waiting for it to work, he looked at the scrappy notes he had mechanically copied down while Urchin was talking. Only part of his mind could have been wandering.

—Part is bad enough, isn't it? Oh God, what shall I do? It's sleeping badly that's doing it, it must be the shortage of sleep, but I daren't take more pills than I'm taking already. The silent noise in the house at night, the creaks of settling floor-boards which between waking and sleeping I mistake for footsteps, calling out and thinking for one slim instant Iris will reply and it will all have been a nightmare. Not because I love her so much losing her had made me desperate, just because I got used and can't adapt to being alone again. Maybe I should shut up the house and move to the hospital; after all the place isn't mine anyway, bought with Iris's inheritance. But to lie awake under that cracked bell every night...! Has Alsop noticed? I suppose he must have. Thank God he hasn't taxed me with it directly. Wants to see how I can keep personal problems from interfering with my work, no doubt. So far: yes. Better able to concentrate on the diploma course without distractions ("there may be said to be a continuous spectrum between the isolated traumatic experience and the disorienting environment which may give rise to schizophrenic responses") and the routine of every bloody day ("do this please Nurse ask Matron if she would kindly do that Nurse I wonder if you'd oblige me by doing the other Dr Alsop") and of course there's Urchin, but . . .

The notes on his pad danced before his eyes, evading his clumsy attempts to grapple with them and deduce the content of his next question.

—I don't know. Maybe he isn't satisfied with the progress I've made regarding Urchin. After all I haven't told him the whole story yet, just in case I'm wrong because being wrong about her on top of everything everything . . . Or perhaps he hasn't inquired too closely because he's decided I'm a write-off. How can one be sure with a slick bastard like him?

He looked at Urchin, and a sudden wave of affection rose in him.

—Good girl, keep it up. You're all that stands between me and ruin, did you know that? Ace in the hole, pull you out one of these days and dazzle everybody with my sleight of mind, "such insight, Dr Fidler, such perspicacity, this major contribution to the theory of gabblephobia!"

"Tell me more," he said aloud. "Tell me more about . . ." And couldn't remember what the subject was, but she saved him the trouble, and talked on, the button having been pushed.

—Meantime: maybe I should take a holiday or something. But to spend a fortnight in some place I've never heard of, nobody to speak to night after lonely night except people I never saw before and never want to see again! If I could go where Urchin lived before she came to Chent . . .

Bit by bit, now the dam had been broken by his chance inquiry in her own language, he was assembling a picture of Urchin's world. Turning back the pages of his notebook, he found that although he might have copied down key-words and abbreviated sentences automatically during the past several sessions with her, on a second inspection they conjured up with present-time vividness the entire statement to which each corresponded.

—It's like my own life, isn't it? Forking outwards. And she's trapped in a dead end.

The idea, with the overtones of forking, was lightning to him, illuminating a whole great landscape of possibilities.

—I see! Yes, I'm sure I get the picture now. Not so much a visitor as an explorer and researcher, but when she had to answer my first question she hadn't enough words to do more than approximate it.

He broke in, regardless of the fact that she was still speaking. "Urchin, when is this 'other time' you come from?"

"I can't explain. It's *away* from this one."

"A long time ago, or still to come?"

—Harmless, to play with words and humour a lunatic's delusions. Nonetheless: strange, somehow fascinating. A way out of this world which traps me. If I could only . . .

"N-no." She was shaking her head in despair. "Not in front, not behind. *Northwest.*"

She turned and gazed at him with pleading eyes, as though beseeching his comprehension.

—Mustn't let you down, girl, or you might let me down, and . . . Northwest? Off ahead but at some kinky weird angle?

He said carefully, "Did you expect to come here?"

"No!" A sudden gleam of hope. "You—all this"—a gesture to embrace the office, Chent Hospital, the world at large—"not in our history."

"What did you expect to find?"

"They"—he still hadn't established "their" identity, but they were apparently some figures of authority—"send to report on . . ." She fumbled for the right term. "On Age of Muddled . . . ?"

"Confusion?" Paul ventured.

"Right! To answer many questions because history had got . . . well . . . broken. To leave written accounts in special places for finding later."

"Were you expecting to go back?"

She hesitated; then she answered almost inaudibly, "It's not possible to go back. Time runs forward at fixed speed, limit like speed of light."

—I'm not sure I follow that, but there's a weird kind of consistency in all these things she's said. . . .

He leafed back through his notes again.

"What is your history, Urchin? Have you found out what makes it different from ours?"

"Rome."

"What?"

The tranquilliser had given him back some of his powers of concentration; he was absently sifting his earlier records in the hope of finding further clues.

—But what to make of all this baffles me. Vague hints about a pastoral world without cities, people living to be a hundred and fifty, the epitome of Utopian wishful thinking!

"Rome," Urchin said again. "You call your kind of writing Roman, don't you? There are very few and bad books about history in the library, but— Wait, I show you." She opened her battered portfolio, which she had brought to this as to all recent sessions.

"Just tell me," Paul sighed.

Disappointed, she let the case slide to the floor. "If you say. Romans were conquerors, beat all others in what you call Mediterranean Sea, came to here even. Left strange writing, strange language. For me history says were people from . . . *aaah!*" She snapped her fingers, momentarily infuriated with herself for forgetting a word. "Middle Asia, that's it. Asia . . . Learn writing in North Italy, near what you say Alp Mountains, cut on edge of piece of wood so." She sawed the side of her right hand across the index finger of her left.

Paul stared at her. Abruptly his mind locked into focus on what she had been telling him.

—Christ, it's ridiculous. Shoemaker said there were traces of Finno-Ugrian influence in the tape I gave him. And the shape of her eyes: an Asiatic overlay on a European bone structure. And she's just described the reason why runic is all spiky and straight while our kind of writing is curved. How far has she elaborated this wild notion of hers?

"Why didn't you arrive where you expected to, Urchin? And where did you expect to come to?"

"Town called"—he missed the name, his ear not being attuned to the sounds of her own language. "Market for meat, cloth, vegetables, thirteen thousand people, ruled by Lord of West Mountain, about to start war against Middle Land

Plain." She recited that tonelessly, as though recounting a dream of impossible happiness. "Instead, here I am. I have thought a lot, being alone in my room. What I think is, time is like ... What is your name for the thing at the end of rivers?"

"Ah—mouth?"

"No, no. When in flat land the water separates into many lines?"

"I get you. A delta." He sketched the forking shape of one on his pad and showed it to her. She nodded vigorously.

"Delta! Start here"—she pointed to the main body of the river on his sketch—"go here, or here, or here. Was Rome in your history, not in mine. I start here"—she indicated the extreme left-hand mouth of the delta—"and came to here"—the first of the branches leading to the right-hand mouth.

—Good lord. You know, if one were to take this seriously, the "other Paul Fidlers" would ...

He looked at her in bewilderment. Since the initial breakthrough when he had somehow got her to confess what she believed to be her identity against the command of "they" who had forbidden her to admit it, the induction of a hypnotic state had become less and less important to make her talk. Now, one could hardly tell whether she had been ordered into trance or not. Certainly the full vigour and vitality of her personality was showing in her bright eyes, her tense voice.

"How did you make the ... the journey, Urchin?"

"Literally, promise you, there are no words to say in this language. In my language there are no words to say engine, rocket, spaceman, which I see on television—no word for television either. Is all different. We learned different things to do, studied different problems."

—A society that somehow diverged from ours, concentrating on time-travel as its ultimate achievement while ours is in jet airplanes and sending rockets to the moon. Did she have this moment in mind the night I first met her, when she went around the cars staring and touching them as though she had never seen anything of the kind before?

With a sudden burst of energy, he said, "Tell me about the world you come from, Urchin."

She looked doubtful. "Listen, Paul, first I explain one thing. When first I know what happened to me, how I got stuck and never can go back home, I wanted to explain who I am and why I came here. But I was forbidden. What you do with that clock and talking gently in low voice, was done to me to stop me telling people where I was going about other later things."

—She's got it all figured out, hasn't she? If somebody were to come from the future to the past, it would make sense to impose hypnotic commands against talking too freely, in case the people of the past took her seriously, did something different from what history recorded, and thus abolished the time she had started out from!

There was a kind of fascination in this, like reading a well-constructed mystery novel for the sake of seeing how the author resolved all the misleading clues he'd planted. Paul challenged her.

"Then how come you're taking so openly to me now?"

"Language had changed between the Age of—you said Confusion, yes?—Age of Confusion and my time. Command was to not answer anyone asking in the old language, but you remembered what we say for 'hello' and this was permitted."

She clasped his free hand suddenly in both of hers, and gazed into his eyes. "Paul, I'm so glad to be able to say these things! It was . . . it was full of pain to sit by myself and know I was the alonest person in the world."

Paul disengaged his hand, trembling.

—I could lean over and put my arm around her and . . . Stop it. Stop it. It's simple transference, it's a fixation like Maurice Dawkins's. Suppose it were Maurice looking at me with those bedroom eyes. For heaven's sake.

"Tell me about your world. Go and sit down in your chair again, too."

Sighing, she complied.

"Tell me about . . ."

—What's the least emotively charged thing I can ask her? Politics, maybe. There's not likely to be much reason for arousing emotions over something that's been irrelevant to our world since Ancient Rome.

"Tell me about the government. Who's in charge?"

Obediently she leaned back and let her hands dangle over the chair's arms. "Is not like yours. Is very peacy . . . ah . . . peacish?"

"Peaceful."

"Peaceful, thank you. For two hundred eighty years is no wars, no mad people, no criminal. Rulers are men who we . . . *selected* for being good and kind. Must be father of family and all children speak in support of them. If even one son, one daughter, aged sixty years at least, says no, they are not chosen. Same way is in all places, because when there are not wars people do not like to be afraid of anyone, and mostly of all not the ones who tell them what to do."

"Didn't you say something about people living to be a hundred and fifty years old?"

"Children born at the time I left are expected, yes."

—A benevolent government, no crime, no insanity, this fantastic longevity ... Why couldn't I have been born into a world like that, instead of this death-trap of H-bombs, road accidents, high taxes, and prisonlike mental asylums?

For a few moments Paul let his imagination roam down paths of wishful thinking. Then he realised with a shock that he had kept Urchin long over the appointed time of her session, and there was a mound of work awaiting him on the desk.

—Almost, I could hope she doesn't abandon this fantasy too soon. To wander off once a day into a vision of perfection: it would be like a holiday. But I daren't take a real holiday.

He clenched his fists in something close to panic.

—Because ... who else would take her fantasy the way I do? Who else would have the insight and compassion to understand how real it is to her, who else would decline to say outright, "The woman's off her nut?" Who but me, haunted by the versions of myself who took the wrong turning down life's roadway and signalled their despair, as she puts it, Northwest across time?

◆ *32* ◆

The depth, the detail, the consistency, grew and grew and grew.

—The place is called what I first misheard as Lion Roar; as near as I can transliterate it that would be Llanraw with a sort of Welsh double L. An interesting dialect survival, presumably from the pre-Roman linguistic substratum in our world, showing Celtic influence. It was a minor miracle she recognised my bastard accent when I demanded of her, *"Tiriak-no?"* It's not a K, it's more a click of the tongue, just as in Llanraw the final sound is nasalised like the French *bon.*

"What does the name Llanraw mean?"

"Nobody is sure any longer, but there is an idea that it means 'rock in a storm,' because it was stormy when the conquerors came to it by sea."

—Rock in a storm! And isn't that what it's becoming to me, the one steadfast thing I can turn to when the world threatens to sink me without trace?

"You said the town you meant to come to when you left your home was a market for cloth, vegetables and meat. But you won't touch meat, will you?"

A shudder that racked her whole tiny body. "In my world, Paul, to kill an animal for meat was a religious thing, long ago. That's why in the Age of Confusion there was a special market, and great ceremonies when the meat was sold. Seeing it openly in your shops made me want to—to return my last food. What would you say?"

"Vomit."

"Yes."

"So you don't kill for food any longer."

"No. We keep ... uh ... pets? I thought that was right. But we let animals go where they want to in the countryside, and if there are too many we go and give them drugs so there are not so many young ones."

"What about the animals that are fierce and dangerous?"

"What kind of animals?"

"Well—big animals that do eat meat, that kill other animals because that's the diet they've always had."

"In Llanraw there are none. In far lands where there are few people, we let them do as they wish."

"But there was a religious ceremony when animals were killed?"

"What you would call the butchers were ..." A snap of the fingers. "Men in charge of the religion!"

"Priests?"

"I think so. And afterwards they must go to a river and wash the blood off and say they are sorry to the spirits of the animals."

—Like Eskimos, that. The range of her vision is unbelievable!

"But this was long ago. It's wasting work to make meat for food, and cruel too. More people eat food grown off one piece of ground than eat animals which ate the food off it. Is this clear?"

"Yes, perfectly clear."

She stared wistfully out of the window. "Those same hills in my world, they are planted with high beautiful trees and the fields with flowers taller than you—blue, red, white, yellow. When the wind blows you can smell the flowers at the seashore, there in the west." She hesitated. "It was hardest to say goodbye to the flowers, know I would not see them again."

Paul gazed at her, awed by the courage it would take to cast oneself adrift from everything familiar—not simply parents and lovers, but the very sounds, scents, colours of the customary world.

"And to go above the sea of flowers in the air, to see the wind making them shiver! Once we drifted four whole days and nights before we had to put out the . . . the heater? Oh, I did not explain! A big round hollow thing with warmer air in it that is light and lifts up into the sky."

"A balloon. A hot-air balloon."

"Yes." She was almost overcome by the memory, that was plain. "In summer, with little wind—four days before we saw the sea and had to let the balloon come down."

Paul shied away from asking who the other member of the "we" had been.

So, now, two sets of notes were being compiled: the slimmer for Alsop's attention and eventual inclusion in the general hospital records, giving only the baldest indication of progress—"Patient today was communicative under hypnosis and further success was achieved in enlarging her vocabulary in significant areas"—and the fatter, now numbering hundreds of pages, documenting the strange and lovely world of Llanraw.

Under heading after heading he listed the explanations Urchin had given him, becoming almost drunk on the visions the words implied.

"In Llanraw parents do not punish their children. If a child does wrong the parents ask themselves what they have done to set a bad example. A child is regarded as an independent and responsible individual from the moment it learns to talk comprehensibly, and its education and life's work are adapted to its intrinsic capabilities. Pushing a child into work for which it is not fitted is regarded as cruel, and there appears to be none of that craving for vicarious status which mars so many childhoods in our world."

—Mine too. Bright or not bright, they shouldn't have driven me, bribed me, compelled me up the educational ladder.

"In Llanraw marriage consists in a vow taken before the assembled community that the couple will accept the responsibility of bearing and raising children and remain their best friends for as long as they live, to whom they may always turn for help and advice. Conception without such previous public pledges is regarded as offensive to the unborn child and the administration of an abortifacient is compulsory. Owing to the seriousness with which parenthood is undertaken, there is no excess population pressure, nor any social pressure on young people to marry and bear children as frequently happens in our world, thus ensuring that too many children are subconsciously resented by their parents."

—And if something unpleasant happens to the child, like a nervous breakdown from overwork, they never tire of reminding him how much he owes them for fulfilling their parental duty towards their ungrateful offspring.

"On the other hand, in Llanraw the general attitude towards sexuality is enlightened and permissive, and physical expression of affection is taken as a matter of course."

—I wonder what my father would think if I tried to kiss his cheek.

The day came, not long afterwards, when for the first time he checked himself on the point of losing his temper with a refractory patient, and the thought crossed his mind: *That's not how they'd do it in Llanraw.*

His anger faded. Calmly and reasonably he sorted the difficulty out, and when it was over he felt a warm glow of self-approbation.

He developed the habit of seeing Urchin daily after lunch, except on Mondays when he went to help Alsop with his clinic in Blickham, and gradually sent for her earlier and earlier until he was having to go early for his meal if he was not to risk indigestion from gulping it down.

On a day in June which had brought a sudden blast of summer heat he went into the staff wash-room to rinse his hands and tidy up before eating. He was overdue for a visit to the barber, and on catching sight of his hair in the mirror he attempted without success to make it lie down. Comb still in hand, he glanced sideways out of the open window, and stared at the sunlit countryside.

—How would those hills look covered in a sea of flowers? And what kind of flowers, exactly? Sunflowers? Taller than I am, she said. But in so many different colours ... I rather picture them as being like enormous poppies, with flat gaudy petals that flap in the breeze.

The door opened. Guiltily he darted his comb to his hair again, ashamed of being found standing idly contemplating the scenery. The newcomer was Mirza.

"Morning, Paul," he said, letting the cold tap run fast to fill the hand-basin. "Had any news from Iris?"

"No," Paul said, in a tone calculated to imply that he didn't much care if he did or not. Mirza's eyes darted towards him and away again.

"Forgive me saying so," he murmured, "but you can't completely hide the effect it's having on you. You're looking awful."

—Bunkum. I saw myself in the mirror just now and I look okay, considering. And what the hell business is it of Mirza's, anyway?

"I'm all right! Sorry to disappoint you. But you used to tell me often enough that being married to Iris was bad for me—do you expect me to be worse off now?"

Mirza cupped a double handful of water and dipped his face. Spluttering, he reached for a towel.

"Well, I haven't noticed you ... ah ... taking advantage of your unlooked-for reversion to gay bachelor status."

"Oh, stuff it! It's all very well for you with your endless string of casual tarts, isn't it? I'm not built the way you are. You don't wipe away five years of marriage with—with a swab of that towel!"

"There's no need to bite my head off," Mirza said after a pause.

"There's no need for you to come the heavy father with me either. What started this, anyway? Have you been hearing complaints about my work going to pot, perhaps?"

"As a matter of fact, no."

"Good. I'm getting more work done in a day, and more studying too, than I used to manage in a week with Iris pestering me. So what did put this idea into your head?"

"I took a look at you," Mirza said.

"What?"

"You're losing weight, you have bags under your eyes big enough for weekend luggage, and—well, this isn't the first time you've lost your temper over nothing."

"Nothing!" Paul echoed, and tried to laugh. "Yes, I suppose losing one woman would seem like 'nothing' to you. You always have half a dozen more lined up!"

Mirza tossed the towel back on its hook and sighed. "Don't go on trying to be bitter. It doesn't suit your temperament. All I'm asking you to do is not to pretend you're unaffected. People take it for granted that the bust-up of a marriage is a disaster. Why shy away from their sympathy, when it's perfectly sincere, as if you thought they were—what shall I say?—looking down on you for being upset?"

Paul didn't answer for several seconds. Eventually he shook his head.

"Do you ever find yourself envying your patients, Mirza?"

"Envying them? Heavens no!"

—To go away from here, to float off into the empyrean at the mercy of the wind and drift uncaring above the flowery land-sea of Llanraw . . .

"Why not? The insane have one great advantage over the sane: when things get too much for them, they're taken in charge and looked after. The sane have to sweat it out by themselves."

"If that's really what you think," Mirza said, "you have a damned low opinion of your friends. What are friends for if they're not to help you sweat out your problems?"

"Some problems are one's own personal property," Paul muttered. " 'Marriage according to the law of this country is the union of one man with one woman to the exclusion of all others. . . .' Oh, the hell with it."

"Agreed," Mirza said promptly. He stepped to the window and peered out with an expression of exaggerated pleasure. "It's far too fine a day for wrangling. Hell of a view in this direction, isn't it? Makes me almost sorry to be going back to work in a big city, with the rest of the summer still to come."

"What?" Paul tensed in dismay. "You're not leaving Chent, are you?"

"I am indeed. You knew I'd applied for another job, didn't you?"

"Yes, but . . ."

Mirza turned and gazed at him levelly. He said at length, "I'll tell you one reason I can never imagine myself envying the patients, Paul. They can't arrange to leave Chent when

the place becomes too much for them. I've had my bellyful
of Holy Joe, and it's touch and go whether I serve out my
notice or tell him what I really think of him and walk off. A
patient who did that would be jabbed full of drugs and
maybe even snakepitomised to get rid of the troublesome bits
of his brain. Imagine being stuck here for the rest of your
life; imagine never being able to leave but in your coffin."

He spun on his heel and marched out, leaving Paul aghast
at the venom in his tone.

—I never realised he felt so violently about this place; he
was always so full of banter and mockery.... It's the way I
feel, pretty near, but I can stomach it until I've completed
two years—I think. I shall go on trying, anyway. But it was a
stupid thing to say about envying the inmates. How must
they feel! How must *Urchin* feel, looking back to the free air
of Llanraw! Being put in here is enough to make you crazy
whether you're crazy or not to begin with. Urchin growing
prematurely old shut up in Chent, mourning her lost and
lovely home, slopping around in dirty clothes with her hair
matted and her nails black, stinking the way the older patients stink, not talking except to answer back when the staff
address her ... My God, what a waste, what a *waste!*

◆ *33* ◆

Paul had not been given to talking much at meal-times lately,
but the news of Mirza's impending departure depressed him
so much that he was more taciturn than ever. Natalie made a
couple of attempts to draw him into the conversation, which
he rebuffed; after that he was aware of her eyes and occasionally Mirza's darting his way as though to ask what was
wrong.

While waiting for his dessert course, he suddenly decided
he could not stand company any longer. He pushed back his
chair and strode out of the room. There was no one on the
landing outside the mess. On impulse, instead of returning to
his office, he put his ear to the door and listened.

He heard Natalie say, "Well! Paul's in a funny mood, isn't he?"

"You could try being a bit more sympathetic," Mirza said. "After all, the poor guy's marriage has gone on the rocks, and that's not something you get over in a couple of days."

"Still the same trouble, hm?" Phil Kerans said with a chuckle. "I thought something might have gone wrong with his star patient. He hasn't been so eager to discuss her lately, I've noticed."

—And why the hell should I? Hoping for some dirty childhood memories, maybe, to compensate you for your Irish Catholic repressions?

Without realising it, Paul found he had jerked the door open and taken a step inside. Everyone was staring at him in astonishment.

"Did I . . . uh . . . did I leave my cigarettes in here?" he improvised.

The excuse seemed to strike them as thin; at any rate, their eyes all lingered on his face for longer than he liked before Mirza, who had been sitting next to him, reported that there was no sign of any cigarettes.

"Must have left them in my office, then," Paul muttered. "Sorry."

When he shut the door again, he was sweating—not from the heat of the day.

—What possessed me to do that?

Heels tapping on the stairs, he hastened away to the privacy of his office.

—At least, in another few minutes, Urchin will come and we can talk about Llanraw. "Something gone wrong with my star patient!" If the fat mick only knew . . . But I've done hardly any of the work. All I can take credit for is sneaking under her defences by accident. If she'd been less persistent, say in learning English, if she'd let herself be overwhelmed and lapsed into despair as I might have done in the same situation, I'd be done for. I wouldn't have even one reason for struggling on.

On the shelf where it had remained since the day it arrived, the clock ornamented with the skull-faced figure of Time waved him a greeting with its scythe. Because it too had contributed to saving him when he feared he might sink without trace in the quicksand of his troubles, he had long ago conceived a kind of affection for it. Dust had settled on the polished statuette; he took a tissue and wiped it before sitting down.

His cigarettes, of course, were in his pocket as they had been all along, but for fear of someone coming out of the mess and seeing him he had refrained from lighting one until the door was safely shut behind him. He did so now, and the phone rang in the same moment.

"Dr Fidler? Oh, good. Hang on, I have a call for you. . . . Dr Alsop, I've found Dr Fidler for you now—go ahead please."

—Not coming in today, or something?

"Good afternoon, young fellow! Look, I've had lunch early today and I can come over to you a bit ahead of schedule— in fact I'll be leaving Blickham as soon as I've finished talking to you, be with you in twenty minutes or so. But since I have the extra time in hand, it struck me that I ought to have another look at Urchin. It must be . . . oh . . . almost three weeks, isn't it?"

Paul's heart seemed to turn into a leaden weight.

"I think you said you were seeing her daily at the start of the afternoon's work, correct? Well, don't have her sent up before I join you. I want to have a word with you first."

Paul didn't reply.

"Hello? Are you there?"

"Yes, I'm still here. Sorry."

"Well . . . See you shortly, then."

Click.

Paul sat frozen, the phone still in his hand, for a minute or more after Alsop had rung off.

—Blast the man! What business has he got prying into my affairs? I show him notes that tell him everything I think he ought to know. Won't he take my word that I'm making steady progress? Doesn't he trust me?

The ash on his cigarette lengthened until a chance movement dislodged it down his chest. He blew it away and it scattered as dust over the papers on the desk. There seemed to be a lot of them today.

—And if he comes here and starts questioning Urchin and she tells him . . . I haven't found out everything about Llanraw yet. I couldn't bear to break it off now. On the other hand, I . . .

The turmoil of his thoughts quietened. His hand was quite steady as he reached for the phone again.

"Nurse? Who is that? Oh, Nurse Kirk! Would you be so

kind as to let Urchin come up here straight away, please? . . . Yes, I'm sorry, I know it's still lunch-time, but there's no need for anybody to come with her—I'm sure she can be trusted to find her way on her own after all this time."

Waiting, he finished the cigarette and lit another. Shortly there was Urchin's usual gentle knock at the door. He told her to come in, settled her in the chair facing him, put her into trance—by now, after daily reinforcement, the induction consisted in no more than a dozen words before she sighed and let herself go limp—and addressed her with the calm assurance that he was doing this in the best interests of his patient.

"Urchin, Dr Alsop wants to come and talk to you this afternoon. You remember Dr Alsop?"

"Yes."

"Urchin, what do you think would happen if you told him about Llanraw? Do you think he would believe you?"

A hesitation; then a shake of her head.

"And if he didn't believe you, what do you suppose he would think?"

She shuddered. "That I'm crazy!" she forced out.

"I'm afraid so." Paul leaned forward with an urgent air. "So listen to me very carefully. When anybody else but me is in the room, you will forget about Llanraw. When anybody but me is talking to you, you will not say anything about Llanraw. You will not answer any questions about where you come from or how you came here. In another few moments I shall wake you up; you will go out on the landing and sit in the window-seat until I call you back in here. When you come back I will put you into trance again, but you will not talk about Llanraw if anybody else is in the room!"

Alsop was frowning as he came in. Shutting the door, he said, "What's Urchin doing out there on the landing by herself? I thought I asked you not to send for her until I'd had a chance to speak to you."

"I'm sorry," Paul shrugged. "She comes up here on her own now—she's quite trustworthy—and I suppose she looks forward to her daily session with me. When she turned up I simply told her to hang on for a few minutes."

"I see. Well, anyhow, what I want to say won't take long." Alsop lowered himself into the chair which Urchin had been using a little while previously. "I've been running over your recent case-notes, including Urchin's, and they won't do, Paul, they simply won't do."

A pang of alarm drew Paul's nerves taut.

"I know about your wife, and all that," Alsop pursued. "I sympathise, believe me. That's why I've been putting off my comments until now, hoping you'd recover without my having to prompt you. But while you're not actually in arrears with your notes—it might be better if you were—you're turning out the most uninformative bald *scrappy* stuff I've ever seen. And Urchin's a case in point. No doubt some of the sketchiness of your other notes is due to the amount of time you're devoting to her; well, I'd accept this, provided only that you were making such rapid strides towards a cure for her that these long daily sessions were likely to come to an end in the immediate future. As far as I can tell, though, they are more likely to continue."

He drew from the pocket of his coat an envelope folded double. "This is the sum total of the notes you've shown me about her. Apart from minor details, you could swap the latest of them for any other six or eight weeks old and never know the difference."

"But I am making enormous progress," Paul said. "How is one to define a 'cure?' If you're expecting me to restore her memory in full—"

"It's not stated anywhere here that you've proved she's amnesiac."

"Good lord, half these sessions have been language lessons, not therapy! Until I was certain we both meant the same thing by any given word, I couldn't make my mind up. But now I'm satisfied. She is suffering from amnesia, the cause of which I haven't completely determined, but she's now capable of fluent communication about her recent experiences and in my judgment the best thing is to grant her gradually increasing liberty, keeping a watchful eye out in case of a recurrence of that unforeseen outburst at Blickham General, in the hope that exposure to a less rigid environment than Chent will encourage her to relax and come to terms with the repressed material."

The words poured out glibly enough, but Alsop's face remained set in a dubious frown. "You haven't even established her nationality?" he suggested.

"Uh ... well, no. Beyond a comment from the philologists that the language she speaks is an eastern one."

"There's something funny about her," Alsop said with decision. "Her amnesia, if that's what it is, is too . . . too all-embracing. If it related to some isolated subject, that would make sense. But . . . Well, never mind." He rose and moved to the side of the room. "Call her in and go through a normal day's session with her. Just ignore me and pretend I'm not here."

Palms sweating, Paul complied. He mentioned Alsop to Urchin as she sat down, and she gave him a mechanical smile; then he performed the induction as he had done earlier, and spent about ten minutes racking his brains for questions to ask her that would both satisfy Alsop and evade the subject of her origins.

Dismayed, he suddenly noticed that Alsop was gesturing for his attention. There was nothing else he could do except instruct Urchin to relax and sit still while he turned to the consultant.

"This isn't getting you anywhere, young fellow," Alsop told him briskly. "You want to hammer away at the key areas—sensitive subjects like sex and violence, background material like the family she comes from. Let me ask her a few things and show you what I mean."

Trembling, Paul had to counteract the standard order in the induction—"You will hear no voice but mine"—which he normally dispensed with but had included today because of Alsop's intrusion.

—She's so used to talking about it in this room at this time of day. Will my spur-of-the-moment command to keep her mouth shut hold good?

He caught himself biting his thumb-nail as Alsop launched into his interrogation, and thrust the hand into his pocket; it would be fatal to betray signs of agitation.

Relief welled up as he listened. Determinedly, Urchin was evading every attempt Alsop made to get her to discuss her home and family, although whenever he switched to some more recent event she gave ready answers.

—Bless you, Urchin. This is . . . this is loyal of you. I do my best for you, and you certainly show how much you appreciate it.

Next, however, Alsop swung away on a new tack, and Paul's burgeoning relief — dissipated.

"You remember in the woods where you first met Dr Fidler," Alsop said, "there was another man just before that. You do remember?"

She gave a vigorous nod.

"What happened when he saw you, Urchin?"

—Jesus God. I've never talked to her about Faberdown. What was I thinking of? That ought to have been in all my case-notes. No wonder Alsop isn't satisfied! "Papa Freud he say . . . !"

"I . . . I came to say hello, and he said something I didn't understand and took hold of my arm and wanted to . . . I don't know the word in English. Push me on the ground and have pleasure from me."

"So what did you do?"

"I was first very surprised, not understanding what he said. Then he hurt me, push me over—*pushed*—so I realised I must fight him. He was heavy. I did this," pantomiming clawed nails raking his cheek. "Then I hit him. He moved back, but when he started again I knew I must stopping him."

"How?"

"Hit him on a tree," she muttered, almost inaudibly as if ashamed of the violence she had used.

"And before you saw him," Alsop continued, "what happened then?"

Silence.

"Were you walking in the woods, or in the fields?"

Silence.

Alsop pressed her for a little longer. Eventually he sighed and relinquished control to Paul, who ended the trance and sent Urchin away, glad to have got it over with.

"I see your difficulty," Alsop admitted after the door had closed behind her. "Nonetheless, that's a line you should have been pursuing a bit more intensively—working back from the earliest time she remembers clearly. But the sharp cut-off, contrasted with the accuracy of her memory of what one might expect to be a highly charged incident immediately following, makes me wonder about brain damage. We never did get those skull X-rays, did we?"

Paul shook his head.

"Do you think you could persuade her to lie down quietly and let them X-ray her now?"

"Yes, I'm sure I could."

"Right, better make the arrangements as soon as you can. The whole thing is very puzzling, but there are definite signs that she's co-operating, I suppose, which is encouraging. . . . You'll bear in mind what I said about your scrappy case-notes, though, won't you?"

"Yes. I'm very sorry. But it is losing Iris which has upset me so much."

"You don't think you ought to take a week or two off?" Alsop suggested.

"Thanks very much, but ... no. I'd only mope by myself and probably end up worse rather than better. This way I at least have my work to occupy me."

"There are other things in life than work, you know," Alsop said. He got to his feet. "Still, I agree that solitary moping would be bad for you. When can you have the X-rays done?"

"It would be best if I went with her, I think, as a precaution." Paul flipped the leaves of his desk diary. "I'm not on duty this weekend. Perhaps I can arrange for it to be done on Saturday morning, like the first time we tried."

"Haven't you got one of your whatsit committee meetings this Saturday?"

"Blast—so we have. I'd forgotten to put that down. Never mind, though; there'll be time afterwards. Dr Holinshed prefers to keep the meetings short."

◆ *34* ◆

—I'm scared.

Paul sat silent, listening to the meaningless voices of the other members of the Operating Committee as they discussed a complaint from the union to which most of the maintenance staff belonged about patients undertaking too many repair jobs around the hospital. He was making little attempt to follow what was said. Wordless, the concept of being afraid was shaking his head as the maddening cracked bell of the hospital clock shook its tower.

—I've told her, explained to her, repeated to her, that there's nothing to fear from the X-ray equipment; I've shown her plates of heads and hands. I think she understands. But if she breaks down again, they'll ... No, I don't want to think of what they'll do. But what did she imagine the equipment was, when she panicked? She won't confess that.

Roshman was talking: a roly-poly man, very Jewish, horn-rimmed glasses seeming to rest as much on his chubby red cheeks as on his nose, his hair thinning over the scalp so that his comb drew it into parallel strips between which the skin was visible.

—I've stood off Alsop for the moment, but I made a dreadful mistake not asking Urchin about Faberdown and putting all the details into my summary notes. He's after something neat and tidy and conventional which will give him everything he wants: the superior feeling that comes from telling one's juniors that father knew best all along, the relief of knowing that there isn't going to be any trail-blazing paper to make the junior's name more important than his.

A change of subject. This time Paul ignored it altogether.

—I want ... What do I want? I think, to put a little of Llanraw into this sick world. On this very spot where stupid droning voices buzz like flies hammering window-glass, flowers taller than a man breathing scent to the distant sea. I hope to bequeath them a whole person, lonely, but strong with an inner vision. What would Holinshed understand about Llanraw, where the men in authority are those who are best loved, not those who most crave power?

Holinshed, about to announce the next item on the agenda, grew aware of Paul's gaze fixed on him and raised his head.

"You wanted to say something, Dr Fidler?"

"Ah ... no. No thanks. It's not important after all."

Suspicious, the medical superintendent's hard eyes scanned his face at length before resuming their focus on the documents in his hand.

—To be cut off from Llanraw: torment. But to have it to remember, at least: I envy that. I recall a sort of echoing tunnel, a house with a mile of like ones either side, schools that trained me to answer the questions of a stranger through the second-hand medium of ink, a woman who knew her son to be brighter than average and every spare second breathed on his shine and rubbed it new, another who perfectly understood how the former felt but would not give me the chance to undo the harm in another generation. Out there on the far fork of time's delta, is there a Paul Fidler like the myriads I've heard complaining on their dead ends of disaster, but happy? If he's there, he will think no thoughts with my brain. I'm unattuned to happiness.

He began to draw on the back of his agenda. He designed a sort of map of lines fissioning outward from a central stem. From the bottom upwards he labelled them; naming the first junction "Failed eleven-plus," he put a sketch of a road-sweeper's barrow against it, and at the second—"Expelled"— the broad arrow, sign of prison. There was no real system in the labels he attached to the forks; he could have included a hundred of them had there been room.

At the top, the present day, there were a score to deal with. Eventually, however, each last one was marked with some appropriate symbol of disaster; when his imagination ran dry, he fell back on conventions and drew a gallows and a skull. Thoughtfully he traced back the line, looking for any course he might have taken that promised better, not worse.

—Here? Iris breaking our engagement? Yes, that's the only one as far as I can tell. I'd have been upset, but then . . . then I'd have met some sensible young nurse at the first or second hospital I worked at, and we'd have got married and she'd have gone on working until I was appointed to a fairly well-paid post and then we'd have started on our family and maybe this very moment I'd be looking forward to taking my wife and baby son out for tea in a little village somewhere, in a beat-up old Austin, and we'd be laughing and making plans and . . .

"Dr Fidler, are you proposing to continue the meeting by yourself?"

Holinshed, with maximum sarcasm, shuffling his papers into a file-cover while everyone else dispersed towards the door. Blushing, Paul made to do the same, but Holinshed snapped his fingers and gestured for him to wait. He complied nervously.

"You were scarcely paying attention, Dr Fidler," Holinshed reproached him directly the others had gone out of ear-shot, apart from Miss Laxham tidying up the table. "You might just as well not have attended the meeting, I feel."

Without waiting for Paul's reply, he stood up, his expression severe. "Indeed, your work in general has hardly been outstanding during the past few weeks. I have been reluctant to comment, but so many people are bound to notice if you display this casual attitude during our committee meetings that I feel I must tell you to pull yourself together."

—Smug bastard.

"Have you ever been married?" Paul demanded.

"I know about your wife's ... ah ... departure. That's why I've been giving you the benefit of the doubt lately."

"Have you?"

"I don't see what that has to do with it."

"If you had, you'd understand a little better. Perhaps."

"If I follow your meaning correctly," Holinshed snapped, "then I should also request you to consider the consequences of having yourself closeted daily for long periods with a young and not unattractive female patient. And before you—as I believe the current phrase goes—blow your top, let me stress that while I would not for a moment credit you with improper intentions, patients in a mental hospital do find malicious gossip a favourite pastime. It would be advantageous to all concerned if Dr Rudge were to relieve you of Urchin's case."

"To all concerned?" Paul echoed, shaking. "To all except the patient, that's more like it. The patient comes first, to my way of thinking."

"Are you not aware," Holinshed murmured, "that the young woman is now generally referred to throughout this hospital by a ... well ... scandalous nickname? I don't mean a humorous name comparable with 'Soppy Al' for Dr Alsop or my own epithet of 'Holy Joe!' "

—Good grief. I always thought he was sublimely ignorant of Mirza's inventions.

Aloud, Paul said, "What nickname? I've never heard of any."

"They call her ..." Holinshed hesitated. "They call her the fiddler's bitch."

The appointment for the X-ray this morning was at half past eleven. An ambulance was waiting before the hospital, not far from where his own car was parked, to take Urchin into Blickham, but it would be another few minutes before it had to leave.

Paul stood beside it in brilliant sunshine, grateful for the excuse to slip dark glasses on and hide his eyes from the ambulance driver with whom he had to exchange casual chat for the sake of appearances. Since there was no need for him to return to Chent today, he intended to follow the ambulance in the car and drive straight home afterwards.

"Beautiful day," he half heard. "Taking the wife and kiddy out this afternoon. Go for a swim in the river, perhaps. If the weather holds." A critical squint at the sky. "Just my luck if they make me hang around in Blickham till the sun goes in."

—Fidler's bitch. It couldn't be something Mirza coined. Please not. I could strangle whoever . . .

"They ought to be here any moment," he said mechanically. "Yes, I think that's Nurse Davis bringing her now."

—None too pleased, though. Row with boy-friend? Saturday work when the sun's out?

"Good morning, Urchin!"

"Good morning, Dr Paul."

—Has she been called that? Wouldn't hurt her. Wouldn't know the English overtones of "bitch."

There was a sense of pressure in his head, as though his skull were fragmenting into a pattern like dried clay under the heat of the day and would spill his secret thoughts naked for all the world to see when it ultimately spilt.

"You're coming with us, Doctor?" Nurse Davis asked, her voice uncharacteristically sharp. The driver was opening the rear doors to let Urchin climb in, which she did with a wistful glance at the gardens around.

"I'll join you there. I'm going in my car."

"I see." A bite on her lower lip, disappointed.

"What's the matter, Nurse?"

"Well . . . I just hope they don't keep us too long." She hesitated, then burst out in a fit of frankness. "I'm supposed to be off at lunch-time, see, so I arranged for a friend to meet me, and I thought maybe if you were riding in the ambulance . . . But it doesn't matter."

She climbed up after Urchin and the driver shut the doors with a thud. The sound made echoes in the emptiness of Paul's mind.

—Eager for her date, the executive-type young man, maybe. And taking the wife and kiddy for a swim in the river. Me? The summer sun on textbooks making my head ache. This is the worst summer of my life. Mirza going away, Iris gone, the child . . . probably gone. I have nothing left but the vision of a non-existent world called Llanraw, and they will take even that from me.

He was scarcely aware that he had covered the distance between Chent and Blickham General; his perceptions faded, and came back to him only when he was helping Urchin from the ambulance on their arrival. Then she looked up at the clear blue above and sighed.

"Something wrong, Urchin?" he demanded, nervous for fear his calming and persuasion was about to collapse before the impact of her blind terror.

"I wish . . ."

"What?"

"I wish I could go out and see," she said, and responded to Nurse Davis's impatience, walking quietly beside her into the building to keep the time of the appointment: a pathetic sagging doll in a plain rather ugly cotton dress and clumsy heavy shoes.

—It's beginning to tell on her. To look through bars at the summer sky: isn't that enough to wear down anyone?

The same young houseman was on duty as last time, and he was equally harassed. He was no less apologetic, moreover. Today the schedule had been shot to hell by a horse that had kicked two men, trampled another, and had to be destroyed—but the only weapon available had been a shotgun, and an innocent bystander had been peppered in the leg.

It would mean a wait of at least half an hour.

For a long moment Paul thought about barred windows and Llanraw. His eyes were on Nurse Davis's face, hating the way her ever-smiling mouth now set in a disappointed line, and hearing in imagination the cry of a child promised a trip in the country but growing fractious with delay.

He said, "Go and tell the driver to run you home, Nurse. I'll bring Urchin back to Chent in my car."

—I said it. I must have been preparing to say it while I was on the way here. That was why my mind seemed to hold nothing at all. There's no law, for heaven's sake! She's not certified, she isn't even legally a voluntary patient, just someone stuck in Chent because it came handy. Watch the brown face; does it look "ah-hah!"?

But all it did was smile dazzlingly.

"Are you sure, Doctor? I mean, is that all right?"

"Go on," he said gruffly. "Before I change my mind."

For a moment he thought she was going to hug him; instead, she poured out thanks and spun on her heel.

The houseman was regarding Urchin dubiously. "*Is* it all right?" he murmured to Paul. "Last time, you know, she—"

"There's been all the improvement in the world," Paul snapped.

"I'll have a male nurse standing by anyway," the houseman said. "Just in case. That is, if you don't mind!"

—Don't let me down, girl. Don't let me down.

She didn't. Wary, they let her look the equipment over first, which she did with something more than curiosity; then she shrugged and settled into the correct position for the pictures to be taken. She seemed relaxed; Paul thought that perhaps only he could detect the effort she was making to appear so.

By the time everything was concluded and arrangements had been made for the delivery of the plates to Chent, the hospital's morning routine was at an end. Nurses going off duty crowded the corridor which they followed to the exit, gaudy in fashionable summer dresses, wispy translucent garments sleeveless and high above the knee, two or three of them accompanied by boy-friends in open shirts and brilliant chokers. They crossed the yard among the parked cars to join a flow of shoppers short-cutting down the street towards the bus station a hundred yards away.

Urchin stopped in the doorway, and Paul, sensing her mood, halted beside her.

After a while, having stared long and long at the passing crowd: "Paul, I have been here months and all I have seen of your world is on the television. I have not even seen one of your towns."

"I'm afraid . . ."

The words died.

—No, whatever the consequences, it isn't right that she should think there's nothing better than squalid Chent and war and prison in this world of mine. There are scraps of happiness. Other patients have relatives to call and take them out at weekends. She has no one. I have no one.

He took her arm and led her past the car, feeling drunk with defiance.

—If a patient can't safely go out in the charge of her doctor, it's not worth being a doctor. The hell with you, Holy Joe. The fiddler is taking his bitch for a walk.

At first he was on guard, alert for any attempt she might make to dart away from him. But very shortly he relaxed and began to enjoy himself. She was so delighted that she almost skipped along the pavement, like a girl on holiday from a detested school. It was the literal childishness of her behaviour that touched him: staring without self-consciousness at the passers-by, stopping every few yards to peer into a shop window and demand explanations of what she saw there.

Blickham was never an attractive town, but today the weather made it less than ugly. He took her down the most inoffensive streets, showing her the Elizabethan town hall and two or three other special sights, but after a while gave up wondering what else to head for. Her uncritical fascination with everything in the town was giving her sufficient reward.

An hour or so later, he began to feel hungry. There was the problem of her rigid vegetarianism to bear in mind, he realised, and thought about that for a minute or two before recalling a Chinese restaurant where he had occasionally lunched with Alsop prior to a Monday afternoon clinic. It was not far from where they had come to now.

Turning to suggest they should eat, he became aware of Urchin at his side, despondent in sharp contrast to her earlier elation.

"Something wrong?" he demanded, alarmed.

"No, no. You were going to say something?"

"I thought we should have some lunch. I know a place where you can have a meal without meat."

Nodding, she walked where he led her, in silence. Eventually, when they had passed several more people, she said, "Paul!"

"Yes?"

"The people look at me in such a strange way. Why?"

Startled, he looked at her himself. Abruptly he snapped his fingers.

—Good lord! In that oversized bag of a dress, those clumping great shoes, she must strike everyone as fresh out of jail or something.

He halted and stared around.

—Mustn't let anything so ridiculous spoil the day for her. She won't know what sizes she takes in anything. What do I do, buy a tape-measure? No, the hell with it. I treat her like a kid. I feel like a father. I feel . . . God damn it, I feel proud.

"Right!" he said aloud. "The next person who looks at you on the street is going to think, 'Wow!' "

"What?"

"Never mind."

There was one large department store in Blickham which

stayed open on Saturday afternoons for the convenience of office-workers and villagers who could only spare the time to come into the town at the weekend. In the women's department he confronted a stately assistant wearing a tape-measure as a girdle to her black uniform dress.

"The young lady here has been in hospital for some time and her . . . ah . . . her clothes are in storage," he lied cheerfully. "Can you fit her out with something suitable?"

The assistant looked doubtful. "Only from the Junior Misses' range," she said. "Over there we have . . ."

Paul turned to follow her gesture. He spotted racks of parrot-brilliant clothes in a corner of the department he had overlooked on entering. Briskly he strode over to them.

—Now let's see if any of the fashionable taste of Iris's London friends has rubbed off on me. I might as well reap some profit from that bloody woman.

His eye was caught by a display of printed cotton underwear in bold black and white checks, lacy suspender-belts, and stockings in white lace, net, floral designs.

—They're wearing that kind of thing nowadays, aren't they? She'll look about fourteen, but I probably look forty by now.

"A set of those," he said, pointing. "And . . . let's see. Blue? No. Yellow, that would be splendid. Show us some yellow dresses. And a summer coat. A nice leaf-green coat."

"Yes, sir," the assistant sighed docilely.

He lit a cigarette nervously while he waited for Urchin to return from the fitting-room. The department had filled up with teenage girls on a Saturday shopping spree. He was the only man in sight, and they all kept staring at him, except a few who apparently regarded him as part of the furniture and disconcertingly made no bones about peeling off their clothes if the fitting-rooms were all engaged and trying new dresses on within arm's reach of him. He tried to think of them as furniture too, but an instinct which had lain dormant in his mind since Iris left was rising up at the sight of so much smooth warm skin.

—I wonder if Mirza knows any of them. Wouldn't be surprised. He must have worked through a fair cross-section of the local inhabitants by now.

"Paul?"

If it hadn't been for her addressing him by name, he literally would not have recognised her. She stood before him shyly, tiny and exquisite, in a skimpy yellow frock over lacy white stockings and a pair of flat tan sandals, eyes shining, hair—grown out longer since her stay in Chent—combed into sleek wings either side of her face. At her side the stately assistant was looking positively smug.

"I'm sorry to have kept you so long, sir, but it struck me the young lady would need shoes, too, and I took the liberty of brushing out her hair into a more stylish arrangement—"

"Don't apologise," Paul said. "Just show me the bill."

The assistant, smirking, moved to the counter to add it up, and Urchin gave up trying to resist the impulse and threw her arms around him.

Two girls at the far side of the room, probably sisters, stared at them. Their expression said as clearly as words, "Sugar daddy!" And in perfect synchronicity both faces turned to a look of unashamed envy.

They were just in time for the restaurant; the next action of the waiter who admitted them was to turn around a sign on the door so that instead of reading OPEN it read CLOSED. But the service was unaffected by their being the last customers.

Inconspicuously, as he hoped, Paul checked the amount remaining in his wallet as he read down the menu.

—Considering the exiguous quantity of material that goes into them, modern fashions are a bit pricy!

"Let me see?" Urchin murmured, holding out her hand.

"What? Oh, this?" He drew out the money. "Don't you have money in Llanraw?"

"Yes, but it's not used very much." She hesitated, eyes suddenly widening. "Ought I to have said that? We aren't alone here."

She put her hand to her head, a little dizzy. "I have a feeling you said I wasn't to talk about it."

Paul smiled reassuringly. "Away from the hospital it doesn't matter. Besides, I mentioned it first."

Examining the bank-notes curiously, she nodded.

"Why isn't it used very much?"

"Oh—because there is enough of everything for everybody. Enough food, enough houses ... You don't live at Chent, do you, Paul?"

"No."

"You know—" She laughed lightly. "At first I thought everyone in this world lived in big buildings like the hospital, and men and women were forbidden to go together. I thought: *tjachariva*, do they not enjoy each other?"

—Not much. Except for lucky bastards like Mirza.

"What was that you said just now?"

"What? Oh! *Tjachariva?*" At the beginning was the sound he had tried and found impossible to imitate; his lips and tongue refused to work that way. "It means 'let it not happen,' I think you might say. We put it before saying something we do not mean to take seriously."

—Urchin in Chent for the rest of her days: *tjachariva!*

An idea struck him, and he tensed. "Waiter! Have you a phone I can use?"

—If I don't come back with Urchin, they're liable to assume she attacked me and escaped!

Ferdie Silva was on duty today. Paul spun him a glib yarn about hoping to jog Urchin's memory with the sight of familiar things in the neighbourhood. To the demand when they would be back, he returned a non-committal answer.

"Paul," Urchin said when he rejoined her at the table, "will you show me the place where you live?"

"If you like." He felt giddy, careless of consequences. "And a lot more besides. I may not be able to offer you a balloon-ride, but you can cover much more ground in a car."

—They told me when I was little that children came from heaven. This person is of another brighter world: not an angel, but at least a sprite, an elf, daughter of Llanraw and not of common flesh.

Walking back to where they had left the car outside the hospital, Paul kept his arm on Urchin's shoulder. She liked that, and every now and again reached up to give his fingers a squeeze. As he had predicted, there was nothing odd any longer about the glances she attracted from passers-by.

It was in this attitude, a few hundred yards before they reached the car, that they came face to face with Mrs Weddenhall.

Time stopped.

When it moved on again, Paul heard himself saying with idiotic gravity, "Good afternoon, madam. Have your hounds caught any good maniacs lately?"

She purpled, and when he began to laugh she snarled at him like one of her own dogs. Urchin was bewildered, but seeing that he was amused smiled likewise. Without a word Mrs Weddenhall marched on.

◆ *36* ◆

He kept laughing at the remembered spectacle of her discomfiture the whole of the rest of the afternoon. Everything was so perfect! The only flaw was a brief one; he forgot that Urchin's experience of travel was confined to the police-car and the sedate progress of ambulances, and when he let the little Spitfire race down the road at seventy with the top open, she was so alarmed she clung to the underside of the dashboard.

Soon enough, however, she learned to enjoy it, and he took her on a whirlwind tour of little charming villages he'd never seen since his first trip to this district, when he had driven around musing about Iris's reaction to the prospect of living in Yemble. He showed her the brawling Teme, rough on its rocks at Ludlow, the stiff-backed hills, the trees greener than her gay new coat in full summer rig, and once when he had stopped and backed up so that she could admire a traditional cottage garden, its roadside wall a riot of aubrietia, arabis, stonecrop and rambler rose, she murmured, "I thought it was all ugly here, Paul—all, all ugly!"

His eyes stung. For an instant he thought he was going to cry.

—I must be sensible, though. I must bring her back responsibly at the regular time for patients with same-day Saturday leave. But why didn't I think of this before? Why didn't I remember that she must envy the people with friends and relatives to call for them and take them out?

She ceased her contemplation of the garden and turned to him.

"Paul, do you live in a house like that one? You said you'd show me where you live."

He consulted a mental map. "We can be there in ten minutes, if you like," he promised, and accelerated down the road.

She was charmed and overjoyed at sight of his home, and struck dumb by the interior. She wandered about the living-room, touching the furniture as if she didn't believe it could be solid, while he stood watching and unable to keep a smug grin off his face. There was something so refreshing about her reaction compared to Iris's. Innocent of prejudices about quaintness and suitability to one's status, she could look at it with an unbiased eye, and she approved.

He toured the whole house with her, having to explain as he went: not the cookery utensils, but the electric stove; not the television, but the telephone, which she had seen in the hospital but never been allowed to use. He amused her by dialing for a time-check and letting her listen to it.

Opening the refrigerator curiously, she inspected a head of lettuce, tomatoes, eggs, butter, with interest, then came to a packet of sausages and sniffed them suspiciously. She turned large eyes to him, and he thought the look reproachful.

"I'm sorry," he said awkwardly. "We don't feel the same way about meat as you do."

She shrugged and put them back. "We have an ancient saying? 'when you go to Taophrah'—that's a big city which once was the capital of what you call Denmark—'you must wear the clothes other people wear.' And eat their food too, I suppose."

Paul felt a stir of surprise. He said, "We talk about Rome that way. 'When in Rome, do as the Romans do.'"

Shutting the refrigerator, she spoke over her shoulder. "Is that strange? We are, after all, also human."

She fingered the taps over the sink, and continued, still without looking at him, "Shall we stay to eat supper here, or will you take me back to Chent?"

"We can eat here if you like. I haven't got much food in the house, but there should be enough for two."

"Do you live here all alone?"

Paul shifted uncomfortably from foot to foot. "I do now."

"Once you did not?"

"Yes, that's right."

She hoisted herself up on the edge of the table and let her legs swing, admiring her smart new white stockings. "You were not happy," she suggested after a while.

"I'm afraid we weren't."

"In this world, I think, people have children when they live together even if they are not sure they are happy and will be good for parents. Have you children, Paul?"

"No."

She gave him a dazzling smile. "Good! I was afraid . . .

But it was silly. I should have known better. You are too kind to make children have unhappy parents."

—If that were only the truth of the matter . . . !

But her mind had wandered to another subject. "Paul!"

"Yes?"

"Am I a prisoner in Chent? Can I go away one day?"

He hesitated. "It's hard to explain," he prevaricated. "You see—"

"Oh, I'm not complaining!" she broke in. "I have been lucky to be looked after when I was a stranger and could not speak English or do anything. But I have tried to learn to talk your language and do the things that people around me do, and . . ."

Paul took a deep breath. "Urchin, how do people think of telling lies in Llanraw?"

"Lies." A twin furrow appeared either side of the bridge of her nose: a sketch for a frown. "We like to say the truth, but sometimes it is unkind. Then we make pretend."

—As she said just now: we're all human.

"I'm worried," he said slowly. "In our world we like to have tidy explanations for everything. We like to be sure about people—where they come from, what they do for a living, what language they speak. You seem to be more of a stranger than anybody else who's ever come here. People are going to want to keep an eye on you."

"Keep an eye?"

"Watch you, make sure you do the right things." He rubbed his sweating palms on his trousers. "If they don't believe you're telling the truth about yourself, they will assume you really are crazy."

She gave a sober nod. "I thought so. Even before you warned me, I had decided not to tell other people than you about Llanraw."

"So you must wait a little longer. When it's definite that you can behave as people here do, you will be allowed to go away from Chent and be on your own. Don't worry—I'll help you every way I can."

"*Must* I be on my own?"

"Oh, you'll have friends, and—"

"Never mind." She jumped off the table. "You haven't shown me what there is up the stairs in this house."

With grave interest she surveyed the two bedrooms, one sparsely furnished for guests. But it was the bathroom which made her clap her hands in delight and cry out.

"Oh! You have one here!"

"A bathroom? Of course I do," Paul agreed, puzzled.

"Can I?" Eagerly she was leaning forward to touch the taps. "I have not felt truly clean since I came to the hospital. There is always a—a *stink*. The bath they let me use is swilled with disinfectant. Dis . . . ?"

"Yes, you pronounced it right."

—Hmmm . . .

He tugged open the bathroom cabinet and produced some of the toilet luxuries Iris had left behind. Drawing the stopper on a bottle of bath-oil, he held it out.

"Is that better?"

"Mmmm!" Her eyes shone.

"Go ahead then. Scrub all you like. Put some of this in the water." He turned on the taps as he spoke, waiting for it to warm up with his hand in the flow. "And—how do you feel about drinking in Llanraw?"

"Drinking?" she echoed in a puzzled voice.

"Alcohol. Ah . . ." He hesitated. Naturally, liquor was forbidden to the inmates at Chent. "Do you understand beer, wine? Something made from fruit or grain that makes you feel cheerful?"

"Oh yes! We make it from grapes."

"Wine, that's what we call it. I have a little sherry downstairs; I'll bring you a glass of it."

He was about to go out when she called after him, "Paul!" Turning, he saw that brilliant smile again.

"Paul, you are very kind to me. Thank you."

—Everybody ought to be. That's why I feel embarrassed.

She had taken off her dress and stockings when he came back with the sherry, but since she had not closed the door of the bathroom he had no warning. He was a little startled at the matter-of-factness of her attitude, and firmly drew the door to as he left her.

—Though since on the first occasion we met she was in the nude, I suppose . . .

He wandered back downstairs, collected his own drink, and went into the kitchen to consider the possibility of a meal. It would be little more than a snack; since Iris left, he had begrudged the time spent in preparing elaborate meals for himself, and made do most of the time on the hospital lunch and something fried up in the evening.

However, Urchin could hardly object to a cheese salad, and there was a brown loaf only a day old. Humming, hap-

pier than at any time since he secured his job at Chent, he set
about preparing the food.

—I love the way little things delight her. To think that
giving someone a bath in reasonable privacy, with a drop of
scent instead of disinfectant, could create such _joy!_ It's like
taking out a kid from an orphanage, showing her a dream
come true.

He had been drinking quite a lot since he was on his
own—more than his medical training told him was advisable,
but it did help him to face the situation without panic—and
when he came to look for wine to accompany the food he
found he had drunk the last bottle. However, there was cold
beer. He shrugged.

—If she doesn't like it, there's water.

He surveyed his handiwork with approval: a mound of
cheese framed by green lettuce, red tomatoes, pale cucumber,
yellow chopped apple and brown dried fruit. With bread, and
perhaps an orange each for dessert, that would be plenty.

He went back into the living-room to fetch himself another
glass of sherry. From behind, as he was pouring it, he heard
her voice.

"Paul?"

He raised his head, and almost dropped the bottle he was
holding. She stood with one foot on the landing, one foot on
the first tread of the stairs, face averted to run her nose with
sensual approval along her arm. She was pinkly flushed from
the heat of the bath, and completely naked.

"Urchin, for goodness' sake! Go and put your clothes on!"

She let her arm fall and stared at him with hurt bewilderment. After a pause she said, "But don't you like to look at
me?"

"Yes! Yes, God damn it, you're a beautiful girl. But—"

"I don't understand people here," she sighed. "Even when
it's warm, always in clothes, and always talking about clothes,
too—never about how their bodies look, or about how to
make their muscles firm ... But, Paul, that stuff you put in
the bath makes me so delicious! I want you to smell, first."

She came leaping down the stairs three at a time, holding
out her hands towards him. Just before she arrived within
arm's reach of his petrified body, she stopped dead, her face
falling.

"Paul, this is ... not right?"

"I—" His voice was thick, and refused to form words
properly. "Urchin, I think you're sweet and charming and

lovely and everything. But I'm your doctor, I'm supposed to be looking after you, and so I'm not allowed to . . . to . . ."

She put her hands on her hips and jutted her small breasts forward aggressively. "It is to look after a woman, to stay away from her, not touch, not kiss? Paul, I have never in my life since I was thirteen years old been without a man to want to touch me for so long as I have now! It will make me really crazy. It is like having a fire in the tummy. I thought today, thank goodness, finally, this is the punishment for mad people in your world and he is satisfied I am not crazy and do not have to be punished any longer, and—"

She raised both fists to shoulder level, closing her small fingers on the air as though she would strangle it.

"And if it does not make me crazy, now I think it will make me dead!"

She buried her face convulsively in both hands and began to cry.

From outside there came the sound of a slowing car. Panic gripped him. He darted to the nearest window, which stood open for the warmth of the evening, and dragged the curtains across it. It was still light outside. The next curtain, and the next, and he was screened from passers-by. Panting, he turned back to Urchin. The car's engine stopped and its door slammed.

—By the skin of my teeth. If one of the neighbours had looked in and seen her . . .

Awkwardly he tried to calm her, but she flinched away; when he made another attempt, she chopped at his arm viciously with the side of her hand, making him cry out for the shock. Curling her lip, she looked as though she might spit at him.

—Oh my God. What sort of trap have I dug for myself now?

There was a rap on the door. He froze, heart flailing at his ribs. His hands shot out and clamped on Urchin's shoulders.

"Urchin, for pity's sake! If they find you here like this with me, they'll send me away and you'll never see me again. They'll lock you up in Chent for the rest of your life!"

She raised lustreless eyes to him. "It can't be true," she said sullenly. "Human people could not live in that way."

There was another bang on the door, louder. He shook her back and forth.

"I swear it! In a little while, Urchin, when they let you go

away from Chent and you're not my patient any more, perhaps then—but now it would ruin me. Please, *please!*"

She freed herself with a ducking twist and began to plod
towards the stairs, head down, shoulders slumped. Paul put
his hand to his forehead and found it slippery with perspira-
tion.

—Move, woman, don't dawdle like that!

Behind him there was the rustling sound of a curtain being
thrust aside. A voice said through the open window, "Paul!
Did you get the clock I—? Oooh! I say! Hello, Iris! It *is*
warm tonight, isn't—? Oooh-*hoooh!* You're not Iris! Paul,
you randy old so-and-so, such goings-on never did expect!"

Chortling at the window, leering and giggling, the flushed
round face of Maurice Dawkins in the grip of his manic
phase.

◆ *37* ◆

When Paul regained the power to move, his first impulse was
to turn his head towards the stairs. Urchin had vanished.

—Perhaps she was never here at all. Perhaps it's all a
dream. I've been walking about in the sun getting delusions
from the heat and the strain.

"Aren't you going to invite me in to join your little party?"
Maurice demanded.

—Everything go smash, fly apart, house fall down, earth
open and swallow me . . .

"Paul, I didn't expect this kind of welcome from an old
friend! Well, I'll come in anyway."

Maurice disengaged the window-stay and pulled the case-
ment wide. With much huffing he put first one fat, wobbling
leg and then the other across the sill.

His hair was all over the place, he couldn't have shaved for
three days, his shoes were filthy and the zip of his trousers
was open an inch and a half. Paul noted these facts mechanically, camera-fashion, while struggling to order his raging
mind.

—Let him talk for a bit, calm him, and get rid of him? Won't work. If he's in this state he'll be out of reach of normal persuasion. How do I get drugs down him? There are packets and bottles and jars of pills here thanks to my own need for them, but I can't expect to make him swallow them. Have to get him drunk. Get him to Chent—no, for heaven's sake, must keep him away at all costs. He belongs in a hospital but now he has more to tell than simply that I once had a breakdown, now he can say I was seen with a female patient naked in my home and . . .

The world slithered, tilted, spun awry.

Face sweating so much it gleamed as if it had been greased, Maurice advanced on him and clapped him on the arm. "It's wonderful to see you again, Paul," he babbled. "I've kept meaning and meaning to look you up, thank you for all the help you've been to me when I was brought down in the past, but I didn't know where to find you until I ran into Iris at Meg and Bertie's the other day and I heard you'd had some sort of bust-up and she was staying with them for the time being so I thought really I ought to come and sympathise with you a bit. Hello, hello, and who's your lady friend—ah? It ain't the one I saw yer with at 'Ampstead!"

Carolling, he lurched forward in a grotesque parody of a dance figure, and the words blended into a disgusting chuckle. Withdrawing, trying not to appear to retreat, Paul saw from the corner of his eye that Urchin had reappeared on the stairs. She had apparently slipped on her dress and sandals only, without taking the time to bother about stockings.

"While the cat's away the mice will play, dance over my lady gay," Maurice continued, approximating the tune of "London Bridge Is Falling Down." "I'm surprised at you, being a doctor, but of course doctors are as human as anybody, aren't they?" He winked and gave Paul a hearty nudge in the ribs. "It was a great comfort to me to know that—did I ever tell you? It meant I was able to put up with my bad phases much better. Of course, I feel on top of the world at the moment, and all the more so for seeing you again after all this time, but—" He lost the thread of his declamation; his wet lips flapped for a couple of seconds before he concluded, "Well, aren't you going to introduce me?"

"Urchin, this is Maurice," Paul mumbled. "A friend of mine from London. Maurice, Urchin."

"One crazy-type name!" Maurice exclaimed. "Caviar is the

roe of the searchin' Urchin—hmmm . . . Lurching? Researching! Caviar is the roe of researching virgins—not true, that, of course, because as I understand it any sturgeon which goes into the caviar business has already lost her cherry stone and all. I keep meaning to lose a stone, too." He stuck his thumb in the waistband of his trousers and gave his pot-belly a rueful look.

"You . . . uh . . . you must be thirsty after your drive," Paul ventured. "How about a drink?"

"Yes, I rented a car from some funny firm or other in an impossible suburb this morning and got up here in what would have been good time except for a damned fool of a driver in a Mini who got in the way while I was overtaking—well, it's all insured, I suppose, but I'm glad I got here before dark because I don't suppose either of the headlights is much good now, one broken and the other sighted on Mars or Jupiter or some planet or other. I thought I'd signal to them later on, send them some Morse code saying hello and good wishes from Maurice but since the collision the car sort of swings when I'm putting the brakes on and I'd probably miss them by miles. Drink! Yes, we ought to celebrate. Long long time no see. Paul, I love you, did I ever tell you that?"

He began to jig up and down on the spot, as though his tense muscles wouldn't permit his limbs to remain still but insisted on contracting randomly. His wide staring grin moved from Paul to Urchin, standing silent and nervous in the background, and slipped for a moment into a look of feral jealousy.

"Sit down," Paul suggested, terrified at the implications of that fleeting expression.

—Thought . . . ? I don't know. Possibly: now's my chance to catch Paul on his own without a woman around.

"I can stand," Maurice said. "I can stand it. I can stand practically everything. *Practically* everything."

His eyes transfixed Urchin and the grin, after its brief return, collapsed into a tight-lipped smile.

"About that drink," Paul said heartily. "I have some special strong ale which I think you'll like. Urchin, come and help me bring the glasses."

She complied without demur. The moment they were inside the kitchen door, she whispered, "Paul, is he sick?"

"I'm afraid so," Paul muttered. He reached for the little bottle of pure alcohol and spilled three fingers into a glass before uncapping the beer.

"Why do you put that in?"

"I wouldn't be able to make him take the dose of tranquilliser he needs. This will make him drunk—he'll get sleepy and perhaps pass out, though when somebody's in that state it takes an awfully long time and there's a risk of him getting violent first."

The beer foamed up to the rim of the glass. He poured the rest of the bottle into a glass for himself, for appearance's sake.

"Want some?" he murmured to Urchin. She dipped a finger, tasted, and grimaced, shaking her head.

"Paul!" she said, just as he was about to leave the room again. "It was true, what you said? You're not allowed to . . . to have anything to do with me? It wasn't because you don't want to?"

"Oh, Christ," Paul muttered. "How can you think I wouldn't want to?"

She gave him a sad smile and reached up and touched his cheek so lightly he could barely feel her fingers.

Maurice had been on a lightning tour of the living-room; half a dozen books were out of their shelves and open, the fire-irons had been picked up for inspection and replaced, and one of the cushions on the settle had been turned over.

"Here you are," Paul called to him, and he danced over to accept the glass.

—I've never seen him camp around so much before. Maybe he's got over his guilt problem and is still stuck with the other one.

Maurice poured the adulterated beer down his throat in a single thirsty gobble and put out his tongue to lick away the moustache of foam it bequeathed to him.

"Ha-hah!" he exclaimed. "None of your London washing-up water, that! Got a kick to it—probably made of worn-out horses, hm! This country stuff!"

"Another?" Paul said.

—If he puts three or four of those away on the trot . . .

"I'll get it," Urchin offered, holding out her hand for the empty glass.

"Another of the same," Paul emphasised, and she gave him a conspiratorial nod.

"Foof!" Maurice perched on the arm of the settle, found it uncomfortable, and leapt to his feet again. "Well, I have lots and lots of news for you, Paul old pal—Palpaul, Paulpal,

marvellous place you've got here, must be earning a bloody
fortune unless it was Iris's old man who facilitated the purchase. Dead now, I hear, is that right? Anyhow, it would be
absolutely ideal for what I have in mind that you simply
must do, it'll make you far more than you can possibly get
from this horrible job you're doing now, you've got to open a
special adjustment clinic—that's what it'll be called, SAC,
strategic application of cunt, do you like that? I thought of it
myself, because you see the point is that people like you and
me, this must have been the reason for the breakdown between you and Iris, never have the good fortune to establish
the right set of reflexes"—a tear began to creep down his
plump cheek, but the flow of words went on unbroken, so
that Paul could not tell where he was pausing to draw breath.

"Got to expose the poor devils to lots of female influence
from the very earliest possible age, you see there's nowhere a
kid can go with his sister for example and because to the lay-
man it'll look like a sort of respectable brothel you're bound
to get lots of wealthy customers who will pay for the privi-
lege of being a voluntary patient and this will help to undermine the social stigma of being in a mental home and also
it'll set up these reflexes I'm talking about with all kinds of re-
inforcements, pin-ups of girls with big wobbling titties all
over the walls and a trained staff recruited from this place in
Mysore that my friend was telling me about and anywhere
else you can hire them and then maybe there won't be this
sort of problem for you and me, you'll really want and be
happy with an uddery cow like Iris instead of having to hunt
for the little boyish types like the virgin sturgeon Urchin
here!"

He thrust out his arm in a dramatic gesture and Urchin
stepped back, her face taut with suspicion.

"It'll be the millennium I don't know why they haven't
done this in Sweden already or maybe they have but you see
someone will have to introduce the idea to this country and
maybe you could have some boys here too sent by their
parents who are getting worried and want them to grow up
the way society thinks is right and hetero and the rest of it
and nobody would know if you sort of borrowed them for
the really recalcitrant cases and is that my beer *thank* you—"

It went down his throat exactly as the first had done, non-
stop.

"Paul you've got to do it you've got to help me to be

normal it's driving me crazy can't you help me start teaching me with this one here it's so like a lovely slim boy I—"

He made a lurching grab for Urchin, the glass crashed to the floor in fragments, and in the next second, after what seemed to Paul's dazed understanding no more than a gesture from the girl, he had measured his length on the floor.

"Oh my God," Paul said emptily.

"Paul!" She sounded frightened. "I—"

"Shut up," he forced out, and went down on one knee beside Maurice. "What did you do?"

"I—I . . ." An enormous, struggling swallow. "To stop him, that's all."

—For good?

The thought chilled him against the heat of the evening air. His hands sought a pulse and found it, but whatever blow she had used had rendered Maurice completely unconscious—not temporarily, like a boxing knock-out, but for heaven alone could tell how long.

He rose, his eyes on her child-small face, frightened despite himself of the power that she concealed. Hardly taking his attention from her except to check nothing was in his path, he crossed the room to the telephone, dialled the number of Chent.

In a moment, Ferdie Silva answered.

"Ferdie, Paul Fidler here. I'm at home. Send me an ambulance. Emergency admission. A former patient of mine in London called Maurice Dawkins, who turned up here this evening in an extreme manic phase . . . No, he's—he's passed out. I had to give him some spiked beer, and it's worked a treat . . . Yes, I have Urchin here. I'll be bringing her back shortly."

He cradled the phone, face a mask of despair.

—But after this, there's nothing else I can do. Maybe the lie about the spiked beer knocking him out won't hold up; I'll solve that problem when it hits me in the eye. We can probably get him sent to London tomorrow, back to his own psychiatrist, before he has a chance to talk to anyone too freely. I'll make sure Ferdie doesn't overlook his homosexuality, plant the idea that anything he says about Urchin is probably a fantasy bred from sexual jealousy, deny everything . . .

He visualised a confrontation with Holinshed and beyond the mere image of the medical superintendent's face could not imagine the results.

"Paul!"

Almost weeping, Urchin had stumbled over to where he stood by the phone.

"Paul, I'm sorry, but I was so afraid of him! I have spent all these months among crazy people, and it has made me frightened of everything they do!"

"It's all right," he said in a dull voice. "Not your fault. Maybe it'll even turn out for the best."

She pressed close to him, head buried against his chest. By reflex he raised his left arm and patted her hair, mind elsewhere. She moved to bring her cheek under the mechanical rhythm of his fingers.

Abruptly, without warning, she dragged up the skimpy skirt of her new yellow dress around her waist, seized his right hand and clamped it with the full force of her convulsing muscles between her thighs. Bewildered, he stared at her without being able to decide he must pull free, saw how her eyes were closed, her mouth open and trembling to the pulse-like gasps of her breathing.

The solitary impression that dominated his thoughts was the sandpaper roughness of her pubic tuft as she rode astride his hand.

◆ *38* ◆

Paul sat in the staff sitting-room, drawing ragged puffs from the latest of several cigarettes. Ferdie Silva hadn't even invited him to assist with the examination of Maurice; for once, moreover, he had displayed tact worthy of Mirza and refrained from commenting on Paul's agitated condition.

After her sudden outburst of uncontrolled sexual frenzy, Urchin had kissed him on his cold closed lips and gone meekly upstairs, to remain out of sight until the ambulance had collected Maurice. Thereupon she had rematerialised, fully clad, carrying the bundle of hospital clothing she had for some reason brought in with her from the car on their arrival. Now she was securely back in the female ward.

—Where they are doubtless gossiping about the fiddler taking his bitch out. To hell with them.

More elaborate thoughts than these fits of resentment were beyond him at the moment. His entire body was absorbed in a sense of diffused lust, more violent than any he had experienced since adolescence. As though his skin had acquired an independent capacity for memory, his hand reported over and over the rasping touch of Urchin's body-hair.

Through the screen of imagined tactile sensation, only one other coherent image could gain access to his consciousness: a pattern like a chain of nerves forking and forking until it climaxed at one of its terminal branches in the beautiful impossible country of Llanraw.

The door opened. Startled, he almost dropped the butt of his cigarette. Ferdie Silva nodded to him and plumped into a chair opposite.

"Everything all right?" Paul croaked.

"He has a bruise on his chest," Ferdie said. "Directly over his heart. Are you sure it was the drink you gave him which knocked him out?"

"I thought it was," Paul parried. "I had some absolute alcohol in the medicine cabinet at home, and he had about half the bottle."

"You didn't hit him," Ferdie persisted, the words flat, not even constituting a question.

—The damaged car!

"I know how that must have happened," Paul exclaimed. "He turned up in a hired car and said something about having crashed into a Mini on the way from London. He might have banged himself in the collision."

"Funny." Ferdie's eyes were focused just past Paul's head, on the wall at his back. "He said he didn't even feel the bang when the other car hit his."

"Is he talking? Didn't you sedate him?" Paul almost jumped out of his chair.

"He came to while I was examining him," Ferdie said. "I didn't want to give him anything before I was sure he was okay physically. But I've given him a jab now and he's gone to sleep like a baby."

Paul subsided. "Did he ... uh ... talk a lot when he came around?" he ventured.

"Not much. But he did say one thing which rather worries me."

"What?"

—The make or break question.

"To be frank, he claims he walked in on you and Urchin making love. I'm sorry, Paul, but I think you ought to be warned."

"Warned!" Paul gave the most convincing laugh he could manage. "Thanks very much, but it's no great surprise. The poor guy is as queer as a coot, and he's had this fixation on me for years. You can't take him seriously, for goodness' sake."

"I wouldn't think of doing so. It's unfortunate, though, that it had to be now rather than any other time he chose to come and pester you." Ferdie paused. "Was Urchin any trouble, by the way?"

"No, she responded very well to being taken out. I haven't seen her so relaxed since her arrival."

"I must say I was worried before you telephoned to let me know what you were up to. I had visions of the same thing as last time—laying the X-ray staff low in droves. Er . . ."

"If you're going to say something," Paul invited, "spit it out."

Ferdie took a deep breath. "She didn't perhaps put you in a compromising situation without your encouragement, did she? That sort of thing can happen so easily, and if your friend Dawkins burst in he could very well have—"

"That's enough," Paul snapped. "No, this is not, simply *not*, so! I'd taken her for a drive all afternoon, we'd come in just a few minutes before Maurice showed up, I'd been fixing a snack in the kitchen and Urchin was in the bathroom. He knows my wife Iris, and his dirty little mind invented an equally dirty reason for Urchin's presence. That's all." He mopped his forehead absently. "Well, I'd better be getting along. Among other things, there's a damaged hired car parked outside my house that somebody is going to be looking for pretty soon, so I'd better get in touch with the police. By the way, I know the psychiatrist who looks after Maurice in London; I'll get on to him too and tell him we're transferring him his patient tomorrow."

"Tomorrow's Sunday," Ferdie said.

"I know it is. He probably won't be at the hospital, but—"

"Paul, I haven't got a spare driver available to take a patient to London on a Sunday! We have a few empty bedspaces; he'll do all right here until he's far enough past his peak to be escorted home by train, or maybe simply discharged."

—No. I cannot, I dare not have Maurice at large in Chent spreading tales about Urchin!

Paul climbed to his feet and stood over Ferdie with his fists clenched.

"Am I the psychiatric registrar here, or are you? Remember, I've dealt with this man before and you haven't. I say he needs to go back at the earliest possible moment to his regular therapist and the hospital he's been in before!"

His swarthy Iberian face paling, Ferdie also rose. He said with equal force, "And I happen to be the medical officer on duty here. I am not going to send my one and only available ambulance all the way to London with one patient on your say-so!"

"Then I'll just have to get someone to come up here and fetch him!"

"You do that," Ferdie said, swinging on his heel and marching towards the door. "That, thank goodness, will be no concern of mine!"

Paul stood aghast as the door slammed. He had never before seen the normally imperturbable Guianese even mildly annoyed. The implications were terrifying.

—He believes the story Maurice told him. He thinks I'm lying and want to get Maurice away before I'm found out. Is he going to put it all in the admission report? I'm done for, I'm ruined. God damn you, Urchin, parading around naked for Maurice to see.

That thought washed away in another surge of actually painful desire. When he recovered, he found to his horror that he had been picturing himself going to the dispensary and drawing a hypodermic secretly, thrusting it into Maurice's heart to inject a bubble of air at a point where the bruise would conceal the mark from casual inspection.

—Never. It's a disgusting idea. But if Maurice were . . .

He ran blindly out of the room, out of the building, as if he could literally flee from such thoughts. At the Needle he stopped and bought a bottle of vodka which consumed almost all the cash he had left since his impulsive spending spree to clothe Urchin.

It was no longer Iris's presence that haunted his home now, but Urchin's. The scent he had brought hot on her skin from the bath seemed to float after him wherever he went; a shadow he mistook for hers darted away at the edge of his vision, and imagination filled his hands with the firmness of her muscles, the sleekness of her skin.

Hopelessly drunk, at four in the morning he found himself encouraging her in hoarse whispers to finish the job she had begun on Maurice, to clamp her steely little fingers on his fat wobbling throat and choke the life out of him so that they might couple undisturbed beside his body on the floor.

◆ *39* ◆

On Monday morning he did what he could to conceal the haggardness of his appearance and went first thing to Holinshed's office.

"Yes?" the medical superintendent said, glancing up. "Oh, it's you, Fidler. I was just about to send for you. Sit down. What is it you want, first?"

The words choked Paul as he forced them past his stiff tongue.

"Sir, I've been thinking over what you said on Saturday morning—about Urchin—and I've come to the conclusion that it would perhaps be best if Dr Rudge took over her case."

"It's a bit too late for that, Fidler," Holinshed grunted. "I already have the admission report here on this man Maurice Dawkins, and it's pretty damning, to say the least of it. You've been caught *in flagrante delicto* with a female patient, and I have no choice but to suspend you from your post forthwith and report your conduct to the General Medical Council."

"You're not going to believe the accusations of a psychotic!"

"If you imagined that Maurice Dawkins was insane, your incompetence must be total and I cannot guess how you ever deluded me into accepting you on my staff. He is and has been since he awoke yesterday—and no doubt was when you misused your status to have him committed—in full possession of all his faculties." Holinshed shuffled his papers noisily. "Dr Silva assures me the matter is beyond doubt."

Paul screamed.

On Sunday afternoon after a great deal of difficulty, he managed to reach his former colleague in London, and informed him that Maurice was at Chent but ought to be brought back to his regular therapist at once.

"Sorry, old chap," the voice at the far end of the line replied, "no go. No point! I'm moving to Edinburgh tomorrow and Charlie's emigrating to America and nobody else here has any knowledge of his case. You have, though. I'll send up his recent case-notes for you; I can't do any more."

"For God's sake—"

"He's no particular trouble, old son. Bit of a loudmouth when he's in the manic phase, of course. You should hear some of the dirty gossip he spread about me around this place. It was kind of flattering—answer to a maiden's prayer stuff—but he got practically everyone believing it for a while."

Paul threw the phone at the wall and it smashed.

In the end Paul decided to ignore the whole business, trust to his ability to furnish glib excuses for any accusation Holinshed might level at him, and continue his work in exactly the same pattern as hitherto. Oliphant brought in some memos from his charge nurse and plonked them on the desk.

"Morning, Doc," he said cheerfully. "Nice bit of nooky on Saturday night, I hope? Heard about it from the ambulance driver. You old so-and-so, you!" He gave Paul a playful jab in the ribs and went out.

"I must congratulate you, Doctor," Matron Thoroday said. "Of course, it's hardly conventional treatment, but what insight to diagnose that this was precisely what Urchin needed! She'll be out of here inside a week if she continues to improve this rapidly."

"Can't say I expected you to take what I said about the therapeutic value of orgasm at its face value in this fashion," Alsop grunted. "However, the proof of the pudding, as they say . . . It's a remarkable development in psychotherapy, to my mind, well worth a short paper in the *BMJ*. If you'd care to use my name as co-author, please do so. I propose to try the technique myself at the earliest opportunity."

"Brave of you," Mirza approved. "Often thought about it myself, to be frank, but I didn't quite have the guts. Also there's the problem of finding a suitable patient. I've got Urchin over in the male wards now, though, co-operating an absolute treat. It's put life back into at least half of the men

there. And she's got such fantastic stamina! She seems positively starved for it; been through about thirty of them already."

Paul picked up Maurice's clock by the statuette on top and
smashed it over Mirza's head.

"Thanks very much, Paul," said Maurice, washed, shaved,
neatly dressed, extending his hand to be shaken. "I don't
know what I'd have done the other day if I hadn't been able
to locate you. I was sure you'd be able to help."

Paul gripped the proffered hand squarely. "It's a pleasure,
Maurice," he said. "Any time. And, speaking of time, did I
remember to thank you for the clock? Most kind of you." He
hesitated. "Will you be seeing Iris, by any chance?"

"I expect so. Bertie and Meg have invited me to dinner tomorrow, and I imagine I'll see her there. I'll tell her you're
getting on okay, shall I? Not too badly despite her going
away, at least not since you acquired this snazzy little girl-
friend I met at your place. One of the patients, I gather.
Look, if she gets out of here and is ever in London, put her
in touch with me, won't you? I doubt if Meg will tolerate
Bertie messing around with Iris indefinitely, and it would be
nice for him to have a complete contrast for the next one. You
can trust me to pass her on unscratched, tee-hee!" He giggled
in his familiar camp manner.

Paul turned to pour him a farewell drink. Into one of the
glasses he tipped a generous measure of cyanide.

When he went to answer the knock at the door, he found
Inspector Hofford there. Hovering in the background was
Mrs Weddenhall, clinging to two monstrous hounds on a
shared leash, while beyond her again were a number of
figures whose faces he couldn't discern—whose only clearly
visible attribute, in fact, was the gun each one carried on his
arm.

"Good morning, Dr Fidler," Hofford began in an apologetic tone. "Sorry to bother you, but as the result of an information laid by Mrs Weddenhall, JP, I have a warrant for
your arrest on charges of assault and battery, malicious false
committal to an insane asylum, harbouring a dangerous lunatic, gross indecency with a person below the age of consent,
being an accessory after the fact to an illegal entry into Britain, not having a dog, gun or broadcast-receiving licence and
disturbing Her Majesty's peace. I also have a warrant to

search these premises in connection with the unexplained disappearance of one Maurice Boris Horace Doris Dawkins, a spinster of this parish. How say you, guilty or not guilty?"

Paul slammed the door in his face, and it was ripped open again by the thunderous blast of twelve-bore shotguns. Through the gap, torn in the door like a paper hoop, leapt Mrs Weddenhall's hounds. They fell on him and shook him like a rat until he died.

Paul pulled his car into the yard of Blickham General Hospital, jumped out without removing the ignition key, and marched over the road to the photographer's studio. Samuels was idly solving the crossword in his morning paper.

"Yes, sir?" he murmured on Paul's entrance.

—It won't be Llanraw, but at least it's away from Chent.

"I was in here on a Saturday morning some time ago, about the beginning of March, I think, to have some pictures taken of a girl I brought in. I'd like three more prints of that picture. Do you still have it by any chance?"

"I believe I remember you, sir. Just a minute." Samuels vanished behind his black velvet curtain, while Paul waited, humming to himself, surrounded by the blind faces of strangers.

After some minutes, Samuels re-emerged. "Here you are," he said, showing a negative. "Not much of a likeness, I'm afraid—she wore that scared expression while I was taking it—but I can certainly give you some more prints from it. How many will you be requiring?"

"Three. How soon can I pick them up?"

Paul walked into the bank and rang the little bell on the counter. To the girl clerk who appeared he said, "I'd like to see my current balance, please."

Armed with the statement, which showed a healthy sum in credit, he marched down to the far end of the counter and rang another bell labelled *Inquiries, Foreign Exchange.*

To the stiff-collared male clerk who answered him this time he said, "I'd like to draw my balance in traveller's cheques. How soon can you have them ready for me?"

At home he kept a rubber stamp with the address of Chent Hospital on it, for use when he had to deal with medical correspondence away from the office. Chuckling a little over the almost hypnotic force which rubber stamps exert on the official mind, he carefully laid it on the back of each of the passport photographs of Urchin. Picking up a pen, he hesitated.

—Joseph Holinshed, MD, certifies that this is a true likeness of . . . ? Mirza Bakshad . . . ? No, of course!

With vast amusement at his own imagination, he wrote in a fair approximation of the consultant's spiky hand: *Certified to be of Iris Elaine Fidler—Enoch Knox Alsop, M.D.*

—" 'E knock-knocks!"

For a second his vision blurred with tears.

—All those things gone now, all wasted: scholarship and lies told to Iris to make her marry me, hope of being a consultant psychiatrist with status and prestige, a little bloody sketch for a human baby ground up in Newton Swerd's garbage disposal unit, daddy daddy come and play with me take me shopping for a lovely new yellow dress and white stockings and a coat the colour of the green leaves on the tree . . .

But for once Paul Fidler in one of his myriad versions was going to thumb his nose at the course of fate.

—Stay, and: "This is Iris speaking, Paul. Maurice Dawkins told me about your goings-on with the fiddler's bitch and I've just posted a letter to your medical superintendent"—lovely resounding mouthfilly title which one day her husband should have enjoyed, sterile as a prepubescent boy clinging to mama's skirts against the hostile complicated world—"asking him to report you to the General Medical Council." Finish. *Slut. Kaputt.* Moreover: "Dr Holinshed, this is Barbara Weddenhall. After seeing Dr Fidler in Blickham cuddling a patient of his in the public street I asked the police to keep watch on his home and they inform me the woman was seen brazenly unclothed there in his presence." Following which: "Fidler, you have been called here to answer charges concerning a patient of yours at Chent Hospital, with whom you have carried on an adulterous liaison seemingly without regard for your professional responsibilities towards her."

Pathway after pathway into the future, each ending in a blind alley of ruin, where the disaster he had eluded for so long finally closed the trap on him and he was condemned as surely as Urchin was doomed to a lifelong stay in Chent.

—A weak personality has no business choosing psychiatry for a career anyhow. I'm sick of reaching after stupid ambitions because at every turn someone is ready to betray me and stop me achieving them: Holinshed hates me, Alsop is jealous of me the younger rival, Ferdie distrusts what I said about Urchin, Iris has left me, even Mirza whom I took for my best friend is abandoning me and going away to another hospital. My bloody stinking parents have pushed me this far, like the Yiddischer jokes "my boy's a good boy he's going to be a doctor." . . . Enough. Stop now. Free. Break loose. Out of Chent the prison. And some day our private secret version of Llanraw.

To the woman in the passport office, blue-rinsed, her eyes cold behind steel-framed glasses, he said, "I'm sure this is going to be difficult for you, and I do apologise in advance, but you see I'm a doctor"—important first point to get across, someone responsible like a doctor or JP or minister of religion has to certify the likeness on a passport photo and who would think of a doctor lying any more than a parson?— "and my wife and I have the first chance we've had since we got married to take a holiday abroad and what I'd like to do is have her included on my passport so we can go off as soon as we possibly can."

"Your wife isn't with you," the woman said.

"I'm afraid not. You see, she's going to have a baby shortly—that's why we're extremely eager to get away at once so she can make the most of the trip before she's too unwell to travel. But I have the right number of pictures of her here, and I brought our marriage certificate too." He laid documents on the desk in a tidy array.

"When do you want to go, then?" the woman said.

"As soon as humanly possible. Tomorrow, probably. Look, I do appreciate that one ought to give plenty of notice for this sort of thing, but hospitals are dreadfully understaffed and it's only the sheer coincidence of somebody turning up who can take over my work for a couple of weeks which has allowed us to think of taking a holiday at all this year. The last four years, ever since we got married, I've been so desperately busy we've had to make do with the odd weekend— no chance at all to go abroad, and she's terribly looking forward to it."

The woman looked at the photographs of Urchin. Her expression softened at the childish worry she read on the image of the face. She said, "I'll have to talk to my superior officer about this, Dr . . . ah . . . Dr Fidler, but I suppose there is just a chance we might be able to help you out."

At five-thirty he marched into the entrance hall of the hospital, armed with his deceitful proofs of identity. Natalie was just on the point of going out.

"Paul! Where in the world have you been all day? Holinshed's been raising the roof, Alsop was ringing up the whole afternoon to find out why you weren't at the clinic with him, and—"

He walked straight past her, leaving her gasping.

Ferdie Silva was the next person he encountered: "Holinshed is looking for you, Paul—where've you been?"

—Keeping out of the way of you, you dirty-minded suspicious bastard.

But he judged it safer not to speak the thought aloud.

Afterwards, he never remembered clearly how he had carried it off—by sheer effrontery, perhaps, the tone of authority in the voice with which he instructed the nurses to do as he wanted overcoming their lingering doubts due to the half-heard rumours that must have been circulating through the hospital today. The car was a mile down the road before anyone put two and two together, including Paul himself, who dazedly glanced sideways and saw Urchin wriggling to draw her new bright yellow dress down around her shoulders in place of the horrible hospital bag in which she had come out.

He didn't believe it could be true; when for occasional instants it seemed to him that it was, he felt a spasm of naked panic and relapsed into the reassuring hope that it was an illusion, another of the vividly imagined courses of action leading to disaster which had plagued him all his life.

But she sang at the top of her voice, an eldritch off-key melody belonging to no school of music he had ever heard of, while the car streaked through the gathering dusk, and that night he enjoyed her body in a shabby Dover hotel which for the space of an hour or two seemed like an extension into the everyday world of lovely, heartbreakingly lost Llanraw.

◆ *40* ◆

The town was called Louze. It sat at the end of a road to nowhere, some twenty miles east of Marseilles: an overgrown and deformed fishing-port with a native population of three or four thousand, doubled at the height of the season and perhaps a little more than doubled on Saturday nights when Marseillais came out in their droves for a gambling session at the sea-girt casino terminating the harbour mole.

One deformed quadrant of buildings faced the harbour, hotels at either end, everything between a café, a restaurant or a souvenir shop. From there, what were more alleys than streets staggered backwards into the countryside behind, their curious random directions being dictated by the lie of the ground. Crowning one of the two miniature promontories that cut off further expansion, there was a caravan and camping site; beyond that again, luxury villas were scattered wherever access could be gained to a morsel of beach.

Today, abruptly, the mistral had risen to bring the first promise of autumn to the Mediterranean coast; it was picking up the sand by handfuls and chucking it at anyone who came within reach. The cars that crept by in low gear had their tops up, their windows closed against the wind. The sunbathers had abandoned the shore to a few children playing with a huge bright ball.

At a table outside a different café from the one where they had sat the day before and the days before that, Paul and Urchin sipped slowly at two glasses of *vin blanc cassis*. They had chosen—or rather, Paul had chosen—the other café as the least frequented of the many facing the harbour. When they had come out this morning, they had found it shuttered, its season finished. The sight had hit Paul like a blow; the strange new wind had seemed to speak to him, wheezing jeers that each blended into a contemptuous laugh.

—Tomorrow, this one closed up. The day after, all of them?

Their road had come to an end here not because he chose the spot—he had never heard of Louze before signposts named it for him—but because it was in this town they had to start living off the car.

Somehow he had stretched his money through a summer pilgrimage. Urchin's first pure delight at simply being free of Chent had quickly been alloyed with dismay; discovering passports, frontier regulations, hotel registration, all the invisible shackles the world of her adoption used to bind its citizens, she was horrified, doubting her ability ever to endure such interference with her right of choice. Ashamed for his fellow creatures, Paul determined to show her another side of the picture, and displayed for her the charm, the magnificence and the luxury his own world had to offer: the cliff-hung gem of Rocamadour, the medieval walls of Carcassonne, the fortified cathedral of Albi fantastic in its rose-red sunset garb, the fashionable expensive coast resorts where a single drink might wipe out their budget for the day, the winding rocky *corniches* around the Estérel . . .

Eventually he would have to choose between crossing another frontier, which so far he had been afraid of doing in case the deception he had put over on the passport authorities had been reported, and taking steps towards a permanent residence here—equally dangerous. But not today. Perhaps next week.

He had let his beard grow, and it suited him, giving a new strength to the bones of his forehead and the deep-sunk pits of his eyes—deeper still now, for he had long lost the first contentment which had carried him through the hottest summer days. Always, at the beginning, there had been the force of passion to blot out the inevitability of the future; they had made love more often than he had dreamed possible, nightly in cheap *routiers* hotels, by day in the shade of trees or on the rocks of river-banks, drawing on the free energy of the sunlight to restore them when their spirits flagged.

Urchin exquisite in the skimpiest bikini she could find for him to buy, the envy of men on the most fashionable beaches, wondered aloud with a hint of sadness how anyone could be so foolish as not to swim naked—so he found her a cove where there was no one to see and complain, but she cut her foot on a sharp stone scrambling down to it. He had thought of l'Île du Levant, but the French Navy had claimed it for a base and closed the camp-sites down. . . .

—There is no perfection anywhere in this my world. In

Llanraw there has been no war for centuries; they would not know the purpose of a weapon.

There had been the four beatniks they met in a tiny resort as unrenowned as Louze, pleased at having evaded the immigration authorities' ban on visitors with no visible means of support by wearing presentable clothing through the customs at Boulogne, then selling what they had on and hitching south in torn jeans and sandals. They planned to sleep that night on a beach outside the town boundary; Urchin, delighted at meeting people not fettered to the law and by-law of this unfamiliar world, had insisted on keeping company with them, and to please her he had bought them food, wine and a bottle of rough brandy. So there had been a night under warm stars when he had thought the girl who came swimming fish-pale through the shallows to embrace him must be Urchin, but was not, and the next time was again not, but the first's companion, and in the morning Urchin was singing and glowing and he was afraid of himself and the days to come.

"It was almost like Llanraw," she said to explain her satisfaction, and, hearing her invoke the magic name, he had been unable to express his own unease: this other world not being like Llanraw at all.

—I brought her away from Chent at the cost of a life's ambition and hard work because she is the only free person, free in the mind where it counts, whom I have ever met. But in my world who is freest? The rich man who can buy what he wants, up to and including immunity from the law, as witness Newton Swerd and my child (son? daughter?) gone down an impersonal drain. Perhaps the day will come when the free rich irresponsible bastard with the Ferrari and the limitless horizons . . .

That was one of the thoughts the mistral brought chill from the sea, which yesterday had smiled, now glowered at him grey with frills of white froth.

Another:—In all these months, not once blood on the spear. I asked; she evaded; I listed the technical words, lectured, gave a course in female biology, and she evaded again. The virgin's breasts, so small my hand engulfs them, the hips of a boy not a girl despite the narrowness of the waist which makes them seem feminine in proportion, imply a freedom Iris would envy her. I think . . .

Against this one, alcohol, blessing the liberal laws of France compared to the time-now-gentlemen-*if*-you-please of the Needle in Haystack, but it stole through anyway and put on words like clothing.

—I think Urchin, in whose face you can read experience and wisdom enough for her to borrow Iris's passport age of twenty-six, is in her body a prepubescent child. And sterile.

What he would have done faced with the imminence of a baby under these circumstances, he had no idea. All consequent thoughts were formless, looming at the back of his mind like thunderclouds seen lately on the horizon of this balmy sea. Before he could discern their actual nature, there would have to be a rebirth of Paul Fidler as total as that which had preceded his departure from home, work, and ancient hopes, and he shrank from that second reconstructive agony.

—*Tjachariva*. Let it not happen. Let it drift on, somehow, by a succession of miracles, till I no longer care, till I have been reworked into a new strange person whose core of being is not shaped around a certain incredible girl.

And here, as of today because he had heard a chance remark from a couple passed on the way to this café, was the latest of the disturbing points he shied away from: a girl, her accent suggesting she might be German, had said to her French boy-friend in the latter's language, *"J'espère que ça n'arrive pas!"*

—And Shoemaker the philologist told me about a girl who claimed to understand Martian, only it was bastard French.

He gulped the rest of his drink angrily, as though the idea were a fire in his belly and he could put it out with liquor. Urchin's glass was still half full; as was his usual habit, he reached for it to finish it. But her hand caught his wrist to prevent him.

"I want it," she said.

He looked at her. There was an expression on her face which frightened him. Lately, since he had had to explain about getting rid of the car so that they would have enough money to carry on with, she had been drinking nearly as much as he was.

—Why? If I knew I think I would refuse to tell myself.

He made no demur. He was coming to realise that he was always afraid of this inexplicable person to whom he had chained his life, then thrown away the key. A week or so ago he had had the first of what now amounted to almost half a dozen nightmares, different in details, sharing always the common image of her turning on him as she had turned on

Faberdown, on the nurse at Blickham, on Riley and at last on Maurice Dawkins, making some sudden hurtful move that he was powerless to guard against, leaving him sprawling on the ground while she . . . went away.

Risking it, he had traded on his British medical degree, vouched for by his passport, to obtain some sleeping tablets, and last night he had been free of the bad dreams, but at the cost of being logy this morning.

"I'd like to go for a swim," she said abruptly. "I like a rough sea."

"Go ahead, then," he muttered.

—It would help if I could find some single physical thing I could do better than she does. While I paddle awkward in the shallows, she goes out of sight, her stroke peculiar, a little like a crawl but with a different rhythm, or dives from rocks that make my nape crawl and explores the underside of them until I'm ready to believe she's hit her head and drowned. And as to what I've learned from her in bed . . . She'd have learned to drive equally quickly, I'm sure, but I clung to an excuse about foreigners having too much trouble with red tape when she asked about it, certain this would make her drop the suggestion. Although now we've lost the car, what difference does it make?

She had drained her glass, but made no move to go for the swim she had talked about. Across the promenade from where they sat, a policeman was strolling at leisure, swinging a long baton, his eyes on the boats in the harbour and not on them. Nonetheless Paul flinched. Some day soon there might be a hand on his shoulder; he had compounded his offences when he sold the car.

There was no market for it through regular channels. Apart from the need to get official clearances, which would have meant too many bureaucrats examining his papers, thanks to Britain's stupid insistence on driving on the left the car's controls were wrong for Continental use, and this reduced its price to a fraction of its value at home.

At last a man he suspected of being a petty criminal, met at the casino here in Louze, had made him an offer the night his plan for keeping them going let him down. He had heard from one of Iris's wealthy friends about the professional gamblers who can survive a whole season at Monte Carlo on their daily winnings, never trying to stretch their luck beyond the budget for the day's food and lodging. He had been looking presentable enough on their arrival at Louze to ask for a visitor's ticket at the casino, his beard by then being long enough to comb into neatness. Applying what he had learned of the professionals' caution—backing only the opposite colour after a run of five or six the same, doubling up if he did not win the first time—to Urchin's admiration he won enough to pay for their room and meals for six successive days. Then he grew overconfident, fell down on a freak run of eleven blacks, and lost even the sum he needed to renew his membership.

So the car went for a pittance to this sympathetic fellow gambler.

Leaving . . .

"Are we going to sit here all day?" Urchin demanded petulantly.

"I feel a bit dopy," Paul told her. "Go for your swim and let me sit here a while longer."

A couple of young men, in sweaters against the cool wind, walked past. They whistled at Urchin, who was wearing only a hip-long beach-wrap over her bikini. She smiled and got up, crossing the road towards the beach. Paul kept his eyes on the young men to see if they would follow her, but they walked on.

Alone, he brought out from under the table Urchin's portfolio with the handle of braided string. It contained what he hoped might be the key to getting out of his present mess. He had thought of teaching English to earn some money, but so had everyone else, and his French was poor; he had inquired about casual work, and found out about labour permits and other alarming rigmarole, and decided he dare not expose himself to the investigation of the French authorities. But there was one unique secret he shared only with Urchin.

He had employed it as armour against his fearful forebodings since a night shortly after leaving England when he had been plagued by a fit of panic over what he had done. On impulse he had brought away with him Maurice's clock, and it had been carried into each of their overnight rooms to supervise their love-making. Looking at it, he had been reminded of Llanraw. He had soothed Urchin into trance almost without intending to, and found solace in what she told him of that miraculous land.

Since then he had grown to crave it like a drug, although he tried not to make it an imposition on Urchin. When he detected resentment in her face at what he could make her do—for the months of reinforcement of the hypnotic state had enabled him to put her under with a single word—he postponed the moment. To console himself he one day wrote down what he could recall of the descriptions she had given, and from that conceived the idea of writing a book.

—That'll put Soppy Al's nose out of joint! But I daren't use my own name, or Urchin's; I'll have to change everything so that it's unrecognisable, but at least no one else has ever heard of Llanraw . . .

Daydreams blossomed as he leafed through the sheets he had filled with notes: Llanraw's customs, geography, clothing, art, even a sketch for an understanding of the language. He had tried to make Urchin teach him to speak it, and had been impressed by its logic compared to the ambiguity of English, but he was a poor student and had learned only a few phrases when he desisted for fear of angering her with such drudgery. Nonetheless the directness implied by their common greeting, not "How are you?" but straight out "Who are you?" seemed infinitely desirable beside the mealy-mouthed forms of his own mother tongue.

Since taking the giant step of running away with Urchin, he had escaped some of his recurrent visions of disaster, and in their place was able to enjoy periods of optimism whose wildness did not seem in the least incongruous. Now, with the pages before him on which he had caught at least a pale reflection of Llanraw, he imagined a publisher trembling with delight, writing a huge cheque on the spot, telephoning daily to know how soon the manuscript would be ready, setting up press conferences, selling screen rights . . .

Beyond that: critics raving, readers queueing to learn about the ideal world from which Urchin hailed, clubs and societies forming to try and enact in their members' lives the ideals to which Llanraw was dedicated . . . By then he would be beyond reach of the consequences of his earlier acts; he would pay some fines, perhaps, for putting Urchin on his passport under a false name, but the judge would weep as he pronounced sentence, mourning the shortcomings of his country and assuring Paul that if only it had been like Llanraw this farce would have been unnecessary.

He slowly realised that on the other side of the road the policeman had reappeared, and his gaze now was fixed on this café. A tremor crept down Paul's spine. He called for his bill, shut up his notes in the portfolio, and walked as steadily as he could manage in the direction Urchin had taken.

He found her on the beach with the two young men who

had whistled at her earlier, wrestling each in turn to fall on the sand. They had warmed up with the exercise and taken off their sweaters, and Urchin shouted in delight as her arms locked around their sun-tanned muscular bodies.

The prospect of having a row with Urchin made him terrified. Rows were something that belonged to the epoch Paul-and-Iris, not the epoch Paul-and-Urchin; at the back of his mind, too deeply buried for him ever to have expressed the thought in words, lay the assumption that Urchin would understand the magnitude of the sacrifice he had made for her sake and devote herself to him as though he had purchased her.

He fought it, daylong; moody over their noontide meal he thought of lean carefree youths attuned to leisure, safe from problems that made him a worrisome companion, and said little; later he summoned energy and they walked to the camp-site and back in the clumsy grip of the mistral. He thought by then he had evaded the risk of what he feared, and at dinner was almost his normal self.

But that night, when Urchin lay back naked on the bed contemplating the ceiling and he was at the wash-basin noisily scrubbing the taste of the day's cigarettes away with a minty paste—she had confided that she found the stale smoky tang unpleasant, the first fault she had ever admitted in him—she said suddenly, "I think I like most that one Armand."

"What?" He turned, mopping at white foam drooled down his chin.

"Armand." She gave the name almost exactly the terminal sound of Llanraw, and the expression of dreamy pleasure on her face made his heart sink. "You know—the taller one with brown eyes."

"I didn't get close enough to find out what colour his eyes were," Paul told her curtly.

She gave a sweet lascivious smile and closed her eyes as if to visualise Armand. She said, "You will if you wish. I think he is a little like the ones we met at—what was the place called? I forget. The two men and the two girls we spent the night with. Such people remind me so much of Llanraw. To-morrow I will see him without his friend Henri—I promised. And tomorrow night, if you like, I will teach you a . . ." She hesitated, her eyes blinking open again. "A custom? A . . . No: more like a game we have there."

"What sort of game?" Paul said, his voice rasping harsh past the tingling of the strong paste on his tongue.

She giggled and did not answer.

"You didn't ask me if you could see him alone tomorrow," Paul said after a pause, afraid of what the words might lead to yet unable to prevent himself uttering them.

"Ask you? What for?" She raised herself on one elbow and clasped her hands before her bare breasts to stabilise her body.

—I keep telling myself: the only free person I ever met. But freedom at the expense of . . .

He said, "Why do you want to see him alone, anyway?"

"Why do you think?" The hint of scorn in the voice was perfectly mimicked from some unknown involuntary teacher back at Chent. "He has a beautiful body and strong muscles."

Paul was silent for a while. At length he said, "And what about me?"

It was her turn to fall silent. He prompted her: "Well?"

"Paul, the night we spent on that beach you did not—"

"You know what I'm talking about, at least!" Paul broke in.

"Am I supposed to be stupid? But why do you talk in that unkind voice? Is it not true that he is"—she snapped her fingers—"*beau*. . . , Handsome?"

"So what?"

—There suddenly seems to be a total barrier between us, almost as complete as the barrier that shuts away disturbed mental patients. . . . No, stop it.

He regained his self-control with an enormous effort. He said, "You want another man just for a change. You're bored with me. Is that what you're trying to say?"

"Paul, your voice is so hard and—"

"Is it?" He took a step towards the bed; he still held the wet towel with which he had wiped his chin, and she flinched as if expecting him to strike her with it.

"You are afraid," she said. "Aren't you? You think you are not man enough to interest me all the time, and this makes you frightened. Paul, for—for goodness' sake! Here or in Llanraw a human being is a human being, and there is nothing to be ashamed of in this simple fact, that we *are* human."

She swung both legs to the floor and sat with her hands clasping the side of the mattress. "*What* makes you afraid? I am one single human person, and so are you. I will not go away with Armand tomorrow because I am amused by him and find him handsome. I don't know yet if he is kind, like you; I don't know if he is gentle, like you. Perhaps he is selfish like most people in your world—who can say?"

"But you're determined to find out!"

"Why not?" She cocked her chin arrogantly. "I ask you again, what are you afraid of? You have lived in England with another girl, you have been with two others that I saw myself. Do you think there is no other woman in this world for you? It is a bad place, but it is not all the same as Chent Hospital!"

Paul felt the muscles of his face clamp into a mask of bitterness, locking away any words he might have hoped to speak.

Not seeming to notice, Urchin went on, "So I'm sorry you did not find someone today as I found Armand. Never mind."

"Never mind!" The dam holding back his voice shattered, but all that passed it was that raging echo of her own words.

"Yes 'never mind'—a good saying! We have such a saying in Llanraw." She twisted lithely and leaned back on the pillows as though all discussion were at an end. "Paul, you must know from being with me that there are some things we have learned in Llanraw which seemingly you do not think of here. I am—what do they say in English?—I am a handful for you. Yes, I see why they say it: something picked up which leaks out between the fingers. I tire you. I wear you out. You were tired today because of it."

"I was tired because I took some—"

"Paul!" The name was scarcely louder than a whisper, but it carried such force he stopped in mid-sentence. "Paul, in your world everyone, even you, seems to want to be ashamed of things which are not their fault. I don't *blame* you for it, so don't make excuses." She held out her arms, smiling. "Come to bed. Tonight I will not be ... ah! ... *demanding*. Tomorrow night I shall see if there is something of Llanraw in Armand, ask him to come to this room with us, and I shall teach you a game, as I promised, that we have in Llanraw."

The world shuddered on its axis. Paul, fighting the tremblor that made it swirl about him, turned to the wash-basin and at last hung up the towel, pleating it to the length of the rail with exaggerated care. Not looking at Urchin, he said, "You mean you want two men at the same time."

"We will try and find you a girl if you prefer, but—"

—It isn't true. I've slipped off the pathway of real life and found myself in one of the ruinous dead ends where the other Paul Fidlers live.

"But," she was continuing, "I did not see any I thought hopeful. Last week, now, there was a tall blonde whom I—"

"You're crazy," Paul said, and meant it with the whole of his being.

—That reached her!

She sat bolt upright on the bed. She looked frightened. "Paul, you know that I have had to show you many things that the body likes even though you are a doctor who has studied its nerves! You said they were good things, you shook and moaned and gasped and said you loved me."

—True, damn it, true. From a finger's end she can milk more ecstasy than Iris from my whole suffering corpse!

"I didn't mean to say *you're* crazy," Paul blurted desperately. "I mean what you were talking about was crazy."

"Is this crazy?" She leapt from the bed and touched him in a way he had never dreamed of before she used it on him in a *routiers* hotel on RN5, that instantly brought his nerves tinglingly alive from crown to sole; her fingers found the spot with the same precision she had used to lay low Riley at the hospital dance. "The best thing in the life of a human being is to use the body, and you in this world have never properly learned how! It's your world that's crazy, not me!"

—I wrote that down, almost in those words, I was going to say that in my book about Llanraw!

But a vision of Maurice Dawkins, slurpily repulsive, came between him and Urchin, and he looked at it—which she could not see—with eyes like chips of stone. Before that glare she crumbled on the bed, sobs erupting from the depths of her body to shake her helplessly.

"Paul"—his name, deformed by weeping, was the first coherent sound he detached from the moans she uttered—"I can't help it! I have fought it so long, but they made me this way, and . . ."

"Who?" Paul said, not because he expected an answer he could understand, and she spoke the word he had heard before, in his office at Chent, when she insisted she was forbidden to tell him who she was by command of a mysterious "they."

At the fringe of his awareness something detestable crawled into view; he sensed it without being able to focus his attention on it. Distracted, no plan in mind, he sat down awkwardly beside her and tried to comfort her, stroking her nape and back with steady passes of his fingers. She relaxed little by little, until at last as if the fit of crying had exhausted her she slumped into a sort of sleep.

"Urchin?" he said softly.

She replied in the tone he had heard many times before at Chent and in who could count how many places since where the need to hear her tell of Llanraw had overcome his desire to let her be. The loathsome thing creeping around his mind seemed to chuckle as he realisd he had put her into a hypnotic trance by his caresses, which preserved the single element she seemed to find indispensable: a regular rhythm.

He withdrew the stroking hand and linked its fingers with those of the other to stop them shaking. He said, "Urchin, what did *they* do to you?"

Later, he looked about him at the room. Although they had shared it for all the nights since their arrival in Louze, there was nothing familiar in it bar the hideous clock that he had set, according to habit, where the figure of Time might witness their love-making and sprinkle benisons on them with its wagging scythe. All the rest was strange, impossible, incomprehensible: the wash-basin, the bidet, the cupboard where they had hung their clothes, even the very bed on which they took their pleasure.

Paul Fidler had retreated somewhere out of contact with the lax body that bore his face and name. From a vantage point across a gulf spanned by no named direction, he looked down on the man who had been sitting beside the lovely naked girl now dozing quietly against the pillows.

He saw the hands of that man open a case brought from some distant, fabulous country and without error take from it a short glass cylinder capped with a shiny needle and pistoned with a smooth steel plunger. This he then carried to the basin where there was water; also, close at hand, there was a bottle containing white tablets, which he shook out without counting and broke to dust in a saucer. Mixed with water, they dissolved, were poured into the glass cylinder which they nearly filled.

"Lie still," he heard a voice say; it was connected with the creature who shared his name. "This will make you sleep."

The needle pierced the delicate pale skin of the girl's arm where a bluish vein shadowed it from below, and the plunger drove the liquid down.

There was a silence which seemed to stretch across those same dimensionless gulfs before the hand withdrew the needle, the head bowed, the lips touched the lips of the sleeping girl, and a single drop of blood ran down to stain the coverlid.

❖ *42* ❖

—Intravenously it should be fatal in half an hour at most, but kindly: a gentle slowing of the heart, the brain being already lost to any thoughts but dreams.

Paul wandered down the beach, his consciousness seeming to follow his body at a distance, like a child's balloon trailed on a long loose string.

—There is no such place as Llanraw, never has been, never will be; how was I convinced that there was?

The mistral took small account of night and day. It spoke to him when it whined in the rigging of the boats, and since he paid it no attention showed its anger by tossing sand in his face. He spat out the grains without resentment.

—"They" did this to her, she fought it (at Chent the agony), but in the end they were too strong for her although she had fled beyond their reach . . .

At the casino, despite the onset of the mistral, lights and music.

—Define "they." Against the impersonal menace of the sea at night: easy. The greatest tyrants a race with a history of clever tyranny has ever spawned.

The wind said loud and clear, "No-o-o Llan-raw-aw-aw!" He gave a foolish nod in approval of its insight. He had come to the mole leading to the casino; it was broader than a tightrope, but either side of it the sea was whipped by the wind and if he looked down he felt he was poised over an abyss. Also there were people at the casino and he had the impression that if they saw him they would mock. He turned back and continued along the beach instead.

—Paul the dupe Fidler, who believed a pack of lies so heartily he threw away a marriage, the chance of a child, a career with the prize labelled "Consultant" at its peak . . . Better here on the shore. Quieter except for the wind. The lights out in so many of the promenade cafés. Which way to Llanraw from Louze?

Dry sharp sand filtered into the sides of his shoes and abraded the skin of his feet. He welcomed the sensation as a kind of penance.

—The fact that I forgot, or overlooked: so silly, such a simple thing. That a half-truth is also half a lie. Somewhere not called Llanraw but perhaps away at this impossible angle from now where the other Paul Fidlers also live, is the half-true truth that they are human beings. But in no vision of paradise called Llanraw. In a prison-world ruled by "they" who can take the spark and essence of a person out at will . . .

He drew a deep breath, and the torrent of his thoughts settled to a pace at which he could review what he had been told tonight and, using for a guide facts that he himself had observed and preferred to disregard, sort the truths from the half-truths.

—If only I had asked one question I'd have known, but I chose rather to be blind. I should have asked, "Why does the peaceful land of Llanraw teach its children to kill with no other weapons than their hands?" Under my nose! Under my stupid bloody nose!

He moaned aloud for a little, then checked himself, irrationally afraid of being heard.

—So, more calmly now: there is not a second Eden called Llanraw, where men and beasts live harmoniously in fields of gorgeous flowers and lovers drift on scent towards the stars. There is an inconceivable dictatorship ruled by a handful of men and women who are only restrained from squandering the lives of the masses under them by a single consideration. Bought or stolen skills have made them effectively immortal, and they love their long lives marginally more than they love the total power they might win at the cost of slaughtering a billion in a war where they would risk being numbered with the dead.

—Quarrelling without fighting, jealous but afraid to strike, they grow bored. As a palliative, whim suggests orgy. But the pullulating billions of Man sprawl across the raped face of Earth; it is not only for the rulers, refusing offspring because they will not share their privileges, but for the masses too that sex must be reduced to a simple drug. Hence millions of sterile women, neutered like Urchin, to furnish it in bulk, and in their production every now and then an error of judgment, the mixture made too rich.

—Thus Urchin.

—After a century of satiation the rulers' tastes grow jaded. It is sometimes not enough for them to share the same erotic ministrations as are supplied to the plebs; these fail to arouse desire. There must be other stimulation. There must be young children. There must be corpses. There must be dramatic preludes. For example, a harmless-looking girl must appear to be so overcome by lust for her master that she fights her way through his bodyguards barehanded and hurls herself upon him reeking of sweat and blood to make frantic love while her victims moan their lives out on the floor behind.

—But in the abandon of orgy a joygirl might forget her instructions; carried away by the frenzy of slaughter she might turn her terrible skills on the master himself. To insure against this, orders must be implanted hypnotically deep in her mind, so that with a single word the master can stop whatever she is doing and compel her to wait passively for his next command.

—This can be done. There is little enough left on the ravaged planet Earth except people, of whom there are so many that there is no room for animals, and the desire for meat has been conditioned out of them not through humanitarian reasons but purely because the few surviving cattle and sheep are reserved to the rulers and the plebs have been taught to vomit at the sight of their butchered carcasses. In short, what there is of any desirable thing belongs to the rulers and no one else.

—Among the things they do have are certain machines that focus upon the brain and degrade the personality so that it conceives only the simple thoughts of a moron; it can no longer plot to wreak vengeance against the rulers. Such machines look not unlike the X-ray equipment of a twentieth-century hospital.

—This should have been done to Urchin before she was delivered to her owner (owner! And I thought: "the freest person I have ever met . . .") and would have been done but for a whim on his part. Occasionally he liked to preserve the intelligence of his joygirls so that their conversation might not be hopelessly drab. Having once escaped so narrowly from a permanent idiot twilight in the mind, she had resolved she would rather die than suffer that fate later on.

—In a little while he learned to be afraid of her, for she was cleverer than he was himself. While he was not so stupid as to exterminate his more intelligent inferiors out of hand, he liked to keep them at a distance, confining their opportunities to tasks that would furnish their master with fresh stimulation. He would not have geniuses continually within arm's reach. And he would equally not allow this superlative joygirl to go back among the plebs where they might benefit from her talents. He was too jealous.

—In the nick of time . . .

—There was an infinite universe around the rulers, but the boring prospect of struggling outwards to the stars no faster than laggard light had deterred them from searching there for relief from their ennui. Besides, if they embarked on a fruitless journey of exploration and stayed away until they were sure they could find nothing of interest, they would most probably return to discover that their compeers had stolen their luxuries during their absence.

—But a certain inventor conceived a device alleged to be capable of reversing the flow of time, and a test subject was required to verify his claim. Intrigued, Urchin's owner offered her. She was ideal on two main counts. First, she was exceptionally intelligent and would be well able to observe her surroundings and leave reports, time-capsule-fashion, filling in the blanks of history. Second, since theory did not rule out the chance of history being changed by her intrusion, and since the greatest change would be wrought by the birth of a child who should not have been born, the emissary would have to be sterile.

—Additionally, she was willing to go. She knew that if she stayed her master would condemn her mind to be blotted out.

—Nonetheless, as an extra precaution, they employed the hypnosis to which she had already been made fantastically susceptible to equip her with yet more weapons than she already possessed, and two sorts of armour. Since the era where they expected her to arrive the common tongue had al-tered radically; they gave her a knowledge of it that might pass for a native's. Also they trained her like an escapologist in the subject of evading restraints: locks, bars, shackles, anything. She had put that technique to use, chiefly in order to satisfy herself that she had an escape route if she wanted one, as soon as she could after arriving at Chent. She really had filched something from Madge Phelps—not the hair-brush she had been accused of coveting, but some hair-clips, with which she unscrewed the plate covering the keyhole and later picked the lock.

—By contrast the first kind of armour she was given failed her the instant she encountered Faberdown and realised from his language and clothing that something had gone wrong. It was a carefully faked background enabling her to establish herself in the time she had been sent to if she was questioned by the Lord of West Mountain's police. By contrast with the planet-wide hell she had left behind, she had looked forward to the Age of Confusion as paradisal, despite its local wars and primitive superstition. Stranded, she despaired and hoped by turns. When she was locked up in Chent she took it for granted that she had come to another world like her own where the majority of the population were crowded into giant barracks like cattle and only the chosen few could claim to enjoy their lives, with one extra restriction still more terrible: they were deprived of the comfort of making love.

—Having discovered that those about her were irrational, she began to apply her mind fiercely to unravelling the mystery of what had happened to her. Here there is and has been from the start a half-truth, but now the halfness is not due to deception, only to the foggy mind which will not wrestle the ideas into a pattern. She said tonight that originally she did believe what she once told me, that she had been displaced sideways to another branch of time because even the intrusion of a single individual might so affect the course of her remembered history that her departure failed to take place, an impossible paradox. But later, having learned much she did not know before, about the working of cars, about the time-scale of the history she found in books, she changed her mind and did not tell me for fear of hurting me. She thinks now—or thought this evening—there is only one history after all: no branching river delta, simply a crooked road. They hurled her back along it not for the planned five hundred years, but for something more like ten thousand, to an age when there is still coal, and oil, and unmined ore, being prodigally squandered before our civilisation is ruined by its extravagance and collapses so completely that wandering savages out of Central Asia have to learn the art of writing over again from degenerates notching strips of wood with rusty knives. She thought the great empire which fell in the dawn of time and left a few scattered relics for her own people to find might correspond to Rome; discovering that this did not fit, she deduced that it was before Rome's rise that her history branched off. But ultimately she came to the conclusion that the great forgotten civilisation must be ours.

—She's right, though, about history resisting change. The other layer of her armour worked too well, and hid her inmost mind from me against her will, until tonight. It consisted in a vision of a future so infinitely desirable that even if through persistence, or torture, or sheer chance the people of the past came to believe she was a visitor out of time, they would be afraid to act otherwise than as history would later record for fear of preventing the creation of Llanraw. Almost, they made it more real to her than the truth; so too have sometimes seemed my visions of disaster.

—They were very clever, the bastards who sent her forth. Even in the instant when she finally broke free, they dug her a pit into which, freely, she fell. For I could not bear the comfort she offered me in the last words I shall ever hear from her, though "they" had left her nothing else to give.

—I railed crazily at the mess that I am stranded in for the sake of the lie called Llanraw: a penniless fugitive in a foreign land. And she said piteously, "But, Paul, in your world I think a girl can earn much money if she is good at making love . . ."

The wind was driving the waves like wild animals in stampede. They were washing around Paul's ankles. The shock of their chill brought uppermost in his mind a momentary flash of the person he had once known by his own name, as a capsized boat may be briefly righted by the caprice of the gale.

Shuddering, he turned as though to head towards the town. He stared at its dotted lights, the only symbol perceptible which might define his familiar world.

But instead of taking even one pace towards it, he simply stood where he was, feeling the salt water leach away the doubts and suspicions and uncertainties he had rediscovered a few heartbeats ago. He had thought to arrive at truth when he confronted the incongruities in Urchin's former story; he could not bear to think himself doubly deceived. There was no going back for any reason, even disbelief. *He* could not return to an earlier time.

Resolutely he set his back to Louze again and began to unbutton his shirt.

—I know what I know. I know that because you do as you do, you there on shore behind those yellow cheerful lights, one day your children's children's children will be made barren to amuse a tyrant. I know that they will sweat away a weary drab hopeless existence in barracks bigger than a modern city, scrawny with hunger and disease because what little there is goes always to "them." I could warn you, I could change the doom written in those stars up there . . .

—And I won't.

He let the shirt blow away and kicked off his shoes.

—Count what you took from me, you sons of devils. Count carefully. All chance of happiness when you wished on me pushful parents ("my son's a good boy he's going to be a doctor!"), a marriage ("what makes you so sure it's your child I want to get rid of?"), children ("standing bloody joke in every medical school in Britain!"), the career I'd laboured for ("General Medical Council"), and, latest, most hurtful, beloved stranger Urchin.

He looked dully at his watch. Thirty minutes gone. In the hotel-room, still and white as wax. He took the watch off and hurled it into the sea.

Then, stripped, he waded after it, his limbs numb so that they would not have obeyed his instructions to swim even if he had remembered the desire to, until the wind lifted the sea above his head and he walked on steadily towards lost Llanraw, with a single thought ringing around his skull so loudly he was sure all the people in the world must hear him before that and every other thought ceased.

—So I don't care, damn you! I don't care!